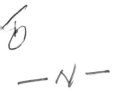

OUTLAW BREED

OUTLAW BREED

Max Brand®

GUNSMOKE

First published in the UK by Hodder and Stoughton

This hardback edition 2009
by BBC Audiobooks Ltd
by arrangement with
Golden West Literary Agency

ISBN 978 1 405 68289 3

British Library Cataloguing in Publication Data available.

Printed and bound in Great Britain by
CPI Antony Rowe, Chippenham and Eastbourne

CHAPTER 1

THE HISTORY OF Philip Slader did not originate on the day when he met the Newells, yet it took a definite turning point at that moment. Looking back for the best time to begin writing the narrative of Phil Slader, this time seems just the day one would want for introducing him.

There was a strong north wind beating sheets of rain against the colder face of Mount Crusoe. From the peaks of the big range, storm vapor came straight out to the south. Over that southern valley the clouds broke off in masses and whirled away toward the gray horizon.

The sun was not totally obscured. It shone through in warm patches and gave many golden moments during which the Newells looked up to the crags of Mount Crusoe and thanked the providence that had directed them to buy their land on the southern side of the range instead of the region of these tempests.

They had come so lately to this section of the land that they had not yet learned that one spoke there of a pitching horse instead of one who bucks. But John Newell knew as much about cows as could well be crowded into one mind, and since he came into the land well provided with funds, there was no doubt that he would succeed. The very first men from whom he bought cows agreed afterward that this was no tenderfoot. He knew beef when he saw it and he knew a right price from a wrong one. However, he began moderately, hesitating to show his hand or commit himself until he learned how cattle wintered in this locality. If all turned out as he hoped, he would invest heavily in the spring. In the meantime, as has been said, he was congratulating himself that he had not bought on the north side of the range. Then the brightness of the day ended; the evening stooped slowly upon them like a shadow leaning from the crests of Mount Crusoe, and with the blackness outside, and the windows trembling and the howling of the storm, they looked often at one another and smiled, half in fear and half in happiness as they tasted the full pleasure of their security.

The fire in the dining room was smoking badly; therefore the dinner table was spread in the kitchen. The family had finished soup and come to boiled beef and cabbage when they heard a knock on the door. Sam Newell, like a boy who knew his duties, rose to answer the summons, but his father called him back to his chair.

"You take a night like this," muttered John Newell, and he glanced apologetically at his wife, "and you can't tell who'll be traveling around."

As he stepped to the door and turned the knob, the wind struck the house so heavy a blow that the door pitched strongly back to the face of Newell. It left him staggered, half blinded with the force of the gale. He did not see, but he heard his wife crying:

"Why, John, it's only a boy!"

Then Newell saw that it *was* only a boy. He was not more than fourteen, certainly, strongly built, and dressed in rags which the gusts of rain had drenched. He made no movement to step inside, but merely tilted his head back a little and looked quietly into the face of the rancher. Newell was startled. They were like the eyes of a man, and not of a young man, either. Such deliberation, such calm power should not lie in the eyes of a man until middle age.

"How's things?" asked the boy.

"Why, dog-gone my heart!" muttered the rancher, and

he took the youngster by the shoulder and pulled him inside.

He closed the door and turned to find the stranger as calm as ever, standing at ease with the water coursing down his clothes. His legs were bare from the knees down, and the smutch of mud, from a recent stumble in the dark, was now washing away from one tanned shin and turning to a muddy puddle around his naked toes.

But what his eyes saw was not the chief interest in the mind of Newell. In the tips of his fingers there was still a tingling feeling of the hard, sinewy muscles with which the shoulder of that boy was overlaid. A trained man, a hard-working man might have muscles like that, but never a child!

"What's up? What's up?" gasped out Newell. "Have your folks sent you here for help or something? What's broke loose to send you out on a night like this, youngster? What brought you here?"

The stranger hooked a thumb over his shoulder. "The light," said he, "and the smell of the chuck."

Here his glance wavered toward the table with its loaded plates and platters. Then he looked back to his questioner; there was no sign of emotion in him except a faint, faint quivering of his nostrils.

Mrs. Newell stood up in her place. Her voice was rich with indignation directed against the entire human race which had allowed a child to reach such a condition as this. She had seen that glance and she knew hunger when she saw it. What mother does not?

"Sammy!" she cried to her son, "take him up to your room as fast as you can jump and get him into some of your dry clothes. Quick, do you hear me? Don't stand there like a booby. Nell, fetch another chair here to the table."

Sammy lurched out of his chair, keeping upon the strange boy the stare of one enchanted. "Come on!" said he. "I'll fix you up," he added, as the boy from the outer night stared back, as though not comprehending.

Then he said: "I see. I'm kind of sloppy, ain't I. Well, I'll fix that!"

He opened the door behind him and slipped out, and though the wind was raging in a veritable screaming hurricane at that moment, the door was closed against it smoothly, gently. Mr. Newell blinked, for he knew what power of arm and fingers such a feat required.

His wife had clutched him and drawn him apart. "John, John," she was whispering, "don't let the children hear—but—did you ever see such a creature in your life?"

"Humph'" said Newell.

"So wild, I mean," said his wife, "and such a look—like a little animal."

"He's a queer one," admitted her husband, "but the main thing is that he's hungry. Feed him up, but I wouldn't be too strong on giving him a suit of Sammy's clothes. The clothes might walk away before the morning—Sammy, mind what you're saying!"

He was squelching a remark of Sammy's to his sister, to the effect that the stranger was "a funny-looking guy. Barber's never bothered *him* any."

"Aw, dad," said Sammy, "I know. But look at that hair of his—clean down to his shoulders, and black and all sun-faded at the ends. Never seen uch a mop of hair."

"Saw, Sammy, not seen," corrected his mother absently.

"Of course, we have to make the best of it," she whispered to her spouse. "But couldn't we send the children upstairs?"

"Rot!" said her husband. "The kid ain't poison, is he? He's not typhoid fever, I hope! Don't be so finicky about your kids, mother!"

There was no chance for further discussion. The door was deftly opened and shut, and in the brief intermission, the stranger snapped into the room with a deft, gliding movement. You would not have said that he jumped. Few jumps could have meant such swift motion. He pointed to his clothes.

"They ain't dripping now," said he, "if that's what bothered you, ma'am."

"Gracious me!" cried Mrs. Newell. "The child has wrung them out. *What* an idea! Young man, would you sit all evening in sopping clothes like those?"

8

"Me? I've done it a million times, pretty near!" said the boy.

"Heavens!" exclaimed Mrs. Newell. "How could you?"

"Why, I've got a thick skin, I guess," said the youngster.

She appealed to her husband with a desperate side glance.

"Let him have his own way," said the rancher, more than a little relieved. "Sit yourself down here next to the stove, son."

"Thanks," said the boy, "but I fit in here pretty good. If you don't mind, none."

He drew the chair around to the farthest and the coldest corner of the table and there he sat down. Mrs. Newell began a noisy protest, but her husband stopped her. He himself had lived in rough countries and among rough men most of his life, and he understood. The place which the stranger had chosen, faced the door!

Something, therefore, was pursuing him. What could that be? If he were a runaway, from what home had this bundle of rags come? On this the rancher pondered while his wife heaped the plate of the waif. Mrs. Newell, feeling that she had been guilty of inhospitable thoughts, covered the breach with much talk.

"Sammy," she said, "reach our new friend the bread plate."

"I can reach," said the waif. Extending a half-naked arm he transfixed the heel of the loaf with his hunting knife and transferred it to his plate.

Mrs. Newell was a little staggered, but she went on: "And give him the salt, Nelly. And you might find something to say to him!"

"I can't see his face to talk to him," said Nelly, aged eleven. "He hasn't taken his hat off!"

Here the youngster removed his hat with the dignity of an Indian chief, wiped his long, sun-discolored hair back from his face, and fell to the serious work of eating. Now that the wide-brimmed felt hat no longer sloped across his face, the Newells saw eyes as black as the hair and the neck and chin and straight-lipped mouth of a man. They had hardly a chance to observe these features, they were

9

so taken by the methods of eating which the stranger put in practice. The bread was used as a helpful wedge by which large quantities were piled upon the hunting knife and transferred to the waiting mouth with an admirable sense of balance, until Sammy broke into a peal of laughter.

"Sammy!" cried his mother.

"I can't help it!" said Sammy. "I wonder how he does it without cutting his mouth."

He laughed again hugely. At this the steady black eyes lifted and were fixed upon him with such strange effect that the laughter died in a single gulp. A heavy breath of silence fell upon the table.

"What might your name be, young man?" asked Newell at last.

"Phil is my name," said the other.

"Thanks," said Newell. "My name is John Newell. And I'm glad to know you. This is Mrs. Newell. And this is my son, whose name is Sam, also. And that is my daughter, Nell."

To each, in turn, as their names were pronounced, the stranger gave one penetrating glance. But though Sammy and Nell stood up to jerk their heads and smile perfunctorily in acknowledgment of this introduction, Phil made no other return than this silence, and these grave glances.

Conversation dwindled again, and all the Newell family became conscious of the howling of the wind outside the house.

CHAPTER 2

EVEN THOUGH Mr. Newell did not pretend he was a man of extravagant culture and politeness, he felt that there was something wrong in an entire family sitting about and shifting their eyes up and down as the practiced knife of Phil rose and fell from plate to mouth. Moreover, the atmosphere became momentarily more depressed. Even though he sat in his own house, Sammy seemed oppressed with something closely akin to fear, and bright-haired Nell watched the stranger with an uncanny fascination. Even Mrs. Newell had changed color a little and sat nervously erect in her chair.

So the rancher stepped into the heavy silence again. "Phil is a familiar name to me," said he. "I had a cousin called that. He was redheaded, though. But what might your last name be, young man?"

The stranger looked up from his plate again. "You won't have no use for it," said he. "I'm traveling on and I ain't coming back this way."

Mr. Newell exchanged glances with his wife—a swift, covert interchange, for even when the eye of the boy was apparently fixed upon his plate, one gained an impression that he saw everything that happened in the room.

"Traveling on, eh?" said Mr. Newell, without pressing the point. "Traveling where, may I ask?"

"I'd tell you, if I knew," said the boy. "All I know is that I'm drifting south. Sort of chilly up this way, eh?"

"Yes," said Newell, "the winters are pretty cold up here, I suppose. And—how old are you, Phil?"

As though this were an unexpected query, Phil looked thoughtfully into space before he nodded and answered: "Twelve last month."

"Twelve!" exclaimed Mrs. Newell. "Why, then Sammy is a whole year older—and my Nell is only a year younger? It doesn't seem possible!"

"Her?" asked Phil, turning his head to the girl beside him. "Her eleven?"

He reached out a brown paw as bigboned as the hand of a man and took Nell by the wrist. It was not a hard grip, but she winced back from him with a little gasp. At that a faint smile appeared rather in the eyes than on the mouth of Phil. Perhaps it was hardly a smile at all, but a mere softening of expression, which enabled Mr. Newell to see for the first time that this was really a handsome youngster. Yet he had been studying the little stranger every instant since his arrival.

"Soft, ain't she?" said Phil. "Like a baby, pretty near!"

He replaced her hand on the table with care.

Mrs. Newell had bit her lip with anxiety when she saw his hand touch her child. Now she exclaimed again: "Only twelve years old! Do you mean that, Phil?"

"I don't lie," said Phil without offense, "except when it's something important. I'm twelve. Why?"

"Only—nothing!" said Mrs. Newell, and she looked appealingly at her husband.

"Why," explained the rancher, "it's only that you look very strong and big for your years, Phil. You'll be bull-dogging the yearlings before much longer!"

"Oh, yes," said the boy. "I started that last spring."

"My!" exclaimed Sammy Newell, "what a—"

The word "whopper" was framed by his lips alone. But he began to look sternly upon this youth. There is a certain pride of place of which all boys partake, and part of

12

that pride is every youngster's certainty that he knows a great deal more and is a great deal stronger than every other boy who is his junior by so much as a month. But nothing of his expression of scorn and doubt seemed to make an impression upon Phil, who smiled back at him, as a grown man might have smiled at an incredulous child.

"It's all a knack," said Phil quietly. "You got to learn the knack, you know. Same as sticking in the saddle. It ain't long legs you need; it's the knack, it's the balance. Ain't that right, Mr. Newell?"

So he shifted the burden of the conversation deftly over the head of Sammy to Sammy's father, and Sammy felt the sting of that alteration without knowing how to resent it in deeds. But a spot of color was beginning to burn in Sammy's cheeks, and there was a flare of danger in his eyes.

Supper ended, and Mr. Newell sent the boys into the next room to amuse themselves while Nell and Mrs. Newell washed the dishes.

He said to his wife:

"I don't like having him here, mother. I don't like it a bit! He may be an honest kid, but he looks to me different —and maybe he's bad. Shouldn't be surprised if we woke up in the morning and found him gone with the best horse on the place! Shouldn't be a bit surprised."

"John," said his anxious wife, "I'm terrible glad to hear you say that. And—John—we got a telephone here, you know! Why not ring up to find out about—"

"Ring who?"

"The sheriff—and describe that boy."

"I'll do it," said Newell. Then he hesitated. "I can't do it. Not about a poor kid that has been blown in out of the wet like this one. He's done no harm that we've *seen*. And maybe he's had no bringing up!"

"Ah," said the wife, "no woman would want to try her hand with him. He's hardened and fixed. Bringing up would never change him. You mark my word. What he is now he was born to, and what he'll be before he dies was written down, too!"

13

Mrs. Newell had risen to an almost prophetic strain. Her husband nodded.

"I feel more or less the same way," he admitted. "I'm ashamed of it, but I can't help feeling a good deal the same way. Where's Nell? I don't want her around that young brute. Where's Nell since she finished wiping the dishes? No use in her seeing such a young wolf. No use at all!"

"I'll call her," said his wife. "My, my, but it does me good to hear—"

She stopped there. They heard the thud of a blow, and then the wild scream of Nell pitched in a key of horror and of fear.

Neither the rancher nor his wife could move. What they saw first was Sam, walking backward through the door of the next room, like one who fears to take his eyes from the thing that he sees. Then little Nell came with a rush and clung to her father, babbling something inarticulate.

As for Newell he could not tell what to think. What he did, was to brush Nelly aside into the arms of her mother; then he drew a gun and stepped to the threshold.

He saw Phil in the middle of the room, his hands gripped into fists, his face white and contorted with a perfectly devilish fury, and a thin trickle of red running down from his mouth.

Whatever it was that the rancher had expected in the way of a horror, he felt that he had enough in this picture. He was a grown man, and there was a gun in his hand; yet he had at first an almost overmastering impulse to slam the door and leap backward into the warmth and the safety of the kitchen.

He controlled himself at once. "Now what?" he asked Phil sternly. "Tell me what you mean by frightening my boy and girl within an inch of their lives!"

A spasm crossed the face of Phil. He put up a hand and touched his mouth. Then, when he saw the crimson on his fingers, he closed his fist again and looked straight into the eyes of Mr. Newell.

"And what happened to give you that?" asked Newell.

"I stumbled and fell against the wall," said Phil.

"Stumbled!" exclaimed Mr. Newell.

There was no good reason why such a thing might not have happened—except to this youngster. For some reason, it was as much folly to expect him to stumble as it would be to expect a mountain sheep to miss its footing.

He strode back into the kitchen. "Now," said Newell, "I'll have the truth, out of this! Sammy, what happened?

"He—he stumbled—and hit his face—against the wall!" said Sammy, white with misery and with fear.

Mr. Newell took his son by both shoulders. "Sammy," said he, "I hate a lie and I hate a liar. Now tell me the truth!"

"I—I thought I would see what he could do. I picked a fight and I hit him—and he didn't hit back! He didn't hit back, dad!"

A cold, little thrill ran through the body of Mr. Newell.

"Maybe he was afraid to," said the rancher. "You've got muscles enough to knock a little sense into his head."

"Afraid? Him?" asked Sammy, and suddenly he clung to his father desperately.

"Dad," he gasped out, "I thought that he was gunna kill me! And I think he will still, before the morning comes!"

Newell moistened his white lips, but he found no word to say. He looked across to his wife, who was soothing Nell. He knew that the same white, sick look which he found on the face of Mrs. Newell was on his own.

It was a little thing. He kept telling himself that it was a mere trifle—a quarrel between children. No matter what reason could tell him, instinct spoke to a different effect. There was no childishness in this strange boy!

He heard a slight rattling at the front of the house, and striding through the blackness of the hallway, he came on Phil, in the very act of unlocking the door, and going out into the night.

There was nothing that he wanted so much as to see the last of that small person, but conscience shouted aloud in the heart of Mr. Newell.

"Phil," he said, "it seems that Sammy was in the wrong —and that he hit you—"

Phil was silent.

"I want you to come back inside," said Mr. Newell.

15

"You've—you've done nothing wrong—and I want you to spend the night here and—"

"It was a funny thing," said Phil. "It seemed to scare her. Why should it scare *her*, Mr. Newell?"

CHAPTER 3

WHEN MR. NEWELL got Phil to go back into the kitchen with him, they found Mrs. Newell, with her two children on each side of her, Nell still sobbing and Sammy still white.

"Now," said the rancher, "I'm going to see that there's justice done here. You struck this youngster when he was here in our house as a guest. And you're going to stand out here and ask his pardon for it Sammy, d'you hear?"

Sammy heard the bitter insinuation and swallowed hard. But he stiffened and strode forth to make the apology. The stranger, who had stood by watching all this with his calm, black eyes, said to the rancher: "Look here, Mr. Newell, d'you want to make him hate me all his life? And d'you want *her* to hate me?"

He pointed solemnly at the girl. For Nell had stopped her crying and was watching this proceeding with a vindictive interest.

Now she brushed the tears from her eyes and burst

16

out: "It doesn't matter! I hate you anyway! I'll always hate you! I'll hate you all my life!"

"Hush, Nell," said Mrs. Newell, but there was more sympathy than anger in her tone.

Phil, watching the girl gravely, finally turned again to Newell. "It's most always like this," said he.

"*What* is mostly like this?" asked the man.

"Nothing," said the boy, shrugging his shoulders. "Well, I'll be drifting." He turned to the door.

However, Newell intercepted him. He did not take hold of him as he would have seized upon another youth. He merely stepped in front of him and spoke as though to a man, saying: "If you leave like this—before the boy has had a chance to apologize—and go out into a storm like this, it'll make me feel pretty cut up, Phil."

"Will it?" asked Phil, his grave glance fixed upon the other. "Will it be like that with you? Why," he went on, making a gesture toward Sammy, "it's all right you know, about that. I was mad for a minute, but I'm over that. I don't mind it. Not at all! I'll shake hands with him to prove it." And he walked forthwith up to Sammy.

It was an uncanny thing to watch and a most unpleasant one. Here was a self-control that might have shamed most men who had reached to full maturity. In such a child it was strange indeed!

Sammy was plainly afraid to stand before the stranger again, but he put forth an unwilling hand when Nell cried: "Don't touch him, Sammy! Don't touch him, please!"

Sammy shrank back. Newell was beside himself.

"Send Nelly to bed," he cried to his wife, "and if you don't give her a good dressing down before she goes to sleep, I'll come and do it myself. You hear me?"

His wife was one who knew perfectly well when it was safe for her to uphold her authority and place in that house, and when it was far better for her to walk in humble silence. Now, as she saw a certain vein swelling in the forehead of her husband, she took Nelly by the hand and walked hastily from the room. Sammy, after one frantic glance at his father, followed in the rear, but he

17

was caught by the iron hand of Newell and forced to turn back.

"I'll skin you alive," said the rancher through his teeth. "Confound it, if I'm to be checked and made a fool of in my own house—and can't teach my own kids manners. Apologize this minute, or I'll make you do it on your knees!"

"I'm sorry!" whispered miserable Sammy. "I'm terrible sorry—that I hit you."

"Why," said Phil to the rancher, "you've done it now! There ain't no chance that I can ever come back to this ranch and find a friend. And," he added to Sammy: "It's all right. I'm sorry that this mess all happened."

Sammy sneaked from the room, and as Newell stood there, with his head hanging, there was a gentle touch at his arm.

"What's wrong?" asked Phil.

"My son is a coward, and my daughter is a vixen! I see it in a flash of light!" said the rancher more to himself than to the boy.

"No," said Phil with equal gravity. "I tell you that that's the way that I mostly make folks feel. The boys, they want to fight. And the girls, they hate to have me near them. I dunno why it is. Except that I'm nacherally mean."

Perhaps the part of generosity was not to believe a word that he had to say, but Newell was no more than human, and he had made many concessions on this night against his flesh and his blood.

"Come upstairs," said he to the boy. "I'll show you a place to bunk. And no matter what else may turn out of this, I want you to know that *I'm* your friend."

"Thanks," said the boy. He raised his head and searched the face of Newell, but he did not seem to find there what he had been hoping for. A little pang of shame passed through the man, as though he had been detected in the act of committing some mean hypocrisy.

However, he felt that something had been gained in the discharge of his debt of hospitality and honor to Phil by getting him up to the spare room and bidding him good night. After that he went to his wife and found her sitting in their room.

"Where is Nell?" he demanded harshly.

But Mrs. Newell merely looked at him with tears in her eyes.

"I see!" said he. "You've let her slip again. You're gunna raise her to be a spoiled woman, like the rest of these American girls. Because she's got a pretty face, you're gunna let her get in the habit of wiping her shoes on folks, chiefly men. I'll not stand it, if I have to beat her black and blue every day of her life."

He hoped, in his heart, that his wife would have some stinging rejoinder, for the pain in his heart needed much spending. But there was no answer whatever. Mrs. Newell merely bowed her head, and the sight of its familiar grayness touched her husband.

He went hastily to the little chamber of Nelly, and when he lighted a match, he found her lying with closed eyes, breathing deeply and regularly, with a faint smile upon her lips. He knew that his daughter was capable of sham; yet when he leaned closer the smile did not alter. There was not so much as a quiver of the eyelids. So he straightened again, with an imperceptible sigh of relief. He could not awaken her. Not from a sleep so beautiful and calm that death itself could not have been more hushed and solemn, it seemed. A religious wonder grew in him that a creature so beautiful should really be his.

Here the match burned his fingers. He dropped it with a murmured oath and stole from the room. When he closed the door gently behind him, how could he know that the delicate smile of Nell had grown to a most impish grin? It had been a close call, this, but she had won again; and she had learned afresh the profound lesson that tears will disarm women, and smiles will disarm men.

Mrs. Newell had been waiting in terror, but when her husband reappeared with a hushed look upon his face, she understood, and she turned away in haste to hide her smile. In five scant minutes the howling of the wind had lulled all the household to sleep, save that in the spare room the stranger sat cross-legged on the edge of his bed, absently

19

raising his hunting knife and letting it fall at a crack in the floor. If it missed the crack it would make an ugly scar in the paint and a thudding noise as well. But it did not miss, time after time, though all his thoughts had wandered elsewhere. At length he, too, turned in, and the house was silent and dark.

It was still dark, barely edged with gray, when Newell arose the next morning. He went hastily to the room of Phil, but the boy was gone.

Down the stairs went Newell in haste. He scanned the cupboard where the few pieces of silver were kept. All of them were in their places. He hurried on to the barn, and there stood all his best saddle stock, tossing their heads and whinneying when they heard the sliding door creak back.

It seemed that the vagabond had taken nothing. He had gone on without farewell, in the dark of early morning, and perhaps it was better that way. Still, when the rancher stood at the door of the barn and looked up to the sky, where the upper wind harried the clouds farther south, he wondered what destination awaited that boy. He wondered, too, how many other things there might be in the world as strange and wild, to the mind of John Newell, as this apparition from the night had been.

It was not a pleasant course of thoughts; therefore he turned hastily to the work of cleaning out the barn and giving the horses their morning feed. The light brightened. He was about to put out the lantern and let the gray of the morning serve him in its stead when suddenly something made him turn around.

He saw a big man wrapped in an overcoat, standing in the doorway, a quirt hanging from his mittened hand—a big, rough man. Newell himself was big and rough enough to suit most needs, but in the presence of the physical size and the craggy spirit of this stranger he felt like a most ineffectual boy.

"I'm 'Doc' Magruder of the Crusoe Hotel," said the big man. "I'm here on the trail of a runaway kid. Might you of seen him? Twelve years old and he looks fifteen, pretty near. Big shoulders and an oldish face."

"Dressed in rags?" asked Newell.

There was enough lantern light to show the flush which came on the stern features of Doc Magruder.

"Ay," he said, "he'd be in rags! As if I didn't give him decent enough clothes to wear. Got no thought, he hasn't, except of putting me in a wrong position with folks. And if I wasn't a known man, Heaven knows what people would think of me! In rags, eh? Ay, the same stuff that he had when his father died, most likely. He'd put that on when he started to run away! But you've seen him, eh?"

"I've seen him," said the rancher, "and if you'll come to the house and have breakfast, I'd like to find out something about him, if you'll talk."

"Tell me one thing. Is he yonder in that house, now?"

"No, he's gone from his room."

"In the night, eh? That would be his way. Most likely you've missed something outside of his company before this?"

"I hunted. Can't find anything gone."

"You *will* find it, though," said Magruder. "Bad blood will out."

"Like murder, eh?" said the rancher, nodding.

"What?" cried Magruder. "What you mean by that, may I ask?"

"Why, you ve heard it said before this, of course."

"Oh, ay. I've heard it said before. But bad blood will out. You can't keep it from showing, sooner or later. And you'll find that he's scooped up something and made off with it. He wouldn't be his father's son otherwise! Not him!"

"Maybe not," agreed Newell.

He was rather pleased, than otherwise. For everything that he had heard, and the very bearing of this stranger, more and more excused the conduct of his own family toward the boy, as though they, being of honest blood with an honest rearing, had felt by instinct the gulf which separated them from the evil nature of young Phil. They were more and more excused, and the vagabond youth was more and more condemned in their places. Newell looked

21

up with a lighter and a lighter heart as he asked: "And who might the father of this boy be, if I may ask?"

"Who might he be, indeed!" asked the big stranger heavily. "Who might he be? Why sir, if it wasn't for the wrinkled look around your eyes—which means range riding or I'll eat my hat—that speech of yours would make me think that you was a dog-gone tenderfoot, and a mighty green one at that! It sure would. But you seen his face didn't you?"

"Ay," said Newell, "I saw his face. And a mighty queer one I thought it."

"You ain't the first that have felt the same way," said Magruder. "Sort of handsome, too, in a way."

"Ay, mighty handsome, except for a sort of a strange, mean look that he had."

"Like his dad!" said Magruder. "Like his dad, except that his old man had the nerve to cover up his meanness with a smile. He was gay, was the daddy of this boy."

"Ay, man, but who was he before I bust with curiosity?"

"I'm trying to get you to guess. Take another try. Think back a few years to the newspapers. They was running his pictures often enough. Ay, and the signboards in the post offices had his face, too. You can't remember? Well, I'll tell you. His daddy was Jack Slader himself. Now tell me if the kid ain't a ringer for him?"

"Slader? Slader?" gasped out the rancher. "Slader, the gun fighter and killer? But—good heavens, man, wasn't it a fellow by the name of Magruder that killed Jack Slader?"

22

CHAPTER 4

IT SEEMED TO Newell that there was some relation between the cold, dim smile of Magruder as he listened to this remark, and the expression in the eyes of the boy Phil, which he had seen there the night before.

Then the stranger said quietly: "It was a Magruder that killed Slader, right enough. And I'm the man!"

The rancher strove to comprehend; he said slowly:

"What I understood a minute ago was that this Phil is the son of Jack Slader?"

"Yes, that's right."

"And—I figgered out that he had run away from you?"

At this, Magruder waved a hand in a large gesture. "It's a hard thing to understand, maybe," said he. "You ain't the first that has pretty near sprained his brain trying to work out that idea, old-timer. But it ain't the sort of a thing than can be told in a minute. You said chuck, and that sounds good to me. I've ridden all night, trying to get trace of the kid. And I'm starved. Let's see the insides of that breakfast that you was talking about before we go any further."

Newell was willing to give more than a breakfast for the sake of information such as this. He conducted his guest hastily to the house, where they found the fire in the kitchen fuming and smoking. Two words to Mrs. Newell set her to work with a glowing ardor. For Jack Slader had been a man of such mark that to entertain his destroyer would have flushed the cheek of the wife of any rancher. In the meantime, Magruder was placed at the table in the dining room, while the egg beater of Mrs. Newell hummed a soft song in the kitchen.

"Mostly," said Magruder, "I thought that folks knew about how things happened. But since you're a newcomer and ain't heard, I'll tell you myself. I ain't going to be particular to you about how I happened to get on the trail of that Slader, after the hound had stole my best cutting hoss. But I'll tell you what, I went after him so mad that I forgot about his reputation. And I still wasn't thinking about his reputation as a man-killer when I got inside of a shack on the Crusoe River, with Slader in front of me. If I *had* been thinking, I wouldn't of dared to fight, I suppose. A couple of days before I'd had to swim a river, and I'd got my Colt pretty wet, and then I hadn't cleaned it quick enough, I was working so hard to figure out a trail puzzle. By the time that I got to that gun, I was tired out, and I give it only a careless oiling up. Well, when I looked at it the next day, it was in bad shape. But still I thought that it would work pretty well.

"However, there I was finally, finding myself unexpected in the same room with big Jack Slader."

"Bigger than you?" asked Newell, filled with admiration as he scanned the Herculean form of his companion.

"Bigger than me? No, I suppose that he wasn't. Not so terrible big in inches. But you've seen the kid, Phil?"

"Of course."

"He looks big, don't he?"

"Ay, bigger than any boy I ever saw at that age."

"So did his dad. Looked bigger than any *man* you ever seen. And yet he didn't measure so much in pounds and inches. That was the puzzling thing about him. That was the main reason, I suppose, that he could keep away from the sheriffs and their posses for so long. You see, when there was no trouble, he could mix right in with any crowd, as small as ever you please, and nobody would notice him particular. But when it come to a pinch, then you would say that he reached out and expanded, and you could of picked him out from among ten thousand by one look at him. There come up a fire in his eye. And even his voice changed and got big and you would of said that he could of took ordinary folks in his hands and busted them the same as you and me could crackle matchwood."

Here the narrator looked off, conjuring up the picture of the famous destroyer, and he winced a little from the very conception.

"I didn't stop to think about what he was," he went on at last, "when I got inside of the room with him. All that I wanted was to tear his heart out. I snatched my gun out and was about to drive a slug through his heart when I seen that he didn't have his own gat clear. It had stuck in the leather as he was making his draw. Somehow, I couldn't pull the trigger. I couldn't kill a gent that was helpless, even when he was a snake like Jack Slader had proved himself to be!"

He paused again, and the heart of Newell began to thunder in his throat. For it was all very well to show mercy to some, but certainly it required a rare nerve to stand in front of such a destroyer as Jack Slader and then to think of insisting that he have his due fighting chances! It was like extending one's naked wrist to a rattler's sting.

"I told Jack that we would both have another fling at the job, and then a mighty funny thing happened. You would hardly believe it, but I suppose that the fact was that Jack Slader had fought so many fights and always won them smooth and easy, that having one setback, like this, and having to take mercy from a gent, sort of sapped his nerve. It watered his blood a good deal, and he got white around the gills and wilted. He asked me what real reason I had for tearing in and wanting to kill him, and when I talked about the hoss, he actually offered to pay ten times its price, and he put the money right out there on the table in clear view of me. Well, sir, if I hadn't been so heated up, I never could of pushed the thing through, because anybody can tell you that I ain't the man to kick a fellow when he's down. I was right sorry for Slader losing his nerve that way. But I'd followed such a long trail to get at him—"

"Wait a minute!" broke in the rancher. "You mean to say that Jack Slader showed yellow when the pinch come?"

"That's exactly what I mean. I would hate to tell you just how crawling and how mean he got before I finished with him!"

"I believe it!" said honest John Newell. "I've always believed that those gun fighters were never the men to stand up in a pinch like a fellow that lived by the law and not with his hands in the pockets of others. I've always believed that one of us was worth any two of them, pretty near!"

"And you're right, absolute!" said Doc Magruder. "A gun fighter does all pretty well. But he's a bully, and when a bully gets hit on the nose as the fight starts, he ain't so gay about mixing in with the other fellow! Anyway, that was the way that even the great Slader turned out. I would like to say that he was a tiger, of course. I would like to say how lightning fast he was, and how I was just a mite faster, and how I beat him by a shade—y'understand? But the fact is that I got to tell the truth.

"He fair crawled and begged me to let him off—because he said that he was weak and sick, and not himself. He offered to ride to town with me and give himself up to the sheriff. Well, I wasn't looking for that sort of work. I say that you got to consider how long I had been on the trail, hungering for a fight with the sneak that had stole my hoss—and stole the lives of a lot of other men, before that! When I got my chance, I couldn't throw it away. Slader deserved to die. I know that. I only wanted to kill him in a fair fight.

"Finally, I got him to the point where he said that we would both put our guns on the little table in the center of the room, and then he would jump for his as soon as I made a move. I agreed to that. We pooled our guns and stepped back, but Slader didn't get more than half a step back before he whirled and dived for those guns. Crooked

26

to the last, you understand! Well, I was watching him from the corner of my eye, but I couldn't match that move. I was a half a second late, but when he pulled the trigger of the gun he had picked, it come down too slow to explode the cartridge, because the gun that he had scooped up in his hurry was my own. That gun had a hammer that was badly clogged with rust.

"I have always held it against myself that I didn't give him still another try. But matter of fact, I was so all-fired mad at him for trying to cheat me and get the jump on me, that way, that I just didn't have the brain to see things clear. I was like a charging bull. I didn't wait to think. I just reached for the other gun and I fired a split part of a second after Slader had made his try for me and failed. Well, sir, that gun that I picked up was Slader's own, and you can bet that one of *his* Colts was sure to be the newest model and the most active and straight-shooting kind! My slug went through his body, and he curled up in the middle of the floor, a dying man.

"Yes, sir, he should have been dead, because I believe that that bullet went right through his heart—or a corner of his heart. At least, that's what the doctors said afterward. But the fact that follows is something that there are witnesses to prove. When they busted through the door at the sound of the shooting, they saw Jack Slader twist himself around on the floor and heave himself up a little. I was leaning over him, and saying: 'Jack, what can be done for you?'

" 'I'm a dead man, Magruder,' says he. 'Curse your soul, I'm a dead man. There's nothing that can be done for me. But for Heaven's sake, do something for my boy!'

"You understand? There was I, standing over the first man that I had ever seen die, outside of a couple of accidents in mines. And I heard that dying man that I had killed, begging me to do something for his boy. What he said sunk deep into my heart. I couldn't forget it none at all. I started out after the crook was dead and I said to myself that If I could find the boy, I would take him home with me, and then I would try to make an honest man out of him.

27

"I did find him, sir. I found him and I took the little tiger home with me. And I've tried from that day to this to try to make him as honest as any man had ought to be. But you've seen him for your own self, sir. You know what he's like. Bad! Mighty bad! Meant for the gallows, he is. Because bad blood will out!"

CHAPTER 5

So SAYING, he shook back his hair and closed his eyes for a moment. With his brows wrinkled as though the pain of his thoughts for the moment overcame him, Rancher Newell regarded him with a proper awed respect; now that the keen hazel eyes were closed he could look at the man with more closeness than he had ventured before, and it seemed to Newell that the leonine face with its square-tipped, auburn beard was the noblest that he had ever seen. Moreover, he was more or less overwhelmed by the knowledge that this man, of his free will, had chosen to devote endless energy and time to the rearing of the wild-cat son of a gun fighter. That self-imposed duty had brought him forth on an all-night ride through a blinding storm—and Newell felt that his own virtues were shrinking to the vanishing point compared with the heroic qualities of the stranger.

After the departure of Magruder, the rancher for a long

time remained at the doorway, staring after the departing form of the big rider on the big horse. The last words of Magruder rang in his ears like a deep, grand strain of music.

"But ain't it dangerous?" he had asked Magruder. "Ain't it terribly dangerous to keep the kid around your house and your family?"

"I've got no family," Magruder had answered him, "and if I can maybe bring this kid to right ways of thinkin' and livin', why, I'm glad to take the chance of waking up, every morning, with my throat cut from ear to ear!"

With that, he had ridden away, leaving the rancher filled with a religious reverence behind him. Then the trailer took up the duties of his work. For actual trail itself, he paid no heed, as though he realized that nothing but chance could give him a glimpse of the footprint of that active and light-treading fugitive. He scanned the country carefully as he advanced, looking far to the right and the left as well as straight down the road. He had before him a long and easy road, just such a one as a traveler bound for the south would be glad to select. He knew the habits of the boy, however, and he felt that young Phil Slader would as soon keep to the open country while pursued, as a lobo would take to hunting in a populated country in the open day. No, where the nearest rough country and shelter from the eye might be found, there would the boy hide himself.

To the right, there was a tangle of willows and other water-loving trees along the course of a little stream. But the thicket was narrow and might be hunted with some ease and speed; moreover, travel would be slow through such screenings of underbrush. It seemed more likely to the hunter that the boy had taken to the broken highlands a mile or two to the left of the valley floor. Here there was little or no vegetation, but all was up and down and the surface of the ground was scattered over with sharp-edged rocks.

To the left, then, Magruder turned, and as he came into the broken lands, he put his horse forward at a stiff trot. For he knew how Phil Slader would be traveling, jogging along with the smooth, tireless gait of an Indian runner. Indeed, there would not be much difference between the speed of the active youngster covering such territory, and the speed of the trotting horse. For it was seldom that Magruder could send it along at a canter.

Moreover, each time that the land rose to a commanding crest he halted for a moment, and with his glasses pitched to his eyes, he swept the country with a brief and cunning survey. Gullies opened here and there, but Magruder, after an instant's survey in each case, took the wildest-appearing gorge which opened even vaguely toward the south. For such, he felt, would be the selection of the boy.

He made a halt to rest his horse and eat a handful of dried raisins. Then he pushed ahead again and in the middle of the afternoon he came across a light print of a set of naked toes at the margin of a little stream. For there, it seemed, some one had kneeled to drink. He dismounted, studied that print for a long moment, and then drew in a sharp breath of satisfaction. It was the print of the boy's foot, he knew and, as he pushed his horse farther along, he wondered at the truly wolfish skill with which Phil had been able to mask his trail as far as this point. Luck more than skill had kept Magruder on the right trail up to this point, as he well knew. But that sign of the boy looked very fresh and new-made, and a definite hope of making the capture that day rose high in the heart of the hunter.

There was another hour of strenuous riding, however, before he came to a pine-covered crest, and sweeping the country before him, he saw a figure jogging steadily and tirelessly not a quarter of a mile before him. Magruder took good heed of the course that the boy was following.

It pointed toward a trail down the side of a mountain, and there was another way of getting to the farther side of the mountain by riding down a shallow gorge on the right and then spurring up the slope to gain the same trail, and so meet the boy face to face. That is to say, all would be well if the course were not too strewn with rough rocks.

He sent his weary mustang into the gorge with a crashing of loosened stones rolling down behind him. He found the bottom of the gully fairly open and got footing, so with quirt and spur he sent the horse storming along its course. Even the rise up the side of the mountain beyond was easy enough, and in a few minutes Magruder had reached the very trail which his eye had picked out before.

It was narrow, but it was deeply worn. And the eye could pick it out easily as it wound across the mountains by the little white streaks and spots, here and there—the skeletons of animals dead a century since, perhaps. For this was an old route by which the Indians for centuries and the Spaniards for generations had crossed the highlands.

But there was no romance in the mind of Magruder. He paid no heed to the lofty beauty of the mountain, and to him the deep voice of the river that curved about the mountain's foot was a mere song of rejoicing in token of the victory that should be his.

In the meantime, he made as sure of everything as he could. He posted the horse, with thrown reins, behind a great boulder which would safely mask it. Then he himself crouched near the base of an old twisted pine that jutted out above the trail. The trunk gave some shelter to his body, and the rising rock also screened him from view, except directly from the trail beneath him.

In this place he waited until he saw Phil Slader work to the top of the ascent and then come at the usual swinging trot down the slope. He was drawn of face from the long and steady effort which he had made in the past few days. Besides, the sun was growing hot, and the rocks threw back the heat with redoubled effect. Beyond all of this the trail had taken a heavy toll by pitching up and down from slope to slope among the hills.

It looked, surely, as though the boy would go headlong past the place where Magruder was crouched, but when he came within half a dozen strides from the place, something must have stirred to attract his attention.

It could not have been anything he saw. Neither was it anything that Magruder, at least, had heard, for the deep, soft voice of the river, swelling ominously from beneath,

31

masked all the casual noises of stirring and breathing. But something, certainly, had come to the ear of the boy, for now he stood alert, with his keen eyes flashing toward the rock and the pine behind which Magruder was hiding. The man himself, though he was peering through the narrowest of slits between the rocks, felt that his very eye might be seen and shrank down.

He himself could see nothing, now, and he had to depend upon a chance ally—the sun, which now stood low in the sky and cast the heavy shadow of the pine tree and of the rock across Magruder as he waited, crouched upon hands and knees. At the same time it threw forward the shadow of the boy as Phil advanced little by little.

Once and again he came to a brief halt and retreated, as though in much doubt as to what he should do. But the way had been long, and the mountainside was steep, both above and below the danger point. Certainly reason must have told the boy that there could be no danger here except in his imagination. So, at the third start, he swung boldly forward and straight past the leaning rock.

Before he was well in view, Magruder leaped. He came like a springing catamount that launches itself wildly and well through the air. But fast though his movement was, and silent, also—Philip Slader heard and saw. He turned like a top when the string jerks it, and the long, keen hunting knife was in his hand. Another tenth part of a second and that knife would have been at work, but the time was not granted him. Magruder, reaching with a long arm and a fist rough as a rock and almost as solid, struck the boy along the side of the head, and dropped him as though with the blow of a club.

He fell backward and lay, slipping over the edge of the trail. A little more and he would have started on a rolling fall for the river, hundreds of feet below. This Magruder noticed, but with no particular horror. He caught the fallen body by one foot, jerked it back into the old trail, and then made a hasty search through the ragged clothes of Phil. There was nothing that could possibly serve as a weapon.

The hunting knife, which lay in the trail had now been

appropriated by the man, and all that remained to Phil, was a little twist of salt, done up in oiled cloth, together with a slender flint. By dint of many an artifice he would manage to catch game of some sort—or steal it, perhaps, where he could. The salt would season his meal. With the back of his knife he could raise a shower of sparks from the flint. It was a small equipment, yet with it the youngster was able to traverse the mountains freely and boldly.

To a city-bred man it would have been a miracle of no small size, but Magruder had known these qualities of young Slader too long to waste time in wonder now. Once he was sure that there was no further weapon in the possession of the boy, he simply set about methodically tying the ankles and the wrists of Philip together. When he had finished, the lad lay in a shapeless, helpless heap on the pathway.

Magruder let him lie. He lighted his pipe and, sitting back on the nearest rock, he puffed quietly at his smoke. He looked down at his captive with as much complacence as though this had been some great grizzly bear which he had brought down by dint of his hunting prowess.

The skin had split along the side of the boy's head, where the hard knuckles of Magruder had landed, but even the trickle of crimson and the swelling lump did not interest Magruder. He watched them with even a faint smile of satisfaction and, glancing down to his hand, he balled it into a fist again, turning it slowly back and forth, admiring its size and its strength.

At length, Phil Slader stirred without a groan and twisted himself at once into a sitting posture. For one instant he looked wildly about him as his brain strove to put him in touch with the realities of his situation. Then he saw big Magruder sitting solemn and silent beside and above him, and understanding came instantly and completely into the boy's face.

CHAPTER 6

IF MAGRUDER WERE familiar with many of the ways of his young charge, a great many of the characteristics of the youngster never lost their fascination for him. The physical abilities of Philip Slader were not such a miracle to him as they would have been to others. Magruder was a big, rough fellow, who was perfectly at home in the mountains—perfectly capable of taking care of himself with little more than Phil required on a long cross-country trip. He, too, had a quick hand, though it never could attain to the snaky speed which already belonged to the boy. He, too, was clothed with strength, and by virtue of his bulk and his maturity, that strength was far beyond the reach of the boy. What Phil Slader could do with eye and voice and foot and hand was no longer of paramount interest to Magruder.

He was more intrigued by the mental and spiritual qualities of the youngster. For instance, to the very roots of his soul he felt the silence with which Phil opened his eyes and looked about him, after having been knocked down and completely stunned, in the open trail.

Silence at such a time as that would have been beyond Magruder, the man. His lips fairly worked in sympathy and soundlessly framed the curses and invectives which he would have poured forth if *he* had been in the place of Phil Slader, and such an enemy had been before him. But to Magruder the greatest miracle of all was the steadiness of nerve with which the youngster was able to look straight up into the face of his captor.

Even now that Magruder sat there in the pride of his strength and the satisfaction of his conquest, he was not able to meet the steady black eye of the boy. His own was forced aside and down, and he pretended to busy himself in retamping the burning tobacco in his pipe bowl, and in shaking the ashes from the top of the glowing coal.

Perhaps it may seem to you that shame had some part in this behavior of the man? It did not. If Magruder knew nothing else in this world, he knew that no one was too old or too wise or too strong to be proud of having captured this will-o'-the-wisp upon the open trail. He had worked long and hard for his part, and he felt that he would like to publish his labor and his success to the entire world. Only the world would never understand. No one, indeed, could ever enter into his mind and understand the thing that he had done except, oddly enough, Phil Slader himself. For *he,* at least, did not underrate himself. It was not outraged dignity and scorn and shame that appeared in the eye of Phil, it was merely the calm acceptance of defeat at the hands of an equal.

"All right," said Magruder, "here we are again."

"Here we are again," said Phil calmly.

"And you've broke your promise to me."

"What promise?" said Phil.

"That you would never leave me."

"When did I give you any promise like that?"

"Why, it's handy for you to pretend to forget. But I know that you don't forget nothing, Phil. I know that pretty good."

Phil regarded the other for a long moment. Then he shrugged his shoulders. "Reach me my hat, will you?" said he. "The sun is sort of hard on the eyes."

"You ain't going to argue, eh?" said Magruder, disregarding this request. "You're above arguing with me, are you?"

35

"I know you," said Phil, "so why should I argue with you? You can think what you want and you can claim what you want, but I know you, Magruder!"

Magruder balled his fist, but as though he knew that there would be no use in attempting physical brutality, he relaxed his hand again.

"You're rare," said he. "Cursed if you ain't all by yourself when it comes to queerness. You know me, do you?"

"Oh, yes," said Phil Slader. "You ain't so hard to learn. Not hard at all."

You could not have called it impertinence, even to an older man like Magruder. It was simply a grave statement of facts.

"All right," said Magruder. "I dunno why I don't pick you up and heave you into the river, though! But you might tell me what it is that you know so well about me!"

"Sure," said the boy. "I don't mind telling you the main thing which is that telling the truth just plain hurts you. You can't do it without pretty near crying, you like to lie so bad."

"Curse your sneaking hide!" cried the man with a snarl.

"No, I'm bad but I'm not a sneak," said Phil, gravely considering his own virtues and faults as though they were the merest intangible abstractions. "I don't lie, either. You know that, Magruder."

"Ain't I taught you to call me Uncle Doc?"

The boy smiled. "We're alone now," said he, "and it don't make no difference."

"It gets you into bad habits," said Magruder.

"Habits don't mean nothing so far as you're concerned with me now," said Phil Slader. "I ain't gunna be living with you now."

"You ain't, eh?"

"No."

"You're gunna break that promise that you give me, four years ago?"

"You keep comin' back to that. But you ought to remember what I said when we talked things over. You said that my father wanted me to go to you. There's others that heard him say the same thing. So I said that I would go, though I couldn't see why. I wouldn't be much use till I was ten. I would stay on two years after that, working at chores, and such, for my keep. And after that I would be free. Four years was what we agreed on, and I stuck by my promise to the day. I don't break my word!"

Mr. Magruder seemed a little put out by the definiteness of these statements.

"I see how it is," said he. "You think that during the last two years you've done enough to pay me back for all of the trouble and the care and the money that I've put out on you. You figure it that way, eh?"

"Look here," said Philip Slader, as calm as ever, "it sure beats anything the way that you talk. A fellow would think, to hear you, that I didn't know you, or that you didn't know me. But we do. I know you, and you know me. There ain't any use whining to me. You can make other folks think that you mean what you say. But I know you, Magruder. You never would of brought me home, no matter what my father said, if it hadn't been that you see how you could use me. Oh, I didn't see through it first. But long ago I knew what it meant, of course. You've had me there like a signpost to draw folks. It seemed queer and generous on your part to take in the son of an old enemy of yours. Folks was talking about you, Magruder. You had never done anything worth while so long as you lived, except to kill Jack Slader. But all that they could remember was that you had finished him. And you wanted to make the most of that. That's why you took me in."

Magruder reached out a hasty hand to strike the mouth which was making these condemning assertions. But his hand was checked as it had been a thousand times in the past by the unmoved expression of Phil.

"You got the brain of a rat," said Magruder, "always working out the darkest and meanest reasons for everything. You wouldn't give no credit to God for making the world. You would only say that He did it when He couldn't think of nothing better to do!"

To this half-snarling complaint Phil listened thought-

37

fully—not meditating on the speech so much as upon the speaker, as though he were letting the true conception of Magruder sink deep and deeper into his mind.

"But it ain't the fact," said Magruder. "It was just bigness of heart that made me take you in, and the whole world knows it, except you!"

"Jiminy," said Phil softly, "I should think it would be a terrible relief to you to know that I understand you for what you are—and to know that it wasn't no use for you to try play acting around me. I should think that it would make you glad, because it would be so restful. But you won't let down. You still got to act up to your part all the time! Well, fire away. I'm listening."

"Why," shouted Magruder, "I ask God to witness me— what good could I get out of a useless brat like you?"

"All right," said Phil, "just tell me why it was that you stopped trying to ranch and opened up your hotel, right after you got hold of me?"

"That?" said Magruder, writhing as though the rock he sat on had turned white hot. "Why, the ranch wasn't paying me. And I thought of a hotel. Nothing strange about that!"

"No," said the boy, "but pretty sudden and pretty pat it come in—right after you got hold of me to draw the crowds for you. Ain't that a fact?"

Magruder merely sat and stared. He tried to speak, but when his lips parted, no sound would come. He seemed more than half strangled by what he heard.

The boy continued: "And they come to you well enough. Every puncher that rides through the country within ten miles of your place, he goes out of his way because he wants to see the man that killed Jack Slader— and that then started in taking care of Jack Slader's son. You get your glory and you get your money too. But if I left, you wouldn't have such an easy time for long!"

"Curse you for a lyin' ingrate!" muttered Magruder. "You'll be saying before long that I *didn't* kill Jack Slader and in a fair fight!"

"You killed Jack Slader well enough," said the boy.

"More folks know that than know you. But how could it of been in fair fight?"

This shot brought Magruder to his feet with a roar. "You doubt *that*?" he shouted like a true believer hearing the first tenet of his faith denied.

"I dunno," said Phil. "I don't see how you could ever of stood up to him, seeing that you're so afraid of me, even!"

"I'm afraid of you, am I?" asked Magruder.

The boy nodded.

"And why should I be afraid?" asked Magruder, dangerously quiet in turn.

"Because," said Phil Slader, "one of these days I might get hold of the news about the real way that you fought my dad. And if I found out that it *wasn't* fair . . . ."

"Well?" said Magruder.

"I'd kill you, Magruder."

They stared at one another, too deeply moved for the use of explosive words. The sham melted from the face of Magruder and left there only cunning and hard malice.

"Well," said he, "I'll tell you this. There's only one thing that keeps me from taking you by the heels and slinging you over the edge of the cliff here to mash on the rocks underneath, and then to wash away down the river."

"The one thing is the way that I'm needed at the hotel," said Phil.

And even Phil blinked with surprise when Magruder answered as calmly as he: "Ay, kid; you've hit the nail on the head!"

CHAPTER 7

AFTER THIS, a pause fell between the two and into the
pause ran the deep voice of the river, humming like a
chanted chorus far below them. But the mask was now
thrown off, and each saw the fact as the other revealed it.

"That's good," said Phil, at last. "Now we're open and
square with each other. Dog-goned if it don't tickle me to
see how plain and open you're hating me with your eyes!"

"It tickles you, eh?"

"Yes."

"It'll tickle you less before I'm through. I say that
you've put your finger on the sore place. I need you at
the hotel. Everybody wants to have a look at the son of
Jack Slader. They know him, by the pictures, anyway.
And they can see him all over again in you. They come
along there to study the makings of a bad man. If it
wasn't for you, my hotel wouldn't take in five dollars cash
in a week!"

"Aye," said Phil. "I know that." He added with heat:
"And there's one thing that the fools don't understand—
that I *won't* turn out crooked. I'm gunna go straight in
spite of what everybody expects out of me. I'm gunna go
straight as a string!"

His enthusiasm was all boyish, now. It faded as the
other replied:

40

"I've told you why I need you and need you bad. I like the easy life there at the hotel. Nothing for me to do. The colored boy does all the care of the hotel. The chink does the cooking. You do the chores, and all that I got to do is to lie back and count out the money, as she rolls in, and play the big man in front of the crowd."

Phil nodded, smiling a little for the first time. "Why, Uncle Doc," said he, "if you'd always be fair and square and in the open with me, like this, I'd pretty near come to like you! It ain't your crookedness that I hate; it's the sneakin' way that you have of pretending to be a regular saint that makes me sick of you!"

Magruder waved this pleasant comment aside. He went on: "I'll be frank and open enough with you, kid. You'll wish for some kind lies, before I'm through with you! You'll wish for them a whole lot! I say that those are the reasons why I need you. Then I'll tell you what's against you. I know that you hate me, I know that some day you're going to turn bandit and crook, just like your old man. It's in your blood—bad blood, and it's sure to come out!"

He smiled a little with a savage satisfaction as he brought out this point, as though he knew beforehand exactly how the taunt would affect the boy. He was not disappointed; it brought a yell of rage from Phil.

"You lie!" cried the son of Jack Slader. "You lie like a coward. Let me get away from these here ropes, and I'll make you eat them words like a . . . ."

He choked with his blind fury and then leaned back in his cords, panting, and crimson of face.

"You'll go crooked," went on Magruder, with the same fierce delight in the pain which he was inflicting. "You'll go crooked, because all of the crooked signs are in you. What makes a man a crook? Knowing that he can shoot straighter and hit harder and run faster than other folks. That's what makes him a crook. He says to himself, why should I go ahead and work my hands off to make a few dollars—no more than the rest of these bums are making? All that I got to do is to lie back easy and let them make

41

their wages. And when they've collected, then I'll just go around and collect from them—with a gun!"

"That's the way that *you'd* work it out!" cried Phil, trembling. "You'd work it out that way, if you had the nerve to try it!"

The big man waved this taunt away from him. "I'm getting down to the brass tacks, now," said he, "and I want for you to listen like you'd never heard me speak before. I say that you're going crooked, and when you do you'll come for me like a cat for milk. I'll be older and slower and not so strong, then. I'm thirty-two now. In another ten years, I'll be forty-two, and there aint so many springs in the muscles and the nerves of a man, when he's forty-two. You understand me? And when you come for me, most likely you'd get me good. You'd murder me, Phil!"

The boy waited, saying nothing, watching with a consuming interest.

"Now," said the hotel keeper, developing his idea slowly, "to keep you from murdering me, one day, the main thing is just to pick you up by the heels and heave you into the river down there. If you're ever found, what'll people say?"

"Don't you say it!" cried Phil, writhing as under lash. "Don't you dare to say it, or I *will* find a way to kill you!"

"They'll only say," said Magruder, choosing his words with a devilish care, "that the son of bad Jack Slader was picked up dead—and a lucky thing that the hangman was saved work by that."

"No!" screamed the boy. Tears of passion and of helpless revolt stood in his eyes. "No," he shouted again. "Curse you, I say no! They won't dare to say it! I've never done a man harm; I've never so much as hit a boy, even if he was bigger than me!"

Big Magruder rocked himself back and forth and chuckled. "You're poison, kid, and you know it. You're poison and the other folks can see what you are. It's written right there in your face for them all to read. But do you have to ask me? Can't you see in their eyes what they think of you? Can't you hear it in their voices when your back is turned?"

The head of Phil dropped upon his breast.

"Now listen to me," went on Magruder. "I want you to understand that I could throw you over the cliff, and nobody would so much as guess what had happened. If they did, they would only be glad that the world was saved from seeing you grow up as bad as you promise to be—and I tell you, kid, that the fear of you as you may be one day would make me a fool *not* to kill you. But there's one thing that stands in my way. There's one thing that holds me up."

"You like your easy time!" said the boy, sneering. "Oh, I knew that that would come out some day."

"I like my easy time," admitted Magruder without the least trace of shame, "and I know that there is one thing that I *can* trust to in you. If I get a real promise out of you, you won't break your word."

"Would you trust the oath of a crook?" muttered the boy.

"I don't try to explain it," said Magruder. "All I know is that it hurts you like the devil to break your promise. I don't know that you've out and out lied in these four years—which is pretty near more than human!"

The boy sat a little straighter.

"Now, kid," said Magruder, "I make you a good bargain. You give me your word to stick by me—not forever, but until you're growed up and my hotel is so dog-gone well established that folks won't *have* to be dragged there to see you. Say you swear that you'll stick by me for ten years at the hotel, and then you'll be free. And besides that, you'll swear that no matter what happens, you'll never raise a hand against me."

"Or else?" questioned the boy.

"Or else I chuck you over the edge of the cliff and lean over to watch you splash down there below. You understand me?"

"Suppose," said Phil, apparently finding this a reasonable bargain enough, "suppose that I find out, some day, that you *did* murder dad, instead of fighting him fair and square?"

"I'd have your oath to protect me, if you was to get

43

such a fool idea into your head," said Magruder. "What's your answer, kid?"

"I couldn't do it," said Phil. "I wouldn't give you no oath. If I found out . . . ."

Magruder, with a shout of anger, caught up the boy and swung him back and forth.

"Now talk turkey and talk it quick," said he.

"I'll see you cursed first," said Phil Slader. "Do you think that I'm a welcher, to be bluffed out like this?"

Magruder flung him down with a groan. "I'll have your oath—for ten years you work for me and never leave me, no matter what happens. For ten years, you're my man, kid. You take care of me—fight for me—stick right by me through thick and thin. And no matter what you might get against me, you pocket it up. At the end of the ten years, you're free to murder me the next day, if you can!"

"Ten years," said the boy slowly, and he closed his eyes in thought. "It's being a slave, pretty near, for ten years," he translated. "But I got to do it, I suppose. Magruder, cut this rope, and I'll shake hands with you on that deal!"

CHAPTER 8

IT IS NOT pleasant to skip ten whole years in a life as eventful as Phil Slader's. There was hardly a month that something did not happen to him, in one way or another.

But there are ways of summing up even such a period as this.

For instance, one might say that he spent the ten years working for Uncle Doc. Or again, one might say that he spent those ten years fighting silently to win public opinion to his favor. Each of those remarks could stand a great deal of expanding.

He worked for Uncle Doc Magruder afield and in the house, and as time went on he became not a dulled attraction, but an exceedingly greater one. For, as he stretched up out of boyhood to youth and then toward man's estate, a keen expectancy began to develop. Here and there were people who pointed out that the boy had done nothing wrong, and there was at least a *chance* that he might turn out as well as another. But for one who retained such flattering ideas, there were a hundred who shook their heads when they looked at the boy and then compared his features with those of the pictures of his father.

"Or worse!" was the common remark. "As bad as Jack Slader or even worse. Because there was something gay about Jack. But there's nothing gay about *this* gent. Mean looking—that's what he is."

Again and again turned up the phrase which Magruder had put into circulation so often.

"Bad blood will out!"

So they shook their heads, and the word went far and wide that if men cared to look upon the face of the next outlaw who would terrorize the mountains, they had better ride their horses in the direction of the hotel near Crusoe, where Doc Magruder was the host, because they would see, in the flesh, young Phil Slader, son of Jack of the same dreadful name!

And they came in steady shoals. One might think that fourteen years would have dimmed their memories. But memories do not dim in the great West—not when they have to do with a figure of such epic proportions as that same Jack Slader. They had heard their fathers and grandfathers speak of him. He was as familiar a picture as ever, and when they rode out, their eyes bright with the memories of him, and saw young Phil, they came away again speaking in voices ominously low.

"The sheriff should keep a close eye on that young man!" was the common opinion.

Then they would carry their doubts and their head-shakings to Sheriff Holmer, the fattest and the most cheerful sheriff who ever groaned on the saddle of a Rocky Mountain trail. From Sheriff Holmer they met no very great encouragement, for he was as apt as not to say to them: "I hear you folks talk. But what'll you have me do? Put him in jail before he's done something wrong?"

"Well, sheriff," they would say, "you know that 'an ounce of prevention is better than a pound of cure.' "

"Cure him of what?" the sheriff would make answer. "What'd you ever hear of him doing?"

"Look at his face, and you'll see what I mean!" they would caution Holmer.

But Holmer invariably replied: "He's the only kid in the county that don't pack a gun, and that don't go shooting."

"Rabbits ain't the kind of game that *he'll* be after!" they said to Holmer.

"Well," said Sheriff Holmer always, in concluding these debates, which were apt to grow extremely heated, "all I can say is that that lad walks quiet and talks quiet and never passes any lip to his elders and never fights. Have you ever heard of him pulling a knife or a gun on any one? Have you even so much as heard of him using his fists on anybody? I tell you that I've kept my eyes open and my ears open, and I ain't heard or seen anything like that connected with young Slader. No two men are alike. Not even father and son. Leave the kid be, say I!"

These friendly speeches on the part of the sheriff did not change the course of public opinion. Let a few think what they would, the great majority were prepared to hear of some dire catastrophe enacted by the hands of Phil.

He knew it, of course. And it was for that very reason that he watched himself with a more than scrupulous care. No doubt he had as many hungerings after a day of sport

46

with his gun as any other youngster in the whole range. But he never let a gun come into the grip of his fingers. Frankly, he was afraid of himself. For who can be so thoroughly sure of himself that public suspicion, long maintained, will not at the last eat into his soul and make him afraid of what may come out of his own hands? The same stern self-control which had prevented him from striking young Sammy Newell on another day, kept him from entering into other quarrels. As a matter of fact, he did not need to be overcareful in this for the simple reason that other young men of his own age refrained from suggesting disagreeable subjects to Phil Slader.

I suppose, on the whole, that there was never a more thoroughly unhappy young man in this world than was Phil, as he lived through his novitiate.

He was twelve and a month more, when he had entered into that ten-year agreement with Uncle Doc Magruder. His twenty-first birthday found him still living according to the letter of his promise. He hated Magruder; he knew that the hotel keeper was making daily capital out of his ward. He knew that a thousand insidious lies were being circulated about him by Magruder's sinister tongue. But still he controlled himself.

Work was his refuge. Magruder had nothing to say against schemes of labor which were for his own benefit. The result was that the forty acres around the hotel were improved as no other forty acres in the whole county, though the county was as large as an Eastern State. There were thrifty rows of apple trees flourishing at a great rate, hardy stock which endured the sharpness of the winters and in the autumn bore a great, red-cheeked fruitage, so many tons of it, in strong barrels, that Magruder could not use all of the fruit for cider and had to send some away to sell in the towns, getting such a price for it that he was amazed. Besides the orchards, there were some smooth acres along the creek which were flattened and checked by Phil with much labor, and brought into bearing of alfalfa.

When water was needed for the various crops during the summer, a neatly arranged dam piled up the waters in the bed of the creek until the alfalfa stubble could be flooded. Beside apples and alfalfa, he kept cows enough to turn out a good supply of butter—far more than the hotel could use. And another handsome profit, from the excess, flowed into the pockets of Magruder. For all of these affairs cost him very little.

At the urgent and repeated plea of Phil, he had finally allowed him a little spare money. With that money Phil Slader had fitted up a forge and blacksmith shop. Plowshares were sharpened there, and the rickety, rolling stock on the little ranch was repaired with fresh ironwork. The neighbors, too, came into the habit of bringing down their broken wagons and their disordered mowing machines to Magruder's place. Magruder's price was no cheaper than that of the Crusoe blacksmith, but the work was better, and besides, it was a pleasure to be able to say: "That rake was fixed up for me last week by Jack Slader's son!"

All of these avenues of revenue constantly increased, at a rate which astonished even the optimistic mind of Doc Magruder. He should have accumulated a fat bank account on the strength of all this income, piled on top of the tidy sums which the hotel itself brought to him, but one of the little weaknesses of Doc was poker, a habit which tends to keep a man's purse as thin in the ribs as a healthy dog.

If you wonder why men did not attribute more undoubted virtues to such an industrious youth, the key was, on the one hand, their natural suspicions of Jack Slader's son, and on the other hand the tales which Magruder was constantly pouring into their ears.

"He's just preparing himself for a break," Magruder would say. "Look at those hands of his! They got to be busy. He'd die if he didn't have something for them to do. Jerking a gun out of a holster would please him a lot better than any other kind of exercise, of course, and since he can't do that, he falls back on nursing the handles of a plow or swinging a sledge hammer. Listen to him yonder. Listen, will you? D'you think that that's a tack hammer that he's rattling out the strokes with so fast? No, sir, that's a fourteen-pound sledge. Wait till I open the window and

48

you'll hear it more plain. Fourteen pounds, and he handles it like a feather—like a feather, gents!

"No, sir, he's got to let off his steam some way, and what the jangling of that iron on iron means is: 'Some day I'll take this out on all the suckers that have let me grow up to be a man! I'll show them what they've done!' Because this here kid is a thinker. Silent and dark is what he is, and always thinking. He ain't busted loose yet. The reason is that though he looks close to thirty, that's because he has the habit of frowning, which had made him more serious. Matter of fact, he's not quite twenty-two. And he wants to come fully into himself before he cuts away! And, in the meantime, he keeps busy with work the hands that he means to keep filled with mischief, one of these days!"

Who can doubt a father when he speaks of the faults which he admits in a son? And who could have doubted big, hearty Magruder, lamenting the sad qualities of the lad that he said he groaned in trying to raise right for fourteen years?

Such were the ways of Phil Slader and such were the speeches with which Magruder rewarded him. Though Phil knew it all, he set his teeth and endured and prayed for the day of his freedom. For when that day came, he wanted to startle this doubting world by a proof of his quiet virtue. On the very day that he left Magruder, he intended to go down to the blacksmith in Crusoe town and there take a position as an apprentice! An heroic resolution? No, for the very fingers of Phil Slader itched with the love of craftsmanship.

As I have said, the history of the ten long years can be sketched in or inferred, if you choose. Now there were exactly three months before the day of liberation should come for Phil. The three months seemed to him so long that he had to grit his teeth to force himself to endure. But his will was iron, and endure he would. He had no doubt of that. Had he not been tempted a thousand times? Yes, and every time he came through the test with flying colors! Three months, then, still remained, when Magruder on an ever-unlucky day hurried out from his hotel one morning and stood looking about him, his eyes filled with a sudden resolution. Finally, he heard a sound that told him where to look—a deep throated voice that called from time to time from the direction of the alfalfa fields beside the creek.

Mr. Magruder struck out for the spot with a swinging stride. His wallet was packed with currency. His heart was light. If he had known anything worth singing, he would have attempted a song on this morning of mornings. So joyous was his spirit that it had even overflowed with kindliness in the direction of the person who, in all the world, he most feared.

CHAPTER 9

HE HAD LOCATED the voice correctly, because when he had passed beyond the orchard and the pasture he could see Philip Slader behind a plow drawn by four horses. He should have had a plow on high wheels with a gauge and lever for regulating the depth to which the share sank, for he was now engaged in the heavy labor of plowing up an alfalfa field for reseeding. No, it would not be planted in alfalfa again, but in some grain, perhaps, to change the quality of the soil before the alfalfa was brought in again.

But, in the meantime, there was Philip, doing the work of a more costly machine with a hand plow of his own contriving. It had a wonderfully deep and well-tempered share, held by a long and narrow plow beam and footing, and that narrowly angled cutting edge tore through the enmeshed alfalfa roots to a great depth. The hotel proprietor, listening, could hear the stout old roots snapping with muffled explosions beneath the rich ground, as the plow cut through them. Six horses could be used more profitably for such work as this, but Philip had only four at his disposal, for Mr. Magruder was by no means anxious to waste money on unnecessary objects. Moreover, Magruder knew that Philip would get the labor of six horses out of four, if he were put to it.

They were doing that, and more, as Magruder now looked at them, with their heads down and their hip straps lifting above their backs as they tugged patiently and together.

They struck some hidden obstacle beneath the surface, some knot of tangled roots or some stratum of extra hard earth. The shock staggered Phil Slader, but he recovered himself and with his voice caught the four horses as they were recoiling from the heavy jerk on their traces. His shout was like a blow of four whips, nicely timed—except that no stroke of a whip ever sent a horse into the collar with pricking ears. They laid down to their work like the tried veterans they were. There was a faint groaning beneath the ground, and then the plow lurched forward, with Philip reeling along behind it, steadying the jerking handles.

Magruder watched, amazed. The fine pulling of the sweating horses pleased him, in part, but after the first glance he paid them no further heed. Their power was one thing, but it was brute power. This strength behind the handles of the plow was a different matter. He had known that Philip was a youth of stout thews. As he watched young Slader staggering down the furrow, meeting the jerks and twists of the rebellious handles, he knew that here was one doing the work of three—a clever driver to manipulate the team and two strong and skillful fellows to hold that leaping, twisting, unlucky plow straight.

Even Philip Slader felt the effect of his exertions. His

face was streaming with perspiration. He reached the end of the furrow; his voice turned the team like so many well-trained men. Then, with a wrench and a tug he tore the plow out and around; he was driving the point in to start the new furrow when Magruder's voice stopped him. He leaned on the handles of the plow, wiped his forehead, and waited. As always, he was neither surly nor snarling, but rather grimly thoughtful and observant.

However, there was such inward sunshine in Mr. Magruder that he could shine even through such a cloud as this.

He said: "This here ground look different than I ever seen it before, Phil. How come it's so much blacker?"

"It's that much richer," said Phil.

"And little white lumps down here on the roots?"

"Nitrogen in those little white lumps. I'll get forty sacks of barley for every acre of this stuff, or call me a liar, Doc."

"Forty sacks!" cried Magruder, honestly astonished. "Forty sacks? Why, that would come over the crops that they brag about down on the bottoms."

"I'm writing it down to the smallest thing we'll get," said Philip. "We might hit sixty."

"Bless my soul!" said Magruder, which was the most innocuous oath that he knew, by long odds.

He added: "But I don't see why you have to rip the heart out of a good field like this! The last crop . . . ."

"Patchy," said Philip curtly. "It's getting patchy. When you get alfalfa stubble that looks like a gent just beginning to get bald, that's the time to rip her up, before she goes all bad. Keep the land working right up to the limit, Doc. That's the way that you'll make money farming!"

"Aye, but it ain't!" said Doc with real emotion. He pointed. "It's you, kid, that's made this land yield so big!"

"Humph," said Phil. "Well, I got to get on with this job, Doc, unless you need me for something. I don't want these hosses to get cold on the job. Bess, there, is kind of sore on the point of the shoulder, and she takes a lot of

52

persuading to make her hit the collar after she gets a bit cooled off."

"Why not carry a blacksnake along with you, Phil? Cursed if a blacksnake ain't by long odds the quickest persuader of a hoss to change its mind from wrong to right! Why not pack one? Ain't you got a chance to use it, hanging onto that plow?"

Philip raised his head a little and looked at the older man in the familiar way, not in contempt and not in disgust, but rather with a thoughtful appreciation of just what Magruder was. It was a subject which never failed to fill him with interest.

"Yes," he said dryly. "That's the reason that I don't carry a whip. My hands are full without it. Well, Doc, what is it? Are you going to get married?"

"No," said Magruder. "I'm forty, but I'm not foolish yet. Came out here to suggest that you take a day off and come to town with me, kid. They're gunna start that rodeo to-day."

"You been drinking," suggested Phil Slader. "You don't mean that you want me to lay off work?"

"I mean it a hundred per cent. A hundred per cent, Phil. You and me are going in to bust ourselves."

"I see," said Phil, nodding.

"You see what?"

"You cleaned up that gang of tenderfeet, last night, at poker?"

"That? Oh, yes. I got something out of them. But . . . ."

"But ain't it dangerous, Doc? Tell me, ain't it dangerous to keep right on trimming the suckers, like that? Every time a real experienced, crooked gambler comes along, he lifts most of your money right out of your pocket in no time. But then the boys come in that have got their coin out of honest work—the gents with the callouses on their fingers—and you hold them up and slip across some of your phony sleight of hand. Why, Doc, I don't see how you get away with it!"

"Get away with what?" asked Doc Magruder, staring, and very much embarrassed. "You ever suspect that I . . . ."

"That you stacked the cards? Yes, and a darned poor job that you do of it. I have eyes, Doc. I'm not blind. And the crimp that you put in the side of that pack when you run it up is big enough for a blind baby to see."

"Why," began Magruder, "matter of fact I never played a crooked . . . ."

The smile of Phil Slader stopped him.

"All right!" said Magruder with a sudden sigh. "You're not going to be bluffed out. But I never trimmed anybody the way that *I've* been robbed. Never! Would be ashamed to hold up folks the way that some of the sneaks have held up me. Criminal, Phil. Darned if it ain't criminal what some men will do with the cards. Now, what about coming to town with me, old boy? What about Crusoe, to-day, and a look at that rodeo?"

"Thanks," said Phil Slader. "But to-day, if you want to give me time off, I'll lay around here and do some tinkering with the forge. The bellows don't work up half the draft they ought to—and I'm thinking of putting a wheel . . . ."

"Curse the blacksmith shop! Sonny, you're coming in with me. And I'll tell you why you're coming. I've seen you grinding out here long enough, and now I want you to come in with me and have a holiday while I pick you out a new sombrero—a real one, old son, that will make you look like something under it!"

Phil Slader shook his head, smiling in his faint way. "I don't understand, Doc," said he. "You're different. You're sort of expanding to-day. You'll rise and float right up to heaven, in another minute. Wait till I get washed up and some other clothes on."

He put up the team and plunged into a tub; in an astonishingly short time, they were in the buckboard, side by side, with the old, down-headed buckskin mare dragging them loyally but haltingly toward the town.

"Now," said the younger man, "tell me what you want out of me to-day, Doc?"

The other flashed an irritated side glance at his companion; then he shrugged his heavy shoulders. "Well," said he, "I won't try to fool with you. It's partly because

I really want that you should come to town and have a little time off and a vacation from the farm work that you seem to like so well. But matter of fact, I'm going to meet a bad actor this here day and pay him twenty dollars that I've owed to him for a long time. Y'understand? A real bad one, son, and he wrote to me when he broke jail that he would expect me in town to-day to pay him back. He didn't say where he would be, either. But I'll have to go in!"

"You're going in," repeated Phil Slader, "and you're going to look up a fellow that you're afraid of and pay him some money that you owe him. And you want me along for a sort of a bodyguard, eh?"

"Yes," admitted the big man. "That's the long and the short of it, I suppose. I want your protection, and I want you to take this here gun . . . ."

But Phil Slader shrank as from poison.

"Doc," said he, "it's hard enough for me to go straight as it is. But if I had a gun, it would make the temptation be too great! Tell me the name of this bucko that you say you're going to meet."

"Well, you've heard of him times enough. It's no less a man than 'Lon' Kirby!"

CHAPTER 10

OF COURSE, PHIL had heard of him. Most other people had. Lon Kirby had not had many years in which to make himself well known. He had achieved his life work, so far, in the scant span of three or four years. It was not that he was any child, but out of his forty years or more he had spent some twenty-five in reform schools or in penitentiaries, and with infancy subtracted, you will see that the remainder is not very large. However, it had been enough for Lon. He was a specialist. He had a fondness for study of a particular kind. The science of safe combinations was the lore which he loved, and he liked to study it at night, with the aid of nothing more than a flash light or a bull's-eye lantern. He had pursued his investigations in various parts of the country, and though his time had been so badly-limited, Lon had achieved certain results that kept him in the front pages of the newspapers. Indeed, it was the boast of Lon that he had never receded farther back than the second page of a metropolitan daily, and this was a record of which he was inordinately vain. It was said that he had taken sums amounting, in all, to several millions of dollars—from various banks. And here he was, loose again!

"When did he get out?" asked young Phil Slader.

"When did he get out?" repeated his guardian. "You don't read the papers, or nothing, do you?"

"No, I don't put much time in on them."

"They don't pack enough news about alfalfa to please you," said Doc, sneering. "But the fact is that he got loose more than ten days ago. And he croaked a guard, when he was getting loose!" Magruder chuckled with a venomous pleasure as he spoke. "He's here now. That's all that I know. He's probably hard up for cash until he pulls off another job. He shook his pursuers off and he got here, curse him!"

Phil Slader regarded him in silence for a moment.

"If you're afraid of him, why don't you turn in a report to the sheriff?"

"Afraid of him?" cried Magruder. "Only the way that you'd be afraid of a snake. Give me any man that'll stand up to me, and I'll handle him, well enough. But this Lon Kirby, he's different. Smooth as silk and more slippery. He'd slip in between them folks and he'd get at me, no matter how hard they tried to protect me and catch him. No, I won't tell the sheriff. I'm not that ready to get a bullet through the back! But I need you, kid. If you won't pack a gun—why, so much the worse for me. But I'm glad to have even them bare hands of yours along. They'll make trouble for that Kirby if he tackles me!"

They had jogged the horse to the top of a small rise of land and now they saw before them a rolling and rising head of dust that shaped its way rapidly toward them out of the distance.

"Well," said Phil Slader, "there's some of the boys that ain't riding toward the rodeo today. Look at that!"

The dust cloud dissolved. Shadowy shapes appeared and then hard-riding horsemen, who swept up the slope and poured about the buckboard.

The fat form of Sheriff Mitchel Holmer was ominously to the fore, shouting: "Have you seen a rider going up the road or across the country in this direction? Seen anybody at all, Magruder?"

"Nobody worth naming," said Magruder. "What's up?"

"The sort of work where we need a hand like yours,

Magruder, to help us out. Here's a trail almost as important as that of . . . ."

He stopped short, looking at young Phil Slader.

Magruder nodded. "I'd like to help," said he, "if I saw that you had a hoss that would pack my weight. But you ain't got one of that type. Tell me—what's up?"

"That hound, Lon Kirby, is loose again—turned loose on us, worse luck! Why couldn't he of picked out some county besides mine?"

"What's he done?"

"What *ain't* he done? Well, I got to get along."

"Bumped somebody off, Sheriff?"

"No, walked into the Crusoe bank in broad daylight and stuck up the whole gang in there—four men, all with guns—but when they saw the rat face of Kirby they turned to water. Did just what he wanted; opened all the safes, handed out the stuff to him. He jammed more than a hundred thousand into a canvas sack and went out and climbed on his hoss. The only shooting they got was at his back, just as he scooted around the corner of the street. Of course, they didn't hit him. He drifted out in this direction—think of it! Broad daylight!"

The sheriff, with a moan, spurred his horse away down the road, and the posse of a dozen dusty, long-faced men followed him.

"They ain't riding with no heart at all," said Phil, looking back. "They'll never catch him at this rate."

"How can you tell?"

"By the way that they're stringing out over the road. Something terrible. They want to be back there at the rodeo, and the sheriff, he's had to gather them up by main force. I figure that not many would be volunteering to capture Kirby. He must be quite a man!"

"He's poison, the skunk. I hate him. Everybody hates him. Got no friends at all! But—a hundred thousand dollars—a hundred thousand dollars! And to think that only a short time ago he would have been glad of the twenty I owe him!"

He closed his eyes with a groan.

"It wouldn't do you no good if you had a hundred

thousand," said the boy. "You'd get in a couple of big games and get excited. You'd drop the first half and then you'd sit in at another game to win back what you'd lost the first time. And the rest of it would follow."

Magruder shook his head. "There's a difference between big things and little things," he said. "There's a big difference. I can throw away the small pieces of change that have come my way. They never amounted to anything. But you know what I'd do with a hundred thousand berries?"

"I dunno. Sit down cross-legged and play with it?"

"I'd soak it all into a good set of bonds, kid. Municipal. That would be my game. You can pick out seven per cent, at that stuff. A hundred thousand iron men, all working every day and every night! Ah, that's the grand thing about money, kid. It never stops. It never gets tired out or old or lame. It never quits, but keeps on piling up a mite more for you every day so long as you live, or them that you leave it all to! A hundred thousand!"

He paused and drew in his breath through his teeth. "That would be seven thousand dollars a year!"

"No!" said the boy.

"It would, though. Figure it for yourself."

"Never thought. Why, Doc, folks commit robberies for a lot less than even the interest on that much cash!"

"Don't I know it? And don't it fair make me sick to think that that much coin is locked up in the dirty hands of Lon Kirby? Oh, but I *do* know it! And it tires me. It plumb fatigues me, kid. I can tell you that. Seven thousand iron men every year is all that I would be taking in if I had that chunk of money that Kirby has managed to grab. That's twenty dollars for every day of my life. Think of that! Twenty dog-gone dollars that I didn't work for, and coming in every day of my life. Secure— no chance of losing it—no chance of gambling it away. Oh, kid, I hate the heart of that Lon Kirby for making a scoop like that, and here I am, worth ten like him, and living out here in the dirt, as you may say. Ain't it enough to bust your heart, pretty near?"

Phil Slader smiled and clucked to the horse. He always

59

drove, for the very good reason that he could get more mileage out of a horse than even the whip of Magruder could manage.

"My heart aches for you, Doc," said he.

"You young whelp!" muttered Magruder. "Well, I hope that this here loss puts a crimp in the pocket money of Alden Turner."

"He's the president of the bank?"

"He is just that, old son. He is just that, and nothing more, except that he's the worst skinflint, and the hardest-boiled pig that ever made life miserable for the folks that might happen to owe him a mite of money, here and there along the way. No good—all mean—iron all the way through. That's the style of that fellow, my boy, and don't you forget it!"

Some rumors to the same effect had reached even the rather removed and unworldly ears of Phil Slader; therefore he nodded and digested the tidings.

He merely said: "But of course you're joking, Doc. If you got your hands on a hundred thousand of stolen money, you'd be sure to take it right in to the sheriff to be returned to the rightful owner?"

Magruder laughed and glanced aside until he saw what was at least a semblance of calm gravity on the face of his companion. And then he burst forth into curses.

"Take it back to the rightful owners!" he cried. "Why, son, folks that are weak enough to let a hundred thousand out of their hands, they don't deserve to have it. A bank that would lose that much of the coin of its customers—why, it's a duty to make that bank suffer, I tell you, because it teaches a lesson to the rest of the banks. I never had no use for banks, anyhow. They run people to death. And that's about all! Push on them reins, kid. We got to get to town!"

Phil Slader obediently hurried the buckskin along, and they presently turned into the long main street of the little town of Crusoe. But there was no echo of the bank robbery remaining here. If any one expected to learn much about anything except a rodeo in this town and on this day, he was sure to be greeted with a disappointment. All was lost and swallowed in the pervading excitement. And every head that they passed, was turned in the direction in which they were riding.

CHAPTER 11

THOSE HEADS BEGAN to turn toward them, after a time, and the boy grew restless. He endured half a dozen gestures that pointed them out. Then he said:

"There's a lot of folks in this town, Doc. They all know that you killed my father. And now that you ain't in any danger of meeting up with Lon Kirby, I'll just leave you here for a while. I ain't anxious to be pointed out as the son of bad Jack Slader that was tamed down by the same gent that killed my dad. I'm sort of sick of that, you know!"

"Are you?" said the big man, with a species of sympathy. "Then run along, old son. You just run along, and I'll take the hoss out to the grounds myself. Meet you back here about . . . ."

"I'll walk," said the boy.

"All right, then."

"Unless you want to buy me that new hat that's to keep the sun out of my eyes?"

Magruder reached into his pocket and sighed.

"Never mind," said Phil Slader, smiling. "You'll be late

for the rodeo and the bucking, if you don't look out. We'll fix up the hat some other day."

Magruder, with a sigh, nodded in great relief.

"All right, kid," said he. "So long. Don't do no fighting. And keep going straight."

He laughed as he said it and drove hastily on down the street.

Phil, standing in the street and looking after the disappearing form of his guardian, had no doubt about the date on which he would receive that promised hat. There had been other promises of a similar nature before this, and usually they came to the same result.

As for Phil, he would have been glad enough to find himself once more back in the alfalfa field, holding the uneasy handles of the big plow, but now that he was in Crusoe, he could hardly turn about and walk the weary distance. It would be too much like turning his back upon a trial by fire. That, indeed, was what such a visit as this amounted to, to him. And as he started on for the rodeo grounds, he was stepping into the very flames.

People seemed to have eyes in the very backs of their heads. The moment that he came up from behind, many eyes were fixed upon him. Men and women glided from his path as though he had been some dreadful force of nature—a thing to be wondered at. Only the children stood to stare at him. And he could hear the comments from them as he passed:

"There's him, now!"

"That's young Slader."

"He's like his dad, only he'll be worse when he gets started, everybody says."

"Jiminy, he ain't so big looking, is he?"

"He's big enough to make trouble, my dad says!"

None of those voices were intended to reach his ears, but the whispers of children are not expertly controlled. For that matter, he had heard the same things many and many a time before. He knew what the people were feeling and thinking concerning him. And as he stepped among them, the resolution grew greater and greater in his soul to conquer, in spite of all of this doubt and silent opposition. He would go straight, if the very devil himself should come to tempt him—the very devil himself!

So thought poor, young Phil Slader as he walked through the streets of Crusoe on the very day when the seeds of mischief were to be planted in him—seeds that inevitably had to sprout and grow tall and blossom and bear fruit.

In this manner, alone even when he was in that gay, chattering crowd, Phil Slader came to the rodeo grounds. The show was already starting. There was a grand parade of contestants of various kinds—ropers, horse breakers, bulldoggers, and what not. Phil Slader, standing well back from the fence, regarded them with an aching heart. He wanted to be in that crowd. He wanted to feel a dancing horse between his knees; to spring into action there before them all and show them certain qualities which he felt surely were in him.

The procession ended in a great chorus of shouting. And Bill and Joe and Jack and Lefty and the rest had the calls of their admirers in their ears, telling them to do well and bravely.

He, Phil Slader, was neither cheerer nor jeered. But he stood alone in the crowd, envying the others with all his heart. He would have been happy, he felt, if he had had only so much as a single friendly face to whom to call. But he had no such friend.

A wild horse race—in which all the horses were untamed, began the program. A rifle cracked to start them. They came in a surging line, with a pony in front—and then a darting mustang lurching into the lead until the five-hundred-yard mark was reached. Aye, still in the lead as they rounded the post which marked the end of the first half of the race.

A scooting, roan-colored, ugly brute of a mustang, that might have carried an Indian of a past generation on its back, so well did it live up to the strain of its ancestors; this was the horse which turned the halfway mark with two lengths of daylight showing between it and the rest. It looked like a certain winner as it straightened out for the finish line.

But here young Phil Slader heard a girl's voice behind him, shrilling musically high above the roar of the crowd: "Go it, Sammy! Go it, old bay! Shake him up, Sammy! Get Rooster going!"

There was such a savage energy in that feminine voice and so much strength and determination, that Phil felt himself plucked halfway around to look at her. At this moment a thing happened which rooted all his attention to the race. A big, gray horse, which had been lost in the ruck, rounding the halfway mark, now lifted itself into such sudden action that it seemed to be magnified in size two or threefold. It dwarfed the rest of the field.

The girl was screaming: "Go it, Rooster! Good old Rooster! Go it, boy! Go it, honey lamb!"

She had stopped calling on Sammy. Indeed, it was plain to the first and most casual glance that Sammy had little or nothing to do with the change. Rooster was running his own race.

There was revealed some sixteen hands and odd inches of glorious horseflesh, head stretched out, ears flattened, foam streaking from his mouth, and that mouth pulled wildly open by the desperate tug of the rider.

Far from jockeying his horse along to get the utmost speed out of it, Sammy sat braced in the saddle, as though he were astride of a thunderbolt just hurled from the hot heart of heaven. His feet were firm and deep in the stirrups, his straining weight was thrust back, and one could see that he feared the power of the horse, once aroused, might rise to such a scorching speed that man, saddle and all would be swept away, with Rooster going wildly on by himself, naked and free.

Rooster needed no jockeying. In half a dozen strides he shook himself free from the pack of horses in the race. In half a dozen more, he shot past the flying mustang which had the lead. As he shot by, the smaller animal bolted to one side in uncontrollable fear. It was as though a tremendous lion had just leaped past his view!

Like a lion, big Rooster went on. He ran by himself. All the sunshine and all the glory was his. Far back behind him came the rest of the horses, worrying their way home

64

unregarded, as best they might. But the center of attention was Rooster, with his rider still braced far back in the saddle and sawing from side to side on the iron jaw of the stallion in a frightened effort to check his final rush.

A wild yell of laughter and delight burst from the throat of the crowd. The laughter was not at the poor rider—they could sympathize with the fear that was in him—but laughter of joy to see such an incarnation of the wild spirit of the West, made visible.

Rooster had won. Far away past the finish line, the winner was finally brought up, not by the hand of his rider, however. He had jammed himself through a line of waiting cow ponies and thrown them into confusion. One was flat on its back, pawing and squealing, and two more were crushed low by his charge. But this impact checked him a little, and before he could straighten out in full flight once more, a dozen ropes were on the gray devil and he was brought under control, while lucky Sammy hastily dropped to the ground.

The rest of the world had ceased, for Phil Slader.

"If a man had a horse like that!" he said to himself. "If a man had a horse like that—well, what couldn't he do? What couldn't he do?"

He went slowly back among the crowd; he wanted to blind himself to the beauty and wild splendor of that creature. It roused in him an emotion that frightened himself and made him feel as though he were standing in an undiscovered country of his soul. In spite of himself, he could not keep from turning again and looking back.

"Good old Rooster!" cried that same girl's voice, so neatly edged that it cut without difficulty through the masculine roar of the crowd. "Good old boy; didn't I know? Didn't I know?"

Phil Slader looked askance, and there he saw her standing on the seat of a buckboard. The horses were unhitched, and moving restlessly back and forth. The wagon was cramped and threatened to be overturned at any moment. In spite of all that, she stood serenely in her place on that seat, laughing and shouting and waving her hand. It was Nell Newell again.

CHAPTER 12

SHE WAS CHANGED, of course. You couldn't pass ten years, or near it, over the head of a child without altering her a good deal. Still, in the main, her heart was unaltered. In the essential person, it was the same Nell Newell that he had first glimpsed on that wintry evening when the wind had howled so loudly and cut so deep.

He had never forgotten her, and yet he had not known how deep she had sunk in him. For the music which we love best is sometimes unnoticed until it is heard the second time.

She saw Phil in the same instant, and she recognized him with even more ease than he had recognized her.

"Hello!" she called, as though they had separated half a day before. "Hello! Yank those horses of mine straight, will you, Phil? Thanks a lot. Jump up here and tell me about yourself, Phil. Here you are. Hello, again! Why, you're not so big as they've been telling me, after all!"

All this she said, as she ordered him to jump up beside her. As he did the thing which she commanded, she shook hands vigorously, and then balanced herself in her lofty station by resting a hand familiarly upon his broad shoulder.

"Did you see that Rooster horse run away with that

race?" ran on the girl. "Oh, but ain't he a jim dandy, though? Oh, but ain't he a sweetheart? Did you ever see such a horse, Phil Slader?"

"No," he said faintly. "I never saw such a horse. He's like a tiger—a regular tiger!"

"They told me that *you* were that way now," said the girl, still smiling and bubbling. "They told me that you could tear things up, just the way that Rooster did when he hit that line of runty cow ponies. But you don't look changed any. Just the same. Glum and thinking about something around the corner! Oh, you're not a very happy fellow, Phil, are you?"

"You make me sort of giddy," said Phil Slader honestly. "But I have to go now . . . ."

"Go? Why do you have to go? I have to keep you here. I *want* to keep you here. I've heard so much about you and I was such a nasty little cat when I saw you the last time—a billion years ago, wasn't it? Oh, what a shoulder you have, though! When I dig my fingers into that shoulder and feel the muscles, I can believe some of the stuff that they tell about you being three men rolled into one!"

And she *did* dig her fingers deeply into the shoulder muscles of Phil Slader until the tips of them came close to the quick and in self-defense he had to tighten his arm which threw up a few great, twisting slabs of rubbery muscle that bulged fairly out of her grasp.

"I better go," said Phil Slader again.

"Do I scare you?" said Nell Newell, laughing down at him and patting that mighty shoulder. "Don't be afraid, Phil. I'm not going to run you away and disgrace you. Only—I'm glad to see you, that's all!"

"I'm thinking of the other side of the question," said Phil Slader. "They're beginning to stare at you—standing up here with the sort of a man that I am."

"What's wrong with you?" asked Nell Newell, fixing her bright eyes on him.

"I'm the son of Jack Slader," said Phil. "D'you understand?"

She merely laughed.

"I know. Slader was the gun fighter."

"He was the gun fighter," said Phil with his usual gravity.

Her laughter went out. She looked steadily into the eyes of Phil, and suddenly Phil remembered that there was no other person he had ever met who could look into his eyes in this fashion. Other people were apt to glance suddenly aside when he fixed his glance upon them. The eyes of others shrank from him as though there were fire in his look, but this girl eyed him with perfectly easy security.

"Did your father kill men, really?" said she.

"Haven't you heard?" asked Phil, much amazed that there was any person in the world who did not know the full details of the story of his parent.

"Oh, yes, I've heard. But that doesn't mean much. You know how people will lie when they get half a chance to make a good story out of anything. I thought that maybe they were making a story out of your dad. Weren't they?"

"I guess not." said Phil.

"You're proud of it, aren't you?"

"Proud of it? Of course not!" He blinked at her, dazed by the very suggestion of such a thing.

"You're not, eh?" said Nell Newell. "Maybe you're ashamed of him, then."

"Why," said the son of the man killer, "he broke the law. He stole things. He killed people. He did all sorts of things that he shouldn't of done!"

"I say," cried the girl in her loud, unsubdued voice, "are you ashamed of him?"

"I don't know. I suppose so!" said Phil Slader. For he had never thought of these things by such a light as this.

"Bah!" exclaimed Nell, snapping her fingers. "If I had a father like that—that tore through other men the same way that Rooster tears through other horses, I'd be so proud of him that I wouldn't be able to sleep at night, I tell you. And you're ashamed of him! Hello, Sammy! Were you scared to death? But I told you that you could do it! I told you that you could do it, and that he'd win, bless him!"

"You'll fall and break your neck," said Sammy with a brother's sharpness. "Get down off that seat, Nelly."

68

She was too filled with questions to stop to argue the point. She sat down obediently in the seat, and Phil Slader jumped down to the ground. He felt that it was time for him to leave them, but still he could not take himself away. He wanted to talk more to this free-swinging, careless girl. He wanted to talk about Jack Slader, but most of all, he had never felt such an overwhelming desire to talk about himself!

The girl was babbling: "How did it feel when he began to run, Sammy?"

"It felt as though I was hitched to a cyclone," said Sammy, taking off his hat and wiping his forehead. "It felt terrible, I tell you. That confounded horse just ran right away with me. I thought that he'd jump out from under me and the saddle and all! I tried to pull him up. Might as well have sawed away at a piece of iron. My shoulders still ache. Needs a giant to ride that horse, and I'll never try it again."

"Sammy!" cried the girl, striking her hands together. "Just after you've learned how to handle him."

"Learned nothing!" said Sammy. "Learned how close I could come to getting my neck broke. I'd give that horse away for ten dollars!"

"No!" cried Nell.

"I would though. I offered him to any of the boys, yonder, for ten dollars. But they didn't want him. They'd seen enough of him in the race, besides what they'd heard of him already. They all know that he's a bad one!"

Said Phil Slader, his heart in his mouth, "I'll give you ten dollars for that horse, Sam."

Young Newell turned sharply around. "It's Slader!" said he. "It's Phil Slader!"

Phil could hardly tell, by the manner of the speaker, whether or not there was pleasure or anger or fear or disgust in Sam Newell. But he himself held out his hand.

"I'm glad to see you, Sam," said he.

Newell shook the proffered hand instantly.

"Why, if you've forgiven me for what I did that night so long ago, I'm mighty glad of it. I'm glad to see you, Phil,

69

too. There's not a day that we haven't talked about you in our house!"

He offered a great resemblance to his sister, now that his face was lighted up. He had the same sunny hair and the same bright, happy eyes.

"If you try to sell Rooster, I'll never, never forgive you, Sammy!" Nell was crying.

"Look here, Nell, don't make such a silly fuss," said her brother. "You know as well as I do that he's no good to anybody the way he is. No good at all, and you know it! He's laid up five men in his day; and he'd of laid me up today except that just when he was about ready to begin bucking, he got the idea of winning that race into his head, and forgot all about me. But if I tried him again, he'd spill me all over this rodeo and . . . ."

"Look yonder!" cried Nell Newell. "There's fellows out there who are not as cowardly as *you* are, Sammy Newell!"

For a dense cluster of excited cowpunchers had been gathered about the gray stallion ever since the end of the race. Now the throng opened and the spectators could see that a man was firmly seated on the back of Rooster.

The horse trotted gently forth, got himself into an open space, and then turned himself into a good imitation of an explosion. The cowpuncher lost his seat high in the air and sailed sprawling until he landed with a thump which, in the sudden silence which covered the crowd, was sickeningly audible even to the spot where Nell and Sammy and Phil Slader stood together.

Some ran to pick up the fallen man. Others put their ropes on the stallion again, but he was not minded to submit tamely. He fought with a devilish intensity until a strong rope was noosed about his neck. At the first touch of it, he submitted as though realizing when a battle was lost beyond all hope. In the meantime, the fallen cowpuncher was seen staggering from the field, and there were no further volunteers to fill the saddle on the stallion's back.

"You see, Nell?" said her brother gloomily. "Of course I'd like to keep Rooster as well as any man. But what use will he be? Just standing around and eating his head off

70

all day long, except when he breaks loose into a pasture and kills another horse, that don't please his fancy . . . ."

"I'm still offering you that ten dolllars," said Phil Slader.

"Philip!" cried the girl, "if you buy that horse away from us, I'll never speak to you again."

But Phil, looking up to her and then to the shining beauty of the horse, had already made up his mind.

"That offer stands," he said to Sam Newell.

"Get the cash for me," said Sam Newell, "and you can take the horse."

CHAPTER 13

SOMETHING ELSE WAS happening in the inclosed ground of the rodeo, but Phil Slader had no eye for it. He ranged through the crowd with the eye of an eagle, searching out faces, and heedless of the glances that trailed after him with constant disapproval.

"Doc," said he presently, drawing up at the side of Magruder, "I want ten dollars."

Magruder turned from earnest conversation with two long-whiskered gentlemen, with whom the leading idea had not been the affairs of the rodeo, but the possibility of working up a quiet little game of poker. When he heard the voice of Phil Slader he started violently and turned with a scowl upon the boy.

"Ten dollars?" asked Magruder. "Ten dollars, kid? And what would you be wanting to do with all that money?"

"I won't be buying myself a hat," said Phil Slader. "I won't be doing that, old-timer, and you can rest easy on that point, if that's what's worrying you."

His smile turned Mr. Magruder's face to ice. A violent shudder ran through his rather corpulent body. Instantly a ten dollar bill lay in the palm of Phil Slader.

With that prize, Phil returned to the Newells. They seemed to have forgotten all about him and his offer. They had pressed their buckboard closer to the fence, and Sammy was yelling frantic encouragement to a cowpuncher who was then in the act of throwing and roping a steer against time. The instant that steer was tied, a ten dollar bill was fluttering in the air in front of Sam Newell.

He took it with an absent-mindedness which cleared at once. "You really want that horse, Phil?" he questioned. "Now, look here. The only other time that I met up with you, I served you a low turn. I don't want to do a worse trick for you now. That horse is poison, old-timer. That Rooster horse is a plain devil, with all the looks and the points and the speed in the world, but with a plain bad heart. I'd hate to see you buy him and throw away your money."

"Besides," put in Nell softly, "I know that you won't want to take him away from me, Phil. I'd plain *die* if I couldn't have a look at that horse, once in a while."

"Bah!" said her scornful brother. "What good does looking do, I'd like to ask you? What good does it do at all, silly? You can't live on looking. You'll never be able to ride him, that's certain!"

"If I were a man, I'd show you," said the girl through her clenched teeth. "I'd master him—or I'd kill him—or let him kill me—but I'd never give up like one of you weak, cowardly, blustering, bluffing, sneaking men! I would . . . ."

"What?" asked Sam Newell, amused.

72

"Nothing," said the girl rather weakly and lamely in conclusion. "I'm tired of talking about it!"

Truth to tell, in the midst of her outburst her glance had fallen upon the stern, dark face of Phil Slader, and suddenly she knew that no matter what truth there might be when her words were applied to other men, they were far, far from true when applied to this son of the mountains. More than that stirred her, too—for it seemed to her that her words were kindling a little fire in the slumbering blackness of Slader's eyes.

"All right," said Phil Slader. "I like you a lot better for giving me this warning and I take it very friendly of you, Sam. But I want the horse."

"Then take him—and I hope you have some luck with him—though I doubt it a lot, I got to say. Are you an extra good rider?"

"I'm fair," said Phil, "but I think that I'll try gentling Rooster."

"Gentling him!" exclaimed Nell Newell. "You should be ashamed, Phil Slader. You should be ashamed! Are you *afraid* of Rooster, like the rest of them seem to be?"

She felt, by the way he jerked up his head, that she had laid her whip upon a too-wild horse.

"All right," said Phil, "I'll try my hand with him, to please you, if you want me to!"

"Oh, I'm not asking you to go get your neck broken!"

"Will you tell me one thing?" asked Phil earnestly. "If you were a man, just what *would* you do?"

"Be free!" said the girl, throwing out her arms. "I'd be free! I'd ride where I pleased, call no man my boss, and eat cake instead of bacon," she concluded, chuckling. "But I'm not a man," she went on with a strain of seriousness. "I'm only a girl. So I'll marry money and be the next *best* thing to a free man—the wife of a rich one!"

"And that's about it," said her brother with a savage air. "You'll wind up by marrying some rich old crook!"

"Why not?" cried the girl. "I don't care where the money comes from, so long as I get it. Life without money is like trying to fly without wings. There's no fun and there's no happiness. There's nothing but grinding, all

73

day and every day, wishing for something around the corner that never shows up. I'd sooner be a sneaking coyote than a man and live the way that most men have to live. If I were a man, I'd be a wolf and no coyote. And I tell you something more. Money is beautiful for its own sake; it doesn't make any difference where it comes from. Steal a million and give a hundred thousand to charity. That makes you *good*—and leaves you nine hundred thousand. Isn't that business, Sammy? I ask you that?"

She laughed as she slapped her brother on the shoulder. But Phil Slader was not laughing when he turned away.

Sammy said to his sister: "You've got to watch the way that you talk to folks. You're pretty hard even on mother and dad and me. It's hard to follow you. But a stranger hearing the way that you talk—why, he don't know where to write you down, Nell. He wouldn't know that at heart you're the safest and the best girl in the world!"

"Am I?" asked Nell. "Am I?"

And she flashed a challenge at him.

"Oh, curse it," said Newell. "I'm not going to argue with you any more. I can't argue with that tongue of yours, because it's double jointed. But no matter what you may be, really, I think that you've put a bee in the bonnet of that Phil Slader. *He* takes you seriously. And I'll bet that the fool goes right out and tries to ride the horse now!"

"I wonder!" whispered the girl.

"It'd please you, I think," cried Sammy, "to see a man even get killed, so long as it was for your sake or for the sake of one of your ideas!"

"Don't be so hard on me, Sammy. But—do you think that he would really do that?"

"Would it please you a lot?"

"Why," cried the girl, "I could love a man that would do a thing like that!"

"D'you mean it, Nell?"

"Don't I, though? I mean it every inch of me!"

"Then that's plain selfish."

"It's not. Not for doing what I wanted him to—that isn't what would make me love him—but doing one big, crazy,

74

fine, foolish thing—like trying to ride a mad horse. I mean that I could love a man who would do things like that!"

Sammy Newell stared at her with the eyes of one who has never charged a windmill, and who never will.

"Well," said he, "I hate to say that I believe you—but I almost do, and I'll tell you what, I'll be considerable relieved when I see you safely married to some good, steady rancher!"

"Will you?" said Nell. "I'll tell you what, Sammy. I may get married, but I'll never get *safely* married. You can lay your odds on that about ten to one. Marriage? Why, it's just a name to me. The man is what counts—and if he changes after I marry him—he'd better look out!"

So said Nelly Newell, and she would have said more, no doubt, had it not been that her brother suddenly announced: "By the jumping jiminy, I think that he's going to try it. Look at him now! He's cutting straight through the crowd!"

Nell Newell jumped up and stood stiff and straight.

"If he does . . . ." she whispered.

"Hello, Nelly!" called a fine, big youth, breaking through the crowd to come closer to her. "Hello, Nelly! I missed you at the . . . ."

"Shut up, whoever you are," said Nelly. "Something important is about to happen out there, if you'll only keep still!"

The youth relapsed into silence, sending a keen glance for explanation at young Sammy Newell, but Sammy merely shrugged his shoulders and made a motion with his fingers around his head, commonly used in school-yards to signify addled wits.

However, there was now a growing union of attention over the entire field. The bulldogging which was under way stopped suddenly. Men were seen running here and there and climbing into the best possible positions from which they could view the approaching event.

And from all sides a universal murmur rolled toward them: "Phil Slader is going to ride Rooster! Can he do it?"

And the universal answer was: "How can *anybody* ride that gray devil?"

75

There was no doubt now, and Nelly Newell was clapping her hands again and again and saying in a voice half choked with joyous laughter:

"He will! He will! He will! Oh, Sammy, he will!"

"Ride Rooster? Never in a million years!" said Sammy.

"Ride him! What do I care about that?" cried the girl.

"What difference does it make whether he really sticks on the back of Rooster?"

"Sis," said her brother, "you plain beat me! Then why in the world should he *try* to ride at all?"

"Just for the sake of the trying, itself. It shows that he has the nerve, while the rest of you men are half frightened to death! Look at him!"

CHAPTER 14

THERE WAS PHIL SLADER, marching through the center of the press of men who were gathered about the gray stallion. Now he stood at the side of the great horse and by his gestures it was plain to all that he intended to ride. It was no wonder that all other activities were instantly suspended to watch. The son of famous Jack Slader was to be seen in action at last! After so many huge prophecies had been made of him, after so many dreadful things had been foretold of what he was and what he could do, they were to see him undertake a little more than any one man could be expected to do.

"He *will* ride the brute," said John Newell, suddenly appearing at this stage of the procedure. "He *will* ride Rooster, I think. Do you know who it is, Nelly and Sammy? It's that same wild boy that we know. It's Phil Slader."

"You're a yesterday's newspaper, dad," said his irreverent daughter. "Besides, you've only read part of the headlines. I'll tell you the real stuff. Sammy, here, has just sold Rooster to Phil Slater for ten bucks! Can you beat that?"

Mr. Newell started, but he finally nodded his head and smiled, saying: "I really think that Phil will be able to ride the brute; I really think that boy will do it!"

The tall, handsome youngster who had vainly attempted to get the attention of Nelly before, now answered this remark.

"He never can do it, Mr. Newell. No other man will ever be able to ride Rooster, when Rooster doesn't want to be ridden."

"Bah!" cried Nelly, flaring instantly as though the challenge were delivered to her in person. "Because Rooster threw *you* on your head half a dozen times—is that any sign? Not a bit! Not a bit! Why, there's always been men who could ride *any* horse. And Phil Slader is one of them. You watch and see!"

Mr. Newell and his son grinned sympathetically at their friend.

"It's up to you to tell her, Dick," they said. "She wouldn't listen to us. Tell her how many outlaw horses there are that never have been rode and never *will* be rode!"

Handsome Dick Chester smiled quietly up at the excited face of the girl.

"I don't *want* to be told. I *won't* be told!" cried Nell Newell.

"You sulky baby!" said Dick Chester. "If you weren't so pretty, I'd want to slap you, honey."

"Slap me! Don't honey me, you rascal!" cried Nelly. "But oh, he *will* win!"

"Well," said Dick Chester. "I'll tell you that I knew an old sand-colored horse down in Austin. He lived staked out in a back lot. So old that nobody could tell when his first birthday might of been. Well, anybody that wanted to put a saddle and bridle on Sandy could of rode him away. Same thing had been true for ten years. All that the owner of Sandy wanted to see was the fun when the riding began. He used to keep a sign tacked up on his front gate about Sandy being a free gift for the first man that could ride him, until the police threatened to prosecute him for manslaughter, y'understand? Then he had to let up a little. But the best riders in the West came to tackle Sandy. Not in the hope of riding him, but to see how long they could stick on his back.

"Willie Armstrong had the record of one minute and forty-two seconds. He had the record for seven years, nearly. Then Pete Van Eyck come along and rode the horse for two minutes and fifty-four and two-fifths seconds, before he hit the sand. Some said that was only because Sandy was getting old. Others said that Sandy would never be old till he died, so far as bucking was concerned."

"What do *I* care about that Sandy horse?" asked Nell Newell with much indignation.

"I just want to tell you," said the big, impassive fellow, "that Rooster is no better at bucking than Sandy, but he's just as good—when he gets his dander up. And he has his dander up today. He's thrown one man already. And I'll put up money that he'll not only throw this Phil Slader, if Slader is fool enough to get into the saddle, but he'll eat Slader when Phil hits the ground."

"Never!" cried Nell.

"Very well," said Dick. "You want to see him ride this horse. I'll make a ten-dollar bet with you that Rooster throws him and breaks him up, besides! Will you take that bet?"

"Is it really as dangerous as that for Phil Slader?" asked the girl, suddenly serious.

"It is," said her father, "every bit."

"Well," said Nell. "I'd like to have the ride stopped—

78

but there wouldn't be any use trying. Nothing could hold Phil back now, I suppose. But, oh—I'd like to know one thing!"

No one had a chance to hear what the one thing might have been. Indeed, she would not have expressed it in words. But she wondered with all of her heart how much of the will to ride the stallion sprang from the desire to master the brute, and how much it was rooted in an impulse to show his strength before her own watching eyes!

A dull roar began with the shout in the center of the inclosure where the horse was held. It spread to the outskirts of the throng and rang deafeningly in the ears of Nell Newell and those around her. Then they saw Rooster dart out with Phil Slader on his back.

For a good hundred yards it seemed that Rooster intended to try to run out from under the saddle. It even looked as though he might do it! The wind of his racing stride tore the hat from the head of Phil Slader and blew back his long hair as stiff and straight as though an invisible set of fingers had grasped it by the flying ends.

But Rooster was not going to rely upon anything as childish as mere speed. There were other spices in the dish which he could serve up for the delectation of the connoisseurs. At the end of the hundred yards he was going fast enough to turn himself into a blur; at the end of that distance he stopped himself in about the time that it takes an arrow to shoot into soft wood and come to a halt.

Phil Slader was braced in the stirrups; he had settled back with a very reasonable expectation that the horse might attempt even such a maneuver as came to pass. But despite all his preparedness, he was snatched from his seat and thrown forward along the neck of the horse.

Rooster spun about like a top. Being already well off balance, Phil Slader was hurled from the back of the stallion, landing upon the ground with such force that the dust spurted up like splashed water. He rolled head over heels through that dust cloud of his own raising.

There was a wild shout from every throat in that crowd, terror in the women's voices, to be sure, and in the

79

voices of the children also. Yet even in these there was a note of exultation. There was something in their blood that was in the blood of the audiences who ringed the amphitheaters in the ancient days.

Rooster wheeled again and charged for his victim, and the hands of Nell Newell flashed up before her face.

"I told you!" she heard big Dick Chester saying. "I told you what Rooster would do—and he's doing it, by Heaven! No!"

The last was a shout of wonder, lost in the cry of the whole audience. Nell Newell jerked down her hands again in time to see Phil Slader rolling to his feet and lurching to the side in escaping the drive of the big gray horse.

He was staggering—that much was sure. It looked so like a tragedy that the crowd was yelling:

"Why don't they get a rope on Rooster?" Or, "Shoot the horse! Shoot the gray before he kills Slader!"

However, there was no one near enough to put a rope on the stallion or attempt such a thing. And there was no gun which was sure of hitting the horse without striking the man. So they saw the big animal deliver its charge and saw Phil Slader lurch out of the path of danger, as if by a miracle.

"It's not possible!" whispered Nell. "It's not possible that he's off the saddle so soon! If Phil Slader is not a man, who is? Who is?"

"Nobody in this world . . . ." began Dick Chester.

"Look!" cried Sammy. "The fool is going to try it again if he can."

As the gray horse shot past the man and saw that it had missed its charge, it threw itself back and reared in a wild endeavor to check its impetus and wheel again at its enemy. As it paused and reared to whirl about, at that very instant, young Slader leaped on its back like some crouched panther and thrust his feet into the stirrups.

It brought a voice like pandemonium from the entire crowd. Rooster began to fight like a madman. Having downed his foe, it was surely strange that Fate should clap the same danger on his back again!

He began, as Dick Chester expressed it, to tie himself

into figure eights and untie them while he was still in the air. He rocked up and down, hitting heavily with forefeet and then with hind; he did the neatest bit of fence rowing that was ever seen in that part of the country, where *everything* connected with bucking horses was known by heart. Then he began to fish for the sun with a whole-hearted enthusiasm that brought every man and woman shouting to their feet.

Even a little range mustang, with a build like a cartoonist's effort at imagining a horse, looks very like a raging lion if it has the brain power and the physical strength to perform the feat known as sunfishing. Imagine Rooster, then, hurling his magnificent body into the air, until he was only a flash of silver, descending again with dreadful force, upon a single foreleg. It sent a convulsive wave through his body, and it jerked the rider like the curl of a whip. What was only a ripple in the horse, became an explosion in the man. It jerked him to the side; it snapped his chin down against his breast. At the very third jump there was a wild yell from a brown-faced savage of a cowpuncher near by:

"He's done! He's done! Slader is finished!"

"Why?" called Nell Newell to the wild man. "Why do you say that? He's still riding and he's riding straight up! And he hasn't pulled leather as yet!"

"He's done," said Dick Chester. "He's done, well enough, but he's given us the kind of riding that we've dreamed of and never seen before."

"Ay, and Rooster is nearly done too!" exclaimed Sammy Newell. "Look at him, Nell! The big boy is about done up from this work!"

No horse could try to turn itself into a bird for minute after minute without feeling the strain, and Rooster, sweat-blackened, but flecked with snowy foam, was undoubtedly on the down grade.

He gave proof of it by changing his tactics. That sunfishing was killing the rider, to be sure. But it was killing the horse, too. Now Rooster altered his form of battle and, rearing, flung himself down and rolled, with a suddenness that made every breath catch.

81

There had been no warning, but Phil Slader was off the saddle in the flicker of an eyelash. As the stallion reared through the dust cloud, Phil was on his back.

"Look!" screamed a big man near by, who had taken a hat from his gray head and was waving the sombrero frantically through the air. "Look at him! That's the quiet boy that the sheriff likes so much! That's the little lamb that ain't never done anything! Watch him. Ain't he a tiger? I ask you—ain't he a tiger? Is it fighting that Rooster wants? Well, he's getting it now!"

Phil Slader, apparently maddened by this treacherous maneuver of the big stallion now clung in his place with biting spurs that gouged the side of the animal. With the biting lash of his quirt, he rained blows on the shoulders of the big gray.

Rooster did not know what to make of this. He had been ridden before, to be sure, but almost always he was ridden only at moments when it was his imperial pleasure that he *should* be ridden. Those who dared attempt to ride him against his will—their hands were generally very well occupied in clinging to their places, with no thought of tormenting his proud self further. He forgot all his cunning for a moment, and burned up priceless strength, giving his foeman an equally priceless respite by leaping out and racing for a full half mile at the top of his speed.

On top of the things which he had been doing, one would have thought that a half-mile sprint, inspired by fear, would have been enough to drop the stallion like a bullet. But it seemed that Rooster grew greater by the use of his God-given speed. Every stride was faster than the one before. As he whirled around the rodeo grounds, he was given an ovation—an ovation for his fierce strength and beauty and for the man who was riding him out. They had come to see a grand show, but this was more than they had ever expected.

The big man with the gray hair near the Newells could not be done talking. "They said that he was a bum copy of Jack Slader, eh?" he snarled. "They said that he was soft, eh! Just a farm hand? Well, look at the farm hand

82

now! Ain't those tiger claws that he's using on the hoss? How could he ever of stuck on, otherwise? Yea!"

He fairly screamed in a savage exultation. "Look hearty at him now, boys!" went on this gloomy enthusiast, "because the next time you see him, most likely it'll be when you're riding in a posse to catch him for the killing of your father or your son or your brother—as I used to ride to catch Jack Slader himself. I tell you that Jack never could of rode a horse like this! Look hearty at him, because the next time he may be stretching a rope!"

The whole crowd fell into a noisy hysteria at this point, for Rooster, having raced like a track sprinter for the half mile, suddenly remembered that in this straightaway running he was simply burning up his own strength and allowing that of his cardinal foeman to be recruited. He left off bolting and began to buck again.

It was his last effort. Just as a staggering, weary runner sees the goal in sight and suddenly picks himself up for a last valiant lunge at the barrier, running as though the race were only begun, so Rooster gave all the might that was in him to shake off the slashing, spurring, clinging menace. He began to sunfish again, and under the sledge-hammer strokes of that buffeting, Phil Slader began to reel and pitch in the saddle like a landsman on the deck of a sea-tossed, small boat.

It was the last of Rooster's strength and it was the last of his rider's also. Twice and again he was unbalanced. He clung to the edge of a fall and scrambled back. There was no question of pulling leather now. With foot and hand and weakening legs he gripped at horse or saddle, and still he could barely maintain his place. He lost a stirrup—and regained it in barely sufficient time to meet the next ship-crack shock.

That was luck, but luck could not be with him all the time. He lost a stirrup again. With the next leap, Rooster whirled himself in the air, and came down spinning. It flung Phil Slader clear of the saddle, outlined him for a moment against the sky and then pitched him headlong into the dust. He lay helpless, stunned, crushed, making no effort to rise.

But Rooster? He made no effort to lunge at the fallen foe. Now, in the moment of his victory, his last ounce of power was expended, and he stood with hanging head, legs braced far apart, foam dripping fast from his gaping mouth, the very picture of exhaustion.

CHAPTER 15

No ONE SHOUTED for Rooster's victory, not even those who had placed their lucky bets upon the horse. They knew how perilously close they had come to losing their money, just as those who had dared to venture their coin at long, long odds upon the son of Jack Slader now knew that they had not made a foolish bet.

"And that," said Sheriff Mitchel Holmer, "is the Slader kid, eh?"

"Aye," said one of his friends, grinning, "and what'll you do about it, sheriff?"

"Heaven knows what I *can* do," said the sheriff, "except to oil up all my guns and then to start praying. Why, here's a kid that has never entered himself in any riding contest. Here's a kid that's never showed himself. And what I wonder is: What is he saving himself for?"

"For something worth while," came the pat answer.

"That's what he's saving himself for. He's not going to be like Jack Slader—in for every kind of deviltry that comes to hand. He's going to be extra special careful in what he does—this same kid! And when he makes his play, it will be for hard cash, you can be pretty sure of that! Hard cash and no small potatoes! That's the style of this here new Slader!"

Not all were busy in making their comments. Some of the men had picked up Phil Slader and poured a dram of brandy between his lips. When the brandy brought back his wits he sat up with a gasp and then lurched to his feet. His numbed legs would hardly support him, and yonder was Rooster, already regaining strength even faster than his late rider; already regaining strength and lifting his formidable head, while he stared ominously at Phil Slader.

Young Slader had no idea of trying the saddle again on this day. He was beaten and he knew it—beaten, too, for the first time in his life, and in fair fight. All other enemies had shunned him from the beginning of his youth. There had been a stamp upon him—the name of that famous father. And on account of it, boys and men had avoided him always.

Now that he had been beaten into the dust by a brute beast, he expected that he would find sneers and scorn around him. But there was no scorn and no sneers. Busy hands were still working about him.

"Take this flask of brandy along with you, Slader," said one.

"Lemme brush off your back," said another. "It's a mite thick with dust."

"It was a grand job that you did, old son," said another. "And the next time out, you'll ride that hoss till he's plumb blind—only, I'd like to be on hand to see the work that you do on him!"

An old, white-haired cattleman came limping up and grasped his hand.

"I've seen all the old-timers and I've seen all the young crop of 'em," said he. "I've seen the game ones come and go, and nothing gamer than the ride you give to Rooster, was it every my luck to lay an eye on, Slader! You remember me, if you ever might be in the need of a friend. I'm 'Pop' Weston. You write that down in your books, and it may come in handy, one of these days—darned handy, m'son!"

He kept nodding very gravely, as he made this little speech, and the addled brain of Phil Slader gradually cleared, letting in the light of the sun and the voices of these men. There was nothing but respect—respect even with a touch of awe in it, it seemed to him. He could have laughed.

It was as though they did not know the thing that had been clear to him throughout the battle with the gray stallion. A dozen times he had been upon the verge of a crashing fall, and a dozen times something akin to luck had saved him. The difference was that he knew it was luck, and they attributed it to skill. That lost stirrup which had been regained, for instance—they thought that that was skill and not merest chance. But let them think what they pleased, he knew that the stallion was his master! So he looked around him with that faint smile which was in the mouth rather than in the eyes, and he took the stallion by the reins and limped away from the field.

He went out past the buckboard where Dick Chester and the Newells were gathered. They gave him a smile and a nod, all of them; awe-stricken smiles befitting mere spectators, when they see one of the heroes of the arena go by them. There was only one gloomy face, and that the most important face of all, to Philip Slader. Nell, her chin dropped upon her small fist, looked vacantly upon him, full of her thoughts.

Phil wanted to say something, but he hardly knew what. He was only sure that the sight of her displeasure was more to him than the buffeting which he had just taken from the stallion.

"I'll tell you," said Phil Slader, "if you think that it ain't fair for me to walk off with Rooster for a small price like ten . . . ."

At that, she came suddenly back to herself and jumped up. "Do you think I care about the money?" she asked.

86

"Or even about who owns him? No, I only want some one who can handle that horse to have him. That's all that I want!"

Phil Slader looked curiously and closely at her. She met his gaze again with more steadiness than any man had ever been able to show.

"You've got your wish, then, Nell," said John Newell. "Because Phil will have Rooster eating out of his hand in a couple of weeks—after a good first start, like this!"

"I don't think so," said Nell, more grave than ever. "It all depends—in that first start. It all depends on who had the most taken out of him in this try—Phil or Rooster. And I don't think that Phil will ever get anything but bumps from Rooster, not until he grows into a different sort of a man from what he is today."

"Nell," cried her brother, "that's out and out insulting, to say a thing like that!"

She disregarded that remark as though it had never been made. "But oh," said Nell, "I thought for a minute that you *would* win. I thought surely . . . ."

She paused again, shaking her head slowly.

"I'm not through with him," Phil assured her. "I'll have another try at him. You can bet on that!"

"When you ride him," said Nell Newell, "you ride him over to see me. Because you'll be the biggest and the best man that I've ever seen, Phil. D'you understand me? The biggest and the best, and I'll want to tell you that face to face!"

A haze of rose obscured the eyes of Phil. Perhaps it was partly because he was very weak, and there was a roaring at his ears. Her voice came to him in waves, as if out of a great distance, and there was such a promise in it that he dared not put the thing into words. He felt more confident and stronger than he had ever felt before. Because there was only one thing for him to do in order to win from her—what?

Ah, well, let the future take care of that! If the one thing had been the moving of a mountain, it would not have deterred him from a wild hope. Yet, he told himself, as he led the stallion away, that even the moving of a mountain might prove a lesser thing than the mastering of this stallion.

The mountain could be attacked every day, a shovelful at a time, or what he could break off with the stroke of a steel pick. But patience and much labor would never affect the stallion. It would never be written that Rooster could be conquered until by some vast expansion of the spirit, Phil Slader met the big gray horse in another struggle and proved himself the greater of the two.

He paused in the distance and looked back. Above the swirling crowds at the rodeo, a vast dust cloud was rising, white and sure in the center, fading to ghostliness at the edges—a phantom Doric pillar. Then another gust of wind tore the dream into shreds.

So it was with this day of his. It had brought him close to the realization of a great thing. He had almost become that superman for whom the girl was looking. Oh, he knew what was in her mind as well as though she had taken him aside and spoken many volumes to him concerning what was in her heart of hearts. He knew and he wondered at her and her vision of what a man should be.

All strength of will and all might of hand and mind— that was what she wanted—power, power, power, no matter how crude and raw its form. That was what she yearned for. And he, by the grace of good fortune, had come within hail of the masterpiece, on this day of days. A few more pounds of power, a little more courage of heart, a little more cunning of hand and body, and he would have mastered the stallion and Nell at the same instant.

Then came disaster. As the phantom column had melted at a touch, so all of his chance had been blown to bits when he rolled senseless in the dust.

He was not weak or childish enough to feel self-pity. He was man enough to wonder that he had ever come so close. But how marvelously well he had understood her—and how wonderfully well she had seen through him. She had known that it *was* a great day for him, that he was at a zenith, that he was laboring his best for her as well as for himself and for fame. Yet he had failed. Being beaten once, he would have to change from his very soul and grow greater, before he could master the big horse.

Such thoughts made the miles shorter. His mind gradually grew clearer: his legs bore him up more strongly. He began to feel once more the bitter heat of the sun and he pulled his ragged, old felt hat lower down over his eyes. It was a different hat from that which he had put upon his head in going to the town. Then, it had been a rag; now it was something more, for kind hands had picked it from the dust where it had fallen. The dust had been brushed from it by another touch than his, and it had been offered back to him as a fallen helmet might have been proffered to a hero returning from the wars.

Yes, he knew now for certain that he was something more than ordinary clay. He knew now that there had been a reason behind the awe with which the world had looked at him from the beginning. He *was* the son, the true son of Jack Slader. Yet, if only Heaven had made him a little bit more—made him a man to conquer Rooster—made him a man to fill the whole eye of the girl!

He reached the abatis of shrubbery which fenced the hotel grounds to the south, toward the town. He passed through the woods upon which the shrubbery abutted to the north and he came again into the sight of the lands which he had labored over so often and which he had made so much of.

Here was his home—for a few months more. Here was the home of Rooster, too. He turned and looked at the tall stallion—and then shook his head in despair.

CHAPTER 16

ROOSTER, NOW QUITE his old self, stood with head raised and ears pricked, staring far across toward the distant horizon, quite overlooking his present owner, as though, like the Arab proverb, he wondered when his real master would come riding down into this world of men!

Poor Phil Slader, staring at the proud monster, told himself that all his efforts and all of his patient labor would never gain this haughty spirit, never prevail upon it to do more than completely scorn him. However, he put Rooster into the barn and straightway employed himself with fixing another bar all around the adjoining little corral, to make sure that the stallion should not leap out and gain freedom by a short cut.

Then he turned Rooster loose. The big horse danced out into the corral, swept the bars with a single glance, and then poised himself in the center of the inclosure, uttering a great neigh. If you had been there to see him, with such a head, so grandly posed, the marvel of his dappled body, the silver arc of his tail and the wind-ruffled brightness of his mane, you would have felt as Phil Slader felt, that this was not a horse at all, but a veritable god of horses come into the hands of Phil.

Out of the distance came the long, wavering howl of a

wolf. Of course it was mere chance that let some wandering lobo give tongue at this instant, but it seemed to Phil that it was something more—the wild giving voice to the wild—the free wolf to the imprisoned one.

However, there was still a good deal of the day remaining; so Phil harnessed his team to the plow and began again on the alfalfa lands. For half a furrow all went well, and then the plow struck a snag. He twisted it around the bad place, but he did not send the horses ahead, again. After a time, he was aware that he had been standing there leaning on the handles of the plow and dreaming.

He forced himself ahead with the labor. But, for the first time, it seemed to him that the sun was sticking in a certain place halfway from the zenith to the far western horizon; it seemed to him as though the end of the day would never come. Hitherto all days had been too short for him!

However, the day ended in due time. The horses were put up. He fed the stallion and saw the great creature disdain the food. Yes, not until the man who had put down the fodder had apparently disappeared did Phil, from covert, see Rooster touch a few straws and then toss up his head, suspicious, dreading lest he had been seen accepting charity from the hand of an enemy!

It moved the man greatly, and he went soberly on toward the house. He felt no exultation in his prize. Rather, he felt a shame. For he knew that by right the stallion should be given freedom to range as he would across the hills, to form a band and pass through a career beautiful and free.

In that moment he formed a lasting resolution. He himself had some scant months remaining of prison life under the control of big Magruder. When that time ended, if he had not subdued the stallion, he would set him free to do as he would—whether that was to range at large or come again under the domination of another man.

When he had made the resolve, he felt far easier in spirit and he went in to take his place at the table for supper.

91

What followed was no easy time for Phil Slader. Magruder knew that the time during which he was to possess this unpurchased slave had nearly drawn to a close. Here was an event which threw his possession into a high light, and he was determined to take the utmost advantage of the fact. That riding of the stallion at the rodeo, impromptu though it had been, had attracted an enormous lot of attention. If cowpunchers had formed the habit, before this, of coming to the Magruder hotel to see young Slader and compare him with the pictures and the reputation of his dead father, there was now a sudden influx of people of all kinds.

They sat on the fence and they watched Phil drive his horses to the plow. They sat at the same table with him and stared into his face until his grave eyes were raised to their own and made them shift their glances with a guilty suddenness. There was one red-nosed old gentleman who said that he represented a circus, and that if Phil cared to undertake a horse-riding job . . . .

"Nothing really so bad, kid. You know how it is. Some old nags fixed up to look dangerous but really not! You dig one spur into them to make them throw a few stiff-legged capers. And you come in with a spotlight on you and the band playing and a swell rig on you—with a silk sash and all that sort of stuff—and the crowd goes wild. You know—Phil Slader, *the* Slader, the only one of his kind now . . . ."

That sentence remained unfinished as the slow glance of Phil rose and steadied upon the speaker.

"Oh, well," said the little old man with the red nose. "Of course, if you feel that way about it there's no use—pass the ham again, will you, Magruder?"

They were hard days for Phil, and one gathering followed another until, about a week later, there was an interruption of an unexpected sort. It was at the lunch table. There were a fat dozen around the board, all eating at Magruder's most fancy prices, when there was a noisy clattering of hoofs on the dust-muffled road, a slamming of the outer door, and a banging of high heels on the passage. Then a cowpuncher broke in upon them, his hat pulled firmly down over his eyes, as though he were still breasting the high wind of a strong gallop.

"Mitch Holmer wants everybody turned out," said the stranger. "He's rounded up Lon Kirby at last. It's the finish of Kirby, and you fellows had better try to get in on it. It's the finish of Kirby, I tell you, if we just get out enough of the boys to round him up and rope him. He's given us trouble enough, and riding enough, but we've got him now!"

Of course, there was a general rising and the sound of many voices.

"Who's done it? What's happened, Jake?"

"I dunno who did it," the messenger replied. "Maybe me. Maybe Bert Stillwell. We both were trying for him with our rifles at the time. But it was a long-range chance, and you couldn't tell who had the luck. Only, all at once there was Lon Kirby's hoss dropped dead, and Lon rolling head over heels in the stubble . . . ."

This brought a yell from every throat. Here was news indeed!

"We rushed Kirby, then," went on Jake. "But there was some bushes near the spot, and he had crawled into them. Then he must of sneaked off down one of the sloughs. Only one chance in a hundred that he would get away from us, but he did. Chances are that he's cut for the hills and the rocks. He knows that part of the country like a book. But he's on foot, and if we can turn out enough gents to comb the hillsides and head him off, he's our meat. He's on foot. Think of that!"

It was a good deal to think about, indeed. One had only to stretch one's hand into the white-hot sun which was pouring through the open window to realize the pain of the man in riding boots who tried to struggle across much of this burning countryside. Every Westerner could appreciate such facts as these. And every man at the table was a Westerner.

They rushed out of that room like hornets from a nest which had just been tapped with a pole. In a trice, down to big Magruder himself, they were in their saddles!

Of course, Phil Slader was not the last to mount. Here

93

was a chance for which he had waited many and many a year. Here was a chance where violence would not be held against him but listed to his credit. And if he were to meet Lon Kirby and shoot it out with him—even if Phil Slader were left dead upon the ground, no one could venture to say that he had not died as an honorable man should—in the attempt to go straight—go straight—go straight!

He paused in the hall just long enough to snatch from the rack an old Colt. It was a gun that he had had in his hand more than once before. He had never carried it, for it was against his principles to carry shooting weapons. Guns were poison; guns were apt to bite the hand that fed them; guns, most of all, were taboo for a Slader with such a father as he must call his own! However, here he was in the saddle, with a Colt in his saddle holster, and the sun-whitened country before him to range through!

First of all, he turned toward the hills, toward which the others were riding, some of them in groups, and some of them one by one, each in the particular direction which struck his fancy as being apt to be the one in which the famous outlaw might have ridden. When he reached the high ground which first lay before him, he drew rein and looked around him.

It did not seem to Phil a time in which to make haste in any way except slowly. Kirby had a long start in minutes. Other hard riders were already combing the hills. What if they were wrong? What if Kirby were riding in a different direction?

Phil turned toward the river. The tangled woods along the course of the Crusoe were an ideal shelter. To be sure, they were very far from the spot where Lon Kirby's horse had been shot down. But a very desperate and cunning man, accustomed to taking long chances, might have taken advantage of the first shallow gully to run from the brush in that direction, and then venture to skulk across the wide stretch of perfectly open country toward the river lands.

That idea had no sooner come to Phil Slader than he tried to put himself in the place of the outlaw, followed by hard-riding pursuers, all ready to shoot and to shoot

94

to kill. Beside him lay a dead horse; there was only the partial and scanty shelter of a patch of brush to avail him at the present moment. In such a case as that, Phil felt sure that only one thing would keep him from making for the distant brush along the river—that would be the lack of sufficient nerve to carry him across the open space which lay between. But no one could ever accuse Lon Kirby of lacking enough nerve for the attempt of any enterprise, no matter how hazardous.

So Phil turned the head of his horse toward the river and spurred the mustang into a hard, pounding gallop. He crossed the next low swale; he dipped the mustang into the gulch and forced it upon the dry and crumbling side of the slough beyond. It was hard work; twice the little animal fell back and had to be sent snorting and plunging to the task once more. However, it climbed out at length, and just as Phil was about to send it on with renewed speed, something like the hum of a monstrous bee whirred past his ear, followed instantly by the loud and smashing report of a rifle.

He did not have to think; something in his heart of hearts told him what to do. With every muscle relaxed, he let himself fall from the saddle, lying in a crumpled heap upon the ground. Certainly it was not a suspicious circumstance that he had happened to fall with his revolver in his hand!

He had been fired upon, treacherously, from behind, and in his soul there was a strong prophecy as to who might have done that bit of work. But he waited, not daring to stir, though constantly scanning the woods behind him—until he saw the figure of the man ride out into the open—Doc Magruder himself!

CHAPTER 17

ON THE FARTHER bank of the slough which separated him from the fallen body of his ward, Magruder checked his horse, put his rifle to his shoulder, and drew a careful bead.

The first impulse of the boy was to roll over with a shout and squirm into safety behind the next stump of a tree. The second impulse was to send a bullet from his revolver at the head of that same Magruder. But the third impulse was the one which he obeyed. No matter what he tried to do, Magruder was not apt to miss a shot at such pointblank range as this. At any range, as Phil had cause for knowing, Magruder was a deadly shot, who kept himself in constant and professional practice. It required all of Phil's endurance and all the will power in his body. But he managed to keep himself quiet through dreadfully long seconds until the rifle was finally jerked down from the shoulder of the big man—and he could see Magruder nod with satisfaction, as though he had made up his mind that nothing but a dead body could possibly have held that awkward position in which Phil Slader lay.

Magruder shoved the Winchester into the pocket along the side of the saddle and rode hastily forward to examine his work more in detail. So he dipped down into the gully, and Slader was instantly on his feet.

His head was a little confused, naturally, owing to the length of time he had lain in such a constrained position. But it was clear enough, by the time that he reached the bank of the slough, to permit him to shove his Colt into the face of Magruder as that gentleman forced his horse up the shelving and crumbling bank. There was a choked gasp from Magruder—and then his big arms went up above his head:

"Phil—for Heaven's sake!"

"Is it for Heaven's sake? I was only thinking about my own sake," said Phil Slader. "How come that you're shooting at me, today, Doc? Nothing else do you for a target?"

"Shooting at you. Shooting at you? Heavens about us—shooting at you? Boy, don't talk like a jackass. And lower your voice. Talk soft! Yonder lies Lon Kirby, I tell you. Dead, I think, but maybe only shamming death! I dropped him from behind—a neat shot—and now I want to see . . . ."

Perhaps it was all pretending. But there was just a ghost of a chance that Magruder was sincere.

"Tell me, Doc," said Phil Slader, "just what sort of a looking man is Lon Kirby?"

"You've seen his pictures," said Magruder, "and outside of his long, lean, pale face—curse him!—he's got about your build, I'd say, Phil."

"Keep your hands up!" said Phil Slader.

"Why, Phil, boy," said the older man, "what the devil do you mean by this? Do you . . . ."

"Nothing I guess. You can put 'em down. But be careful with them. If you move a mite too close to the handle of a gun, I'll kill you Doc. You hear me talk?"

"I hear you talk—but I can't understand you."

"Aye, it must be a terrible shock to you, but keep on being shocked, Doc. I'm dangerous, just now"

"You look it, and—why, you act like I had done something to *you*, son!"

"Go easy, Doc," said Phil Slader. "I'm pretty simple. And I love you so much that it would be hard for me

97

to figure you for any dirty trick at all. But, just the same, I'm watching you, and trying to work this thing out. It was me that you did something to. You missed my ear about a quarter of an inch and then . . . .'"

"By merciful Heaven!" cried Magruder. "You mean to say that you were . . . ."

"Yes, that I was the gent that you fired at."

"And you played possum—and let me—but, Phil, when I drew that second bead at you, at point-blank range . . . ."

"I thought that you wouldn't waste the price of another bullet on carrion like me," said Slader. "Not when there was crows to shoot at on the wing. And it seems that I was right!"

"Heaven knows that I'm grateful that I missed!" said Magruder, "but just for a minute there, I thought that I might of had the luck to . . . ."

"You knew that Lon Kirby is on foot," said the boy, crisp and stern.

"I knew that a bunch of fools had said that he was on foot. But how did I know that he hadn't laid about and taken his first chance to knock one of the boobies off a horse and ride on with the horse?"

Phil Slader hesitated. It was all probable enough, from one viewpoint. Lon Kirby was perfectly capable of having done the very thing that Magruder said he suspected. And Magruder was not the man to hesitate, when he thought that he recognized the rear view of fifteen thousand dollars. That was the reward which had accumulated upon the precious head of Lon Kirby.

However, there were other details which had to be considered, and Phil voiced them slowly, one by one.

"I hate to embarrass you any, oldtimer," he said to Magruder, "but if you was to tell me that you didn't know that cayuse wonder, that I was riding, as well as I know my own hat . . . ."

"Know the horse you were riding? Curse it, Phil. I wasn't out to shoot horses. I wasn't out for that, like the sheriff's men. I was out to kill Lon Kirby, if I could. And I thought that I had done it, for a minute! I thought that the skunk might have tried to get to the woods along the river and that maybe . . . ."

"Wait a minute," said Phil Slader. "I got about two months left before I slide away from you, Doc. You know that. You know that when I get away, the first thing I do will be to cut for headquarters."

"Headquarters?" echoed Magruder.

"I mean—the place where my father was killed. And when I get there, I'm going to start drumming up the facts connected with the killing of my father. I'm going to talk to a few of the eye-witnesses. And you know what I suspect—that there was dirty work in that killing. I say, Doc, that you know I'm going to start this sort of an investigation two months from now—and so maybe it would be a pretty handy thing for you to have me out of the way right now, when there isn't much longer for me to work for you, any way that you look at it!"

"You talk wild—plumb wild!" said the hotel owner. "I tell you, kid, there isn't much longer for you to work *for* me, but there's plenty of time for you to work *with* me. You don't think, Phil, that I've let you work for me all of these years for nothing!"

"No," said Phil, "maybe I just dreamt that, and all the time you've been putting money in the bank for me?"

"Amounts to the same thing, or better. You've furnished the work *and* the brains. I've furnished the land that gave you the chance, and some other things that you needed, such as horses, and the rest. Well, now you've worked up a fine thing, on this here place of mine, and what I have always wanted to invite you to do—was to come in with me as partners—half and half, Phil. You and me, half and half!"

He spoke with a truly Falstaffian heartiness, and Phil Slader squinted hard at him but could not make his glance bore through to indubitable truth.

"I'd like to know," said Phil. "I'd sure like terrible well to be able to tell whether you're halfway square or not. I don't want your partnership. Not for a million! I donate the work that I've done—and I give you half a year before you've let the place go to ruin, straight! However, that ain't my party. But I want to tell you one more thing!"

"Son," said Magruder, "dog-goned if it don't shock me to hear the way you talk to me. It shocks me and it cuts me pretty deep. Makes me feel pretty sad, Phil. But I'm listening. What is the other thing that you want me to hear?"

"I'll tell you straight enough. I want you to hear this. From now on, while I'm with you, I'm going to pack a gun. And the reason that I'll pack that gun is because I don't trust you Doc. I don't trust you a bit, and I want you to know it. I'm going to pack a gun, and the first time that I see you making a pass that looks queer to me, I'm going to up and kill you. You understand?"

"Phil!" cried the older man.

"Oh, I mean it. I mean it straight as a die. I think that you knew me, today, and I think that you knew my horse. And I think that you want to murder me, Doc, before I get out of your hands. Now we understand each other. Maybe I'm a swine to suspect you of this. And maybe I'm just a fool for letting you go, now that I've got it all right. But I'd hate to be outlawed on account of killing a pup like you, Magruder. I sure would!"

So said Phil Slader, speaking slowly and calmly. And Magruder swallowed the insults as though they had been delicious wine. The boy had more to say—much more—but instead of stopping to hear what the continuation might be, Phil reined his mustang back and when he reached the shelter of the trees, quickly whirled the animal away into a gallop.

There was no following sound of hoofbeats behind him, and he could guess that, no matter what Magruder might have in mind, he had done enough for this one day.

So Phil Slader shut the thought of his guardian from his young mind and turned whole-heartedly to the work which was before him—the search of the river woods for the elusive form of that famous man, Lon Kirby.

CHAPTER 18

No DOUBT many a man had gone out before to the man hunt with a lifted heart and great expectations, but surely no one ever road forth with such pure joy as that which filled young Phil Slader on this day of days. In his life, he had been forced to exercise a constant self-control. The hand which yearned, on a day, to knock Sammy Newell flat upon his back, had been tied to his side by the knowledge that all acts of violence upon his part would be wrongly construed by the rest of public opinion. So he had proceeded through these years of young life with more inhibitions than channels of expression—a dangerous condition for any youngster, and above all for a powerful nature like his own. But, knowing that he must pay most dearly the first indication of physical violence, he had controlled himself.

Today he was free. He had before him a quarry which he was free to hunt down, if he could. Therefore, his heart was merry indeed! He forgot his encounter with Magruder and all the trouble which that meeting might create. He lived for the moment, for one thing only.

Phil Slader drove his mustang rapidly toward the Crusoe River, with the murmur of the upper falls growing louder each moment. Yet, when he came to another good outlook which surveyed a considerable sweep of the stream, he paused again and considered. If he had been in the boots of Lon Kirby, what would he have done? Would he have turned upstream, through the dense thickets or would he have gone down?

In either case, there were considerable difficulties. If he turned upstream, he had rapidly rising ground before him; but he had, in addition, the sheltering hills not far away, among whose broken surfaces, when the night came, he could surely contrive to slip away out of the circle of the man hunters.

If he went down the stream, his course would be easier with the falling ground, but he would have no particular goal. Phil Slader was, however, reasonably sure that that was where Lon Kirby must have gone. For Kirby would know that the pursuers were searching the hills for him in preference to all other places. He would go down the stream, working his way painfully through the brush.

Another idea came to Phil. It was all well enough to wade through those tangles of underbrush. But what mileage would a strong man make in a day? Phil knew all about those thickets. Certainly it was no district for speed. Nothing, saving the waters of the stream, worked easily down the valley—and there was always that five-mile current swinging down.

It was this that brought the next inspiration to Phil. Five miles an hour was a reasonably good gait. As fast as even a good walker could maintain over any space of time. Suppose that he, himself, had been forced into that covert, would he not have been tempted to expend a little time in gathering dry driftwood along the banks of the stream, and then let himself float serenely with the Crusoe River until the night came? Then, in a region many and many a welcome mile away, he would come forth and take horse and saddle from the unlucky rancher who happened to have a house nearest to his point of exit from the marshes?

When that thought came to Phil Slader, he decided to act as though it was a certainty. He headed, then, not straight for the river, but far down its course. If the bandit had really taken to the water, he had been some time afloat; so Phil Slader made his mustang maintain a heartbreaking gait for a full hour, then, when he was well down the valley, he turned in toward the stream. At the outer edge of the marsh, he tethered his horse—just deep enough to keep it screened from observation from the outside. Then he struck in toward the water working fast and hard.

It was not a pleasant marsh, even as marshes go. There were stretches of water covered with thick-crusted slime, of a pea-green color. Out of this slime rose stumps and half-fallen trees, covered with the same incrustation and of the same deadly color. At every step, rotten wood crunched beneath his heel. When he paused to listen, he would hear stealthy whispers, here and there, as though other creatures had heard his coming and now were moving carefully away. And now and again, with a light slipping sound, more hidden than a whisper, a snake slipped from a wallowing log and dived through the hideous water.

It seemed to Phil, after a time, that he was not the hunter, but the hunted. Vague motions of panic rose in his heart. Again and again he had to check a foolish impulse to retreat in all haste toward the bright, white sun which shone beyond. And when he looked through that decayed forest and past the acephalous trees, toward the blue of the sun-washed sky, he felt as though the green stain of the bog were entering his own soul forever.

Yet he kept on his way, sometimes slipping into the horrible muck deeper than his waist but wading out again and working his way as much by force of hand as by leaping from log to log. At length he came to the higher ground immediately beside the course of the Crusoe. There he had barely kicked some of the muck and water from his feet and wiped some of the clinging slime away from his hands, when he heard a cheerful whistling coming down the stream toward him.

It seemed to blot out all of his labors at once. He cursed his foolish work and his disappointed hopes, at the same instant. He had come hunting for the fugitive from justice.

103

And instead, here was a gayly whistling man . . . . He had a gloomy desire to locate the source of this whistling. No doubt it came from some boy who was fishing in the waters of the river. So Phil Slader stepped under the arch made by a bowed tree which leaned like an abutment against a taller and stronger brother. Through the arch he peered out over the flashing waters until he saw the music maker approaching.

It was no boy in a boat. The craft was a rudely constructed raft made of a dozen or more sizable logs which were held together with twisted withes cut from creeping vines. It was a sluggish and half water-logged structure but it traveled very nearly as fast as the current which drifted it along, and now, as the current at a curve gripped it, the craft went forward with such impetus that the man had much difficulty in steering safely with his oar. This was no more than a length of the tough outer rind torn from some rotten stump of a tree.

There was a broad, shady beach, on the inner side of the bend—the side next to Phil Slader, in fact—and in attempting to veer his clumsy ship away from the shallows at the edge of this, the stranger gave his vessel such strong paddling that it twisted awry and began to turn end for end, spinning in the current. An instant later, it had slid through the slush at the edge of the beach, and there sat the stranger with his arms folded, very much at his ease, in spite of this misadventure. Indeed, he had not stopped the tune which he had been whistling, even while he was paddling most vigorously!

Phil Slader looked upon him with amazement and with delight. For this was Lon Kirby, at last! This was Lon Kirby's long, narrow face; this was Lon Kirby's build, so like his own, as Magruder had said—not overly tall, but formidably wide of shoulder and long of arm. Indeed, there was more than a little excuse for the mistake that Magruder had made, and Phil was glad that he had not pushed matters to an extremity in his interview with Doc.

The pale, ugly face of the fugitive turned slowly from place to place. One would have thought that he was making up his mind whether or not he ought to accept the dictates of luck, and land here permanently from his little boat. Indeed, he finally stood up and stepped ashore, and began to examine the big rocks which were scattered here and there along the sands of that bend.

They seemed to please him, these big boulders, and he examined them, finally, with so much care that it seemed to Phil Slader, the outlaw must be noting the mark of the point to which high water came. At length, he picked out a stone which was beyond that danger point and he began to work and pry at it. It was far too deeply rooted for his strength.

He tried another and this time by a vast effort, he overturned the stone. He turned up its jagged, massive roots and straightway he dropped upon his knees and began to examine the dirt under the stone and then to scoop it out. He sifted the first handful or so through his fingers, and seemed much pleased with the dryness of the gravel.

At length, when he had been digging for some time, he took a little parcel from his inside coat pocket, dropped it into the hole in the ground and presently set about the labor of erecting the big stone over its former site. It was hard labor, to be sure, but eventually he managed it. Then he began to scatter the dry, white surface sand over the spot, and to brush out all traces, as well as he could by working over the sand's surface with the palm of his hand.

He had seemed the very height of carelessness, up to this point, but now he appeared the very acme of scrupulous exactness. All the while, the wonder in Phil Slader grew greater and greater. For he knew that Kirby could not but be aware of the frightful danger in which he stood. Capture meant no mere trial and polite prison sentence. Capture meant for him certain hanging at the hands of the law—if not at the hands of some over-zealous mob.

Yet here was the man whistling gayly and calmly, as he floated down the river, with life or death in the making. Here he was whistling still as he worked at burying his money. Oh, there had never been such another man as this, since the days when joyous Jack Slader rode and

105

fought and prospered along the frontier and left a certain amount of laughter and of tears in his wake.

It was as if Lon Kirby cast the greater part of the burden of worry upon the knees of the gods. They could save him, if they would and they would damn him if they chose. But as for the little matter of a bit of additional noise—why, if there were any man hunter near enough to hear that whistling, he was near enough to nearly see him anyway!

Such, it seemed plain, must be the reasoning of Lon Kirby, and it seemed to Phil Slader dangerous reasoning enough, but filled with wonderful charm to him. He knew before half of the work had been finished, that he could not march down and present his gun at the head of Kirby. It seemed to Phil, now, that there would be a species of cowardly treachery involved in such a procedure. It would be the casting of a certain reflection back upon Jack Slader—the outlaw, and his son, the captor of outlaws!

So reasoned Phil, faultily, no doubt, but with all of the honesty which he could summon. And he sat in his place and watched fifteen thousand dollars, in the shape of human flesh and blood, finish the burial of the treasure, and then push off the rickety raft, step onto it, and finally drift, still whistling, down the farther bend of the current:

"Charlie is my darlin', my darlin', my darlin',
Charlie is my darlin', the young . . . ."

And the rumbling of the waters and the distant hushing of the great waterfall, drowned the sound of the song maker.

CHAPTER 19

AFTER THAT, as the whistling died out, it seemed to Phil Slader that he had doubtless been a great fool to allow this valuable criminal to slip through his hands. No doubt there was a certain duty that he owed society in apprehending the outlaw; moreover had he not started forth with the greatest keenness, bent upon finding and crushing this very man? But the joy had been in the finding of him and there would be no particular pleasure, so it seemed to him, in simply presenting a gun and ordering him to throw up his hands—and then destroying him if he refused to obey.

At any rate, to capture the bandit had become an impossible thing—all the more impossible because he had been so completely at the mercy of Phil. Yet, now that all sound of him had disappeared, Phil came forth shame-faced and went to the spot where, as it appeared, the outlaw had buried his treasure.

He laid hold upon that same rock which the great Lon Kirby had barely been able to move. To his joy, it came away easily in his hands. It might be that Lon Kirby was a cunning and dreadful warrior, but it was certain that his careless and free life had not given his arms and shoulders the same power that lived in Phil Slader,

107

who had been nurtured by hard work and endless work, all the days of his young life.

He raised that rock and, rejoicing in his might, he carried it bodily several steps, though the huge weight drove his feet deep, deep into the sand over which he walked. In the cavity beneath it there was a thin covering of dry pebbles, and when these had been brushed away, he found the small package which he had noticed before, produced from the pocket of the outlaw. A very ordinary package, indeed, and it seemed impossible that anything of worth could be in it. To be sure, when he had cut away the strings, there was oiled silk to unwrap, first of all, and after that, the sight which he had expected—a stack of bills.

It was far smaller, however, than the stack which he had anticipated!.This was merely of the size of a handful. Yet it was wadded firmly together, and when he detached the first note, he saw that it called for the payment of five hundred dollars!

He was amazed by this; he had realized, dimly, that money of such a denomination was indeed printed by the government, and yet it had hardly seemed a credible fact that five hundred dollars could be wadded, if he chose, into a ball hardly larger than a pea—that five hundred dollars could be tossed into the air by the pressure of his breath, and so carried away in the wind forever, to fill a corner, perhaps, in the nest of a hawk or to soften the bed of the squirrel?

But what was five hundred dollars as he had always thought of it in the past? It meant the wages of a year of labor as a cowpuncher, when he was able to attain to the dignity of such free employment. It meant, moreover, what a cowpuncher's wages would be if they were all saved and treasured up, and not a penny expended for clothes or tobacco, for guns or ammunition, or to buy trinkets to present to a friend's children for Christmas—above all, to supply the ways and means for any true cowpuncher's celebration, which gave a little touch of salt to life! If not a penny were spent in the year, there would be at the end of it, twenty dollars less than the sum which this first bill that he lifted from the stack represented!

For this sum could not all the horses of Magruder be clad in the new harness they needed so much; the blacksmith shop could be refitted completely and turned into a place where, with his strength and craft of hand he could make almost anything that the heart of a farmer could desire? All of this was most undubitably true. Beyond this there was to be considered that for a mere miserable eight dollars he could buy that perfectly good plow from Jackson—that one which had only been damaged by a little exposure to the weather. In addition to this, for merely eighteen dollars he could buy the good two-ton wagon which young Caldwell offered for sale; for twenty-two dollars he could get him the buggy which Greenwich no longer wanted. It had cost a hundred and fifty, new, rubber tires and all—with only a repainting job to be done, which he knew perfectly well how to manage himself! He scanned the limitless possibilities which lay in that single sheet of printed paper.

But no, this was money stolen from the bank. It must be returned therefore, to the place from which it was taken. He conjured up before his eye the form of that admitted scallywag, Alden Turner, president of the Crusoe bank. He could almost hear the oily smoothness with which the phrases would be turned off the tongue of the banker, and the unction with which he would pronounce limitless grace over the head of the brave and honest man who returned this money to its rightful owner. In the conclusion, he would offer some ten or twenty dollars reward . . . .

The lip of the young man curled. There was no one who did not hate Alden Turner, and only the fact that his money made him a necessity to that ranching community, kept him from being a social outcast. However, this was the man who would receive back this five hundred dollars and all the rest of the money.

Young Phil Slader bowed his head in profound thought before he went on with the counting of the money. There was only the one handful of it, as has been said before, but how closely the sheets were wadded together had to be seen before it could be believed. For here was a veritable brick of money. Yet no gold brick was ever so precious. No brick made of indubitable yellow gold was ever a tithe as valuable as this one!

The very next bill beneath the top one was for a thousand dollars and fifty sheets came off in swift succession, each printed for the value of a thousand dollars, calling upon the government of the United States to pay to the bearer that sum in the gold coin of the realm. A thousand dollars in gold—three pounds of the solid, precious metal represented by each thin film of printed paper.

There had never been reading half so delightful to any human eye as was this to the eye of Phil Slader. He read on and on and the story swelled in vast interest as he proceeded. Twenty thousand, fifty, eighty thousand dollars —a hundred thousand dollars, and still more and much more to come! But this was more than even the bank of Alden Turner claimed had been stolen from it. Part of the money could go back to satisfy Mr. Turner and his needs which were all just and legal. But what of the rest?

The sum swelled beneath the hands of young Phil Slader to one hundred and eighty-two thousand dollars before he came to the end of this delightful story told in words which even a fool could have understood with the most complete ease! A hundred and eighty-two thousand dollars.

It was far and far beyond the wildest dreams of young Phil. Perhaps there were few men able to sit down and understand the meaning of such a sum. But Magruder had helped to interpret the meaning of a hundred thousand to him. And here was practically double that grand sum.

His mind began to stretch swiftly away. New vistas opened with suddenness before him. And he saw with a dazzled eye the possibilities of buying, let us say, the "Chuck" Oswald place, now used for cattle only, but with all the possibilities of the rich bottom lands whose blackness Phil had yearned so often to furrow with a plow! Much, much was to be done. He felt that the possibilities slipped beyond the grip even of his mental finger tips.

But oh, was it not a grand thing to contemplate all of this?

And contemplate it he did, for burning, drunken minutes, sitting like a statue in the sands, until his mind turned back to the other side of the picture, which was certainly there, begging for his eye. Upon that other side he read indubitable facts—that no man can receive something for nothing, unless it be by legal gift and legal procedure; no man has a right to appropriate that which belongs to another.

He tried to dodge that point; he tried to evade it by simply refusing to think of it. But he could not turn it from his attention. It ate in upon him like the rays which a sunglass focus on a point of burning heat. This money was not his, and nothing connected with it belonged to him. He had not the slightest claim to anything except the reward which might be offered for the return of the loot. Up to that time, the rewards which Alden Turner was offering so profusely had spoken of the apprehension of the criminal, but never of the return of the money—as if Alden Turner was not fool enough to hope for the return of his cash, once it was lost to him.

Phil Slader wondered, as he turned the question bitterly in his heart of hearts, how much money would ever be returned by the same Alden Turner, in case *he* were to come across it, buried in a hole in the ground? How far would he go to make a return of it to the rightful owner possible? Not a single step, and Phil was as sure of it, as human mind can be sure of anything on this mortal earth.

However, he could not help realizing that the standard of what was good and right was not established by Alden Turner. And he knew, presently, that he dared not take that money upon this day. He dared not!

So he decided that he would leave it there in the hole beneath the rock where he had found it. When twenty-four hours had passed over his head, then he would be far better qualified to decide on this all-important question. Such was the decision to which he had come. And so he got up and, having replaced the wad of money in its place, he strode to the big rock and heaved it up again with an easy might of hand. At that moment, as he turned around bearing his load, the shrubs parted and admitted first the long barrel of a rifle, and behind the rifle the squinted eye and the long, pale face of Lon Kirby! He had circled back to make certain that he had not been trailed.

CHAPTER 20

IT MAKES A great deal of difference on which end of a gun a face appears. Looking at Lon Kirby from the security of the brush, with a Colt in his hand, Phil Slader had not considered him an extraordinary person by any means. Looking at him, however, with that same face cuddled down beside the stock of a rifle and the long, gleaming barrel pointed in Phil's direction, it seemed to Phil that he had never seen greater possibilities for cold-blooded mischief in any human being.

"Just stick up your mitts," said Lon Kirby. "Just drop that rock and stick your mitts up into the air, kid, and remember that I'm watching how you get them hands above your belt and the gun that you got there!"

It did not occur to Phil Slader to disobey. He might have dropped the rock, he considered, and whipped out his Colt as he raised his hands, but before he could do that he knew that he would have been a dead man.

So the stone fell and chugged heavily into the loose

sand of that little beach. And Phil's hands rose to the level of his head.

"Good!" said Lon Kirby, forthwith dropping his rifle over the hook of his left arm. "Now we can talk. I was afraid, for a minute, that maybe I would have to snuff you out, partner, before I had a chance to chat with you for a while. And that would of been a shame, because I've met a lot of gents, big and small, that laid some sort of claim to being called strong men, and I've never found one of the whole lot that could lift pound for pound with me—until I run into you. And you're a stronger man than I am, youngster. Did you see how I had to wrestle around with that rock?"

"I seen it all," said Phil Slader.

"You did, eh?"

"I did."

"Quiet and sassy about it, you seem to me to be. Wait a minute!"

He secured the rifle, with his right hand and arm only, still with his finger upon the trigger; then, pressing the muzzle against Phil's heart, he stretched forth his left hand and plucked out Phil's gun.

"Old-fashioned one, ain't it?" said Lon Kirby. "Pretty old-fashioned it looks to me. But now there is your gun on the ground. And I ask you, kid, if I was to lay aside my own guns, would you fight me here, hand to hand and man to man, and the best man win a rough and tumble?"

A flame burned in the heart of Phil Slader and a flame burned in his eyes. The hands beside his head crooked a little as though already they were closing on the flesh of Lon Kirby.

"Do that," said Phil, "and I'll try my luck with you
. . . ."

"And the winner will die, kid. You understand that that would be the way out?"

"Oh, yes," said Phil, moistening his lips, for his very heart was dry with the thirst for this battle. "Oh, yes, I understand well enough! Throw your gats away, Kirby, and I'm ready for you, man. Will you do it?"

Lon Kirby merely smiled. "I thought that it might be in

you," he said, "but I wasn't half sure. I'm glad to see that sort of stuff. Very glad. But you ain't going to have your chance on me, youngster. I've seen what you can do to the rock. And that's enough."

He laughed openly and then rubbed a stubby-fingered hand—the true hand of the strong man—over his long, pale chin. He pointed toward the little open pit.

"If it wasn't for that thing yonder," he said, "there ain't any good reason why you and me might not be the best of friends. But the way that it stands, I'll have to tie you to a stump here while I go on down the river. Otherwise you might wade out through the marshes, yonder, and give word to the boys that I'm drifting down the river. And they would work up a little reception committee to wait on me when I come out of the brush, eh?"

Said Phil, very thoughtful: "If you tie me up here, nobody would ever hear me holler. You know that?"

"I know that," said the outlaw with a perfect blandness.

"And since nobody ever comes down this here river except once in about every ten years, there wouldn't be much hope of me ever getting loose."

"That's reasonable," said the outlaw, as unmoved as ever.

"And the chances are about ten to one," said Phil Slader, "that I'd sit there against a stump until I starved to death."

"Son," said the criminal, "you speak it out like a piece learned right out of a book. There ain't a thing that you've overlooked except the fact that the mosquitoes, that are getting pretty hot just now and which might eat part of you alive before any help came. But I'll tell you what I'll do, kid. I'll give you a choice between being tied up and, on the other hand, taking a lead pill between the eyes. The bullet won't cost you no pain, and it won't be a much surer way of dying than being tied here to a stump, as you've just pointed out so dog-gone exact."

"You'd do it, I think," said Phil Slader, moved with wonder.

"Sure I would," said the outlaw. "They'll hang me when

114

they get me, of course. And they might as well hang me for one more as for one less!"

He added, in the silence that followed: "What else is there for me to do?"

"A pretty good thing," said Phil Slader. "The thing for you to do is just take my word that I won't squeal on you when you go on down the river."

The other smiled broadly and waved his hand.

"That's a fine idea," said he. "Dog-gone me if that ain't a fine bit of thinking on your part. Why didn't the idea come to me before?"

"You didn't think that you could trust me," said Phil.

"No, but now I got the proof that I *can* trust you, eh? Kid, are you simpleminded?"

"You mean that you can't do it?"

"Why, son, I like you fine, and I would like to do you a good turn instead of a bad one, but, boy, you can't ask me to fit the rope around my own neck, can you?"

"I see," said Phil Slader.

"Well?" said the outlaw.

"There's no use in arguing when you've made up your mind so complete."

"Curse me if you ain't cool!" said Lon Kirby. "Set down and rest yourself and roll yourself a smoke. I dunno when I've got into a mess that I liked less than I like this! Now, why couldn't you be some sneaking, whining yap of a gent, instead of what you are? Why couldn't you fall on your knees and scream for help, when you seen me and my gun? Or why couldn't you of pretended that you didn't know who I was? Or why couldn't you of begged for your life, and, most of all, why couldn't you of throwed up to me how you lay there yonder in the bush and watched me bury that coin—and didn't put a bullet through me when you had a chance? Why couldn't you of been something like that, instead of a white man, so far as I can see? If you was a low sneak, it would be a plumb pleasure to me to drill you and leave you there to rot beside the water till the spring floods come along and washed you down. But the way it stands, you would ride on my conscience for a long time. Darned if you wouldn't bother me in my sleep. And here I am, like a windy old fool, talking a lot too much. And maybe," he added, his eye and his voice turning to iron, "giving you a wrong idea that I'm getting mush-hearted and soft, eh? Maybe doing that for you, son?"

Phil Slader shrugged his shoulders.

"You ain't in the mood for talking, eh?" said the outlaw.

"I know I'm about to die," said Phil Slader, "and that doesn't make your ugly mug any better looking to me."

"Keep your lip to yourself, kid," said the outlaw darkly. "I'm no uglier than some that are a lot better men than you'll ever be, my lad. And I want you to cotton onto that idea and never to forget it. You understand me what I say?"

"Take your rifle," said Phil Slader, "and stand off a mite and do the job. I've got no mind to stay here and be chewed to bits by the mosquitoes before I kick off."

The outlaw calmly stood up and raised his rifle to his shoulder.

"Wait a minute," said Phil Slader. "Just stand back there another yard, will you? And then let me stand up. I got an idea that I'd like to stand to take this."

"All right," said the bandit, nodding. "Are you ready?" he added, as Phil stood up.

"I'm ready, right enough," said Phil Slader.

"Close your eyes, then."

"No, I'll take this with them open."

The finger of the bandit curled around the trigger—but though the soul of Phil Slader seemed to lurch forward as though eager to take wing, there was no explosion.

"You didn't blink!" said the outlaw, and he dropped the rifle into the hook of his left arm. "Curse my soul, but you didn't even blink!"

"What's up?" asked Phil angrily. "Is this a joke, maybe?"

"Joke? Powder and lead don't make good joking, son!"

"Then get the mess over with, will you? I'm tired of it."

"You sort of hunger after 'going West,' do you? Well, kid, I'd like to tell you this: I want to be decent with you.

116

I want to do what's fair and right, as near as I can. And if you was to give me any messages for anybody, I'd be pretty sure that they got what you said, word for word."

"Thanks. I got nothing that I want to say to nobody."

"No? You don't mean it! Not a word to nobody? I see that you're a cold-blooded young devil, then. But you sure are in the mooney period, and you must have a best girl stuck away somewhere in your head, eh?"

"No," said Phil Slader. "No—she doesn't waste any time thinking about me."

"Aye," said the other almost joyfully, "then there *is* a girl, eh?"

"Look here," said Phil Slader, "you might let John Newell's daughter know that I—er—that I didn't have to wink when I seen it coming. You might do that. She would be sort of interested maybe."

"John Newell?"

"He's a farmer near Crusoe. Y'understand, this girl only has seen me twice. There don't have to be anything weepy in what you write to her about me; but just tell her the straight facts, will you?"

"Good," said the outlaw. "I'll do that. And that winds up the list?"

"That's all."

"Your mother is dead, then?"

"Yes, she's dead."

"And you and your father don't get on well together?" Phil Slader smiled.

"If I had my father living," said he, "you'd never send him a message from me."

"No?"

"No, you wouldn't. You would only be praying humble and hard that he would never know that there was such a gent as you in the world—let alone that you had a hand in bumping me off!"

Lon Kirby raised his brows. "You talk like your dad was a high stepper in his own day, kid," said he sternly. "You talk like maybe I would turn my back on him?"

"No," said Phil. "I'm not enough fool for that. I only

117

tell you the facts—that you might stand to him, but you'd know that you'd be beat before you went for your gun."

"Let's hear his name," said Lon Kirby angrily. "I'd like to know that man's name, kid."

"His name was Jack Slader," said the boy.

And he saw the outlaw shrink and gasp as though he had been struck.

"Jack Slader—*the* Jack Slader? Bless me, but you ain't his son?"

"I am, though."

"It's a lie," said Kirby. "You ain't the sneak that's living ever since with the gent that murdered your old man?"

"Murdered him?" said Phil Slader hoarsely. "Murdered him? No, I'm living with a man that beat him in a fair-and-square fight and took me in afterward, I suppose. I'm not living with a man that murdered Jack Slader."

"Wait a minute," said Lon Kirby. "Lemme stand back and have a look at you. Jack Slader's boy? Darned if you ain't! Darned if you ain't! You got his face, too. Rougher, maybe, and not so gay, but you got his face—only you're a bigger man. Jack Slader's son! Where have my eyes been today? Cursed if you ain't almost able to stand duty for his ghost on the day that I first met him. Well—I was a kid then, and he give me advice that should have put some sense into my head, but it didn't! But lemme tell you this— if you're Jack Slader's boy, you know that the kind of a carrion that Magruder is never had the nerve to stand to Jack Slader in a fight—let alone beat him and kill him."

118

CHAPTER 21

THE THING WHICH we half know beforehand is ever more impressive when the truth is fully revealed than the information which is totally new and unexpected.

Phil Slader began to tremble.

"Partner," said he, "you sure are making me want to live. And if you'll prove to me that Magruder didn't kill dad fair and square—I'll get down on my knees and beg you to let me live long enough to find Magruder and kill him. Then I'll come back here to you. You understand what I say?"

"I know—I know," said the outlaw, "but I can't give you the proof, and even if I could, I wouldn't."

"Tell me why, Kirby?"

"Because it ain't right for any man to stand up and take the law into his hands. It ain't at all right, son. I speak that ought to know what I'm talking about. I've killed my list, Heaven pity me, and I've seen some hard-boiled eggs go down eating my lead. But it never give me no joy, particular. I ain't a particular happy man, kid. You leave the law be. It'll do its own work with no advice from you or from me."

"It's let Magruder live these years and grow fat!" said Phil Slader.

119

"Magruder ain't dead yet," said Lon Kirby. "And you take it from me, the way that a man dies is what puts the mark on the way that he lived. Magruder will have a sick way of dying. His finish will be worse than a dog's, or I miss my guess about him."

"You might as well tell me what you know about dad's finish," said Phil Slader.

"I don't know nothing—except that Magruder lies when he says that he beat your dad fair and square and man to man."

"How do you know that?"

"Because I knew your dad. I was a youngster. Too young to be trying my hand at the sort of game that I liked. Lemme see. It was twenty years ago that I first met up with your father. He was young, too. But he wasn't a fool kid, like me. I was sixteen and thought that I was the hardest man that ever stepped into stirrups and yelled for a fight. But your father convinced me a lot different."

He smiled and shook his head, looking back with a foolish fondness into those dimly distant days of his youth. "I was talking big and acting big around that camp," said Lon Kirby. "And I ran slam into your dad, and I got up and cussed him out and told him what I thought about him and dared him to stand up and fight me!"

"Ah!" said Phil Slader, and leaned forward to listen more perfectly.

"He was about twenty-four or five," said the outlaw. "That was young. But he had ten years of it behind him, and that made him old. Besides, he had as much sense as he had nerve, which means a whole oceanful of it. He looked me in the eye and let me talk myself out. And he smoked his cigarette and watched the smoke blow up and curl away against the stars.

"The young kids that were sitting around, they were mighty scared and tickled to hear anybody talk like that to Slader himself. But the older gents, they didn't smile. They didn't even look at me. It was as though I didn't count at all in that picture. They just kept their eyes riveted on Jack, as though he was the one who would do the things that really counted.

"Well, I just talked myself out, after a while, and still Jack hadn't answered me. I felt a little queer about it, but pretty proud, on the whole.

"And when I met Jack Slader the next morning he just smiled and nodded to me, until I told myself that I had made the great man take water! Yes, I was fool enough to tell myself that. And it was two days later that I happened to be standing beside Slader when a rabbit jumped up and ran away.

" 'Take a try at it, Lon,' says Jack.

"I did, and I missed, and then he snatched out his Colt and fired from the hip, and that rabbit jumped in the air and turned somersaults into heaven. I never saw such a shot before, and I'll never see such a shot again.

"I could only stand there and stare, and, of course, I knew why he had asked me to try that shot. Because he knew that I'd miss, and because he knew that he wouldn't, and he wanted to show me what would have happened to me if I had fought with him that other night.

"Well, it made me feel pretty low and mean and shaky. But he took my gun and fired it at a tree—and missed it on purpose.

" 'I think that your gun shoots a shade to the right too much,' said Jack. And he handed the gat back to me. That was his way. He wouldn't make a fool even out of me, much as I deserved it that day.

"Of course, it was a terrible drop for me, but it took me three whole days before I got up my nerve to walk up to the camp fire, where the rest of the gents were all sitting around. And I says:

" 'Jack, I made a fool of myself here the other night. All I got to say is that I'm all the names that I called you. I want to apologize, and I hope that you'll accept it.'

"No idea what it cost me to eat dirt that way. I had to go out and rehearse that speech for days and hours. And even then, when I came to make it, I had to stutter and stammer through it. When I made my little talk, some of the older men nodded and grunted, but the youngsters,

121

they all sneered at me, as though they would rather of died than of done such a thing. Well, Jack Slader he stood right up and took my hand.

" 'Thank you for sayin' that before the rest of the bunch, Lon', says he. 'But there wasn't any need of it. I knew that you were sorry. Though I see that there's some of the young puppies here that don't understand the thing that you've just done.'

"And he looked around that circle slow and easy. I'll tell you that he had an eye that was hard to meet, and glances dropped like leaves in October. After that, he was my friend. He never forced his advice on me about anything, but when I asked him about something, a few days later, he told me that I ought to go home. He showed me where this sort of a life wound up. But I wouldn't believe him. Why, looking at Jack, he was so dog-gone handsome and sort of shining and glorious that I told myself that a life that was good enough for him was plenty good enough for me! And so there I stuck and got to be the thing that he warned me against!"

This speech was delivered slowly by Lon Kirby, with many pauses—not as one who hunts for words, but as one who lingers a little, seeing more and more clearly the pictures of which he was to speak. What he said came from very near his heart. There was a natural silence after this speech.

Then Lon Kirby said: "It seems as though you didn't know your old man very good?"

Phil shook his head. He could not speak.

"All right," said Lon Kirby. "You don't need to be ashamed and hang your head. Because he was the sort of a man that was worth your while getting soft about. He was white, one hundred per cent white, if I haven't been around the world a good long distance, but I've never yet found nobody that would match up with him for a minute! You take my word for it! Nothing that I've said about him was enough. He was a whole size larger than anybody else that I ever met!"

There was another pause, and some of the brightness had died out of the eyes of Phil when the other said: "Now

122

you can get a general idea of some of the reasons why Magruder never could of killed your dad. Magruder is a good fighting man. He's a straight shot and he's a quick one, and he's as good, or he used to be, as I am myself, which is saying enough for pretty near any man. But he never seen the day when he would of stood up to your father—not even for the half part of a second, y'understand me?"

"I understand, all right," said Phil Slader.

"And now," said the other, "it seems that things has sort of changed between you and me. It looks almost as though we had growed friendly—or is it only talk—which is like booze and often goes to the head?"

CHAPTER 22

It seemed to Phil Slader that all the kindness in the manner of Lon Kirby was almost purely adventitious. If that gentleness was founded upon old relations with the great Jack Slader, those relations were much too aëriform to be counted upon heavily. Under the surface of all this gentleness he felt the presence of iron qualities, hardly masked.

So he waited, saying nothing.

As for Lon Kirby, it seemed that he would gladly have heard more talk from Phil, either persuasive or adversative, so that he could find some manner of working himself out of this affair in one way or another. But the silence of Phil threw the whole moral weight of the decision squarely upon him. And he writhed mentally under the burden.

"Now, kid," said he, "I want you to tell me what you expect that I should do here."

Phil Slader thought upon the question for some time and then slowly looked up.

"I don't know," he said at last. "I see that you want to do what's right by me. But this is a stickler. If you leave me free, I may scoot away, you think, and raise the folks to hunt the river for you. If you don't leave me free, it's kinder to kill me, and you feel that that is hardly fair and square to my father. Ain't that the way that things stand?"

Kirby blinked, like one who, after wandering through thickest night for a long time, sees a sudden flash across the sky before him and hears it crash near his very feet. So it was with Kirby. He had lived so much among the crafty and the cunning that to find one example of frankness and honesty was almost more than he could believe. He remained for a long time, studying the face of Phil Slader, but failing to find there any hint of hypocrisy.

"That's the way that things stand," said Lon Kirby at last. "Here's the money, too. That counts. Because you had a chance to count it."

"Yes," said Phil.

"How much was there?"

"A hundred and eighty-two thousand dollars."

"A hundred and eighty-two or eighty-three. Which makes up a pretty neat little wad of money, eh?"

Phil nodded.

"I ain't a miser," said the bandit, "but you got to admit that I have my reasons for treating that money sort of respectful. You might say that it's my all, eh? It represents my savings and my checking account, too!"

Phil nodded again.

"And d'you aim to understand why I buried that coin?"

"Of course. You're taking a long chance, fetching down along the river in this way. You may win through safe enough, but then, again, you may miss altogether. You may run straight into their hands, and if they catch you, you don't want them to catch the money at the same time. Still, this ain't the only place you can hide it."

The other grinned rather more broadly than before.

"I might leave you here and go off down the stream and hide it in some other place, eh? Yes, and you might follow and see the new place as good as this one, kid! You might do that, and you *would* do that. What?"

"No," said Phil, "not if I told you that I wouldn't."

"D'you expect me to believe that?"

"No, not at all."

The bandit shrank again and bit his lip. He stared for a moment down at the ground.

"You look square. You act square," said he. "And I know that your father was the squarest crook that ever cracked a safe or stuck up a stage in the old days."

Here he raised his head again and stared fixedly at Phil. Inspiration had come:

"Kid," said he, "I don't want to make any fool of myself, but the funny idea has come along to me that maybe I've found out an honest man!"

He spoke it with such emotion that Phil Slader gaped at him and answered: "Why, I hope I'm one of the honest people, Kirby!"

"One of them? If you're honest," said the bandit, "you're about the only one. Don't tell me. I started among good folks. I've seen how much sneaking crookedness there was in them. The bad that is in good people is a terrible badness, kid. Look at me. I'm mean and hard and crooked and I know that I'm bad. I can appreciate that badness, and I can appreciate what real goodness should be, too.

"I've had pals, in my day, that I've swore to be true to, and they've swore to be true to me. And I've had them leave me in the lurch—some of them quit me when the pinch come and the guns were about to start talkin'. And some weakened when it come to making a fair-split of the loot. And some double crossed me for no good reason, except because they got jealous of me, or something foolish like that, y'understand? Oh, yes, I've had my experiences. But I haven't found a square shooter and an honest man yet—except Jack Slader—and they had a price on his head!"

He began to laugh and he ended his laugh with a snarl.

"I have no more partners now, kid. Gents never disappoint me, because I never give them a chance. And I'm not going to give *you* the chance, either! Kid, if I get soft about you, it means that I'm getting old and weak, and near my finish! Ain't that a fact?"

"Maybe it is," said Phil Slader coldly. "I don't know you. But I'm not going to beg. And if you're through telling me what a rotten lot other folks are, now tell me what you're going to do with me, will you?"

For he had grown more and more irritated as he listened to Kirby. He knew, indeed, that he was standing rubbing elbows with a miserable death. But he found that the thought did not fill him with fear, but rather raised joy in his heart. He felt more defiance in him than fear. It was that absence of fear that delighted him and filled him with wonder.

But the devil in Lon Kirby was no intangible thing; it was a living and breathing soul, and now it leaped into his face, transforming him wonderfully.

"By Heaven!" gasped Kirby. "Why, you're beggin' me to shoot, ain't you?"

Phil Slader shrugged his shoulders. "You been talking a lot of bunk about the folks that you knew and didn't know, Kirby. And you been saying what gents was honest, and what wasn't. But the whole point that interests me is this: If you can trust me, you turn me loose, and the thing ends that way. If you can't trust me, you pull a gun and shoot me. That's the whole of it. Now, you make up your mind which you're going to do, because I can't persuade you, and I'm not going to try."

"Aye," said the other, glaring at him. "You're pretty near mean enough to be honest, kid. You've got something in you, though—you got some honesty in you—but how much is there? How much is there?"

Phil shrugged his shoulders again.

"How old are you, Slader?"

126

"Nearly twenty-two."

"Twenty-two? Aye, and when was there ever a hundred and eighty thousand dollars' worth of honesty in a kid twenty-two years old?"

The wide shoulders of Slader were shrugged again.

"One chance in a thousand," said the outlaw, more to himself than to his companion. "But I've played chances that long, before this, so why shouldn't I play them again? Why not again? A thousand to one, kid, that you're a crook, but I take the chance on you!"

Hearing him say it so quietly and thoughtfully, Phil Slader could hardly believe his ears. But he saw Lon Kirby stand up and pick from the ground the revolver, which he had taken from his antagonist.

That weapon was passed to Phil, handle first. He had only to press the trigger with his finger and send Lon Kirby to the last accounting—while he himself picked a hundred and eighty thousand dollars from the gravel.

He thrust the Colt deep in its holster and he smiled at Lon Kirby.

"Lon," said he, "if this was to be the . . . ."

"Shut up, kid," said Lon Kirby. "Shut up and don't talk. It looks easy for you to play square with me—just now when you got your chance to live safe and happy. But maybe things won't be so good when you go back home and sleep over this to-night. You'll wake up in the middle of the night, and you'll see yourself dressed up in fancy togs, with a hundred and eighty thousand dollars in your pocket. That's what you'll see, eh?"

Phil Slader made no reply. He could see that the very inmost nature of Lon Kirby had been stirred by the scene through which they had just passed. His heart had been opened, and a stranger permitted to look into the guarded sanctum which exists in the soul of every man. Now he revolted against the familiarity which he had permitted in a stranger and was closing the portals of the inner temples.

"So long," said Lon Kirby. And he turned on his heel.

He crossed the opening until he came within a stride or two of the undergrowth which edged the beach. Then terror seemed to stab him suddenly in the small of the back. He leaped forward and disappeared with a crash out of the view of that potential enemy who stood in the clearing, with a gun behind at his waist.

But after that first crash, there was silence, and whether the other was slinking away toward his raft, beyond the point, or whether he had remained crouched there in hiding to observe the man whom he had put in danger of death and freed again, Phil could not tell. However, he raised the heavy boulder and let it sink again into its former position, covering solidly the treasure of Lon Kirby.

CHAPTER 23

IT WAS NOT until Phil Slader had gone back from the marshes along the river and started for the hotel of Magruder that he began to recollect the other great event of this day. Even so, though he was riding back to face Magruder—who might be a murderer or not, as the case chanced, the crisis between himself and Doc seemed a very slight affair compared to that interview between himself and the outlaw.

Yet the two, in a way, went hand in hand. For the greatest incident in that interview had been the recollections which Lon Kirby had expressed concerning famous Jack Slader.

The picture in the mind of Phil which made up the living representation of his father had been composed of vague remembrances out of his childhood, to a small degree, and to a greater extent of the stories and the impressions which had constantly been brought to his ears since he reached the age of distinct memories. What he recalled in person was a darkly handsome man, usually smiling, with flashing, quick-moving eyes, who appeared when not expected and disappeared again without any good reason. It was a very vague picture, a mass of vague hints with on agglutinate to hold the different impressions together; that was the sense of fear which had always accompanied his father like a shadow—not dread of Jack Slader himself, but an atmosphere of terror in which Jack lived and moved—the dread which is the breath in the nostrils of the hunted man. His mother did not appear at all to the eye of his mind. She was merely a vague sensation of sorrow and of sweetness, lodged far in the back of his mind.

But the greatest part, by far, that he knew of his father was not brought to his mind by memory; it was built out of the impressions which others had carried to him, and those impressions had been chiefly grim things enough. He had seen his father in every attitude of the desperado and gun fighter. He had seen him gun and knife in hand; he had seen him stealing through the night, like a stalking cat; he had seen him revealed in midday with a black mask across his face; he had seen Jack Slader galloping, yelling, through a startled town; he had listened to the explosion of Jack Slader's Colt in many a barroom brawl. Until, at last, a streak of red flame and a smudge of stinging powder smoke obscured in the mind of the boy his own image of the man.

Lon Kirby had fortified one image and torn down the other. This was a reasonable, sane, gentle fellow of whom he spoke. No doubt there were wild moments of passion in such a nature as that of Jack Slader's. There were times of explosion and rage and terrible blindness of battle fury, but there was also this other person, thoughtful, smiling, considerate of others, as he had been so pre-

129

ëminently in his dealings with that terrible young firebrand, Lon Kirby. With what a soothing influence these thoughts came home to the heart of the boy!

He had registered, long ago, a resolution born of a sense of duty, that when he grew older and chances came to him he would avenge the death of his father, if he could ever discover that Magruder had not downed him in fair fight. Now the testimony of Lon Kirby rang in the mind of the boy like a great bell pealing. Magruder, swore the outlaw, could never have handled Jack Slader. Magruder was as formidable a fighter as Lon Kirby himself, according to that gentleman, but even Lon Kirby would never have dreamed of standing for an instant to Jack Slader, hand to hand!

That was a freight of heavy testimony. This was a poundage of evidence which would be hard to balance; yet something more was needed before the scales inclined absolutely against Magruder. The opinion of no man could be enough to force on Phil the necessity of killing Magruder. There must be some more direct proof. And where could that proof be found?

When he got back to the hotel he hurried on to the field and harnessed his horses for the harrow. And as he took them out and prepared for work, the gray stallion neighed so loudly from the inclosure that the work horses fell into a confusion. They crowded against one another. They trembled and tossed their heads and grew wild-eyed. It was as though they had been mere paper images of horses, and the neigh of the stallion was a breath of wind that set them all at odds with themselves.

The work of harrowing suddenly became a silly thing to Phil Slader. He took the horses back to the barn and returned to the corral. There he bridled and saddled the big gray—and he slipped into the saddle.

It was always easy enough to do that. For it was only when the weight of a rider was settled firmly upon his back that the stallion began to fight. Some said that in his colthood he had been ridden with a burr beneath the saddle blanket, put there by the malice of some fool. And ever since he dreaded lest the torment should begin again!

130

When he felt the weight of Phil against him, now, he transformed himself at once into a raging fiend. A few age-long minutes followed before a whirling, snapping pitch jerked Phil Slader from the saddle and hurled him beneath the lowest bar of the fence—hurled him into safety just as the plunging forehoofs of the great horse struck for the spot where he had slid and missed him by inches.

He sat up, when his brain had cleared enough to permit this, and watched through a haze while Rooster raced up and down the inclosure, foaming, snapping with his teeth, shaking an imaginary victim to bits, rearing to strike a foe down with forefeet, or brandishing his mighty heels to let light through another enemy.

Phil Slader looked upon the monster with awe and with wonder. He could never conquer that spirit, he knew. Something had been lacking in him on the first day, when he fought the great fight with Rooster. Some vital and flaring wildness had been missing from his nature to match the irresistible furies of the big horse. The girl, with a trenchant eye, had looked straight to the real inner weakness which none of the men had been able to observe. "What a cunning one she is!" thought Phil Slader, picking himself up out of the dust and leaning against the fence.

There never had been such a horse for size and beauty and strength combined. There never had been such an animal before, he told himself, and, just as surely, instinct told him that he was the born master for the gray. Aye, for into the chamber of the mind where he kept the picture of all that a horse should be, this image of Rooster fitted perfectly. That ideal horse of his, no downheaded weakling of a slavish disposition. It was a wild-hearted tyrant, like Rooster in very deed! But it seemed that the thing which he yearned toward was the thing which he could not master. It was a nightmare feeling of impotence, and he groaned as he thought of it.

If only something might be added to his nature—some extra spark—some breath of fire—then he knew that he would sit upon the back of the gray horse as perfectly at ease as an eagle in the wind. He would know the mind of

Rooster, and big Rooster would know the mind of his master. And all would be well between them!

So thought Philip Slader and felt, an instant later, a little chill penetrating the small of his back. He turned about, and it seemed to him that a shadow moved from behind the window in the hotel which overlooked the corrals. Some one had been standing there, watching, and he did not need to ask who it was.

To make assurance doubly sure, he went strollilng to the hotel. Half a dozen idlers were on the veranda. They made their usual foolish efforts to sting him into conversation.

"This Kirby has more nerve than even Jack Slader used to have!" a voice said.

Phil passed hastily on into the building. He had no wish to remain there and exchange words with these fellows. He went on and met Bob, the negro servant, in the hall. And Bob grinned. He was just looking for Phil.

"Where's Magruder?" asked Phil. "Never mind what you want out of me. Is Magruder here now?"

"Here and sending me after you," said Bob. "He wants you to come right in."

Phil walked into the room which served, by turns, as hotel office and gambling room for Magruder—according to whether he was broke or flush. He had hoped to find Magruder alone at this moment, but, instead, he found three men sitting in the room with him, reading over a document which consisted of several typewritten pages.

"Here he is now," said Magruder. "Speak of the devil and—you know the rest, boys. Now, Phil, I want you to sit down here and sign your name on something. Want you to sit down here and write out your name, because I've got it all drawed up legal and fine. This here paper is a deed, Phil. It's a deed to a one-half interest in this farm. You hear? One-half interest in this farm and the buildings that's on it—including the hotel. How much did you say that these forty acres are worth, Harry?"

"The way the ground is improved, with alfalfa and fruit and what not, and everything trimmed up so fine by the work of Phil," said Harry, "this farm ought to bring a smart price."

"Aye," said Magruder, "it's Phil's work. I want that the credit should go where it belongs. He's slaved day and night, that boy has, and I want you to understand that he never done it because he expected that this would be coming to him. He done it because he loved the work— and what has his work made this worth?"

"It ought to bring three hundred an acre at any man's auction," said Harry gravely. "And maybe more—maybe more!"

"Twelve thousand dollars in land—another ten thousand for the hotel. Phil, I'm going to give you eleven thousand dollars' worth of stuff, if you'll sign this! And I've got the boys here to witness!"

CHAPTER 24

HE POINTED, as he said this, to the three and, above all, to Harry Mansell. For Harry was a universal authority upon all delicate points; he had been to a university, and there he had acquired the training of a lawyer. Or, at least, he had nearly acquired it. At any rate, Harry Mansell had never practiced, but his opinion was more valued among the cowpunchers up and down the range than was the word of any real lawyer with his name in black letterrs upon the clouded glass of an office door.

"I got these boys to witness," said Magruder, "and specially I got Harry, here, to write out the paper so that it would be good and legal and binding, y'understand?"

"I understand," said Phil Slader.

"A darned handsome thing it is, too," said Harry Mansell. "Eleven thousand—I'd put a half of the property at a higher valuation than that, Phil. There's twelve thousand for the land alone. Burn down all the buildings and throw away all the tools and wagons and horses and what not, but keep the land and what's rooted in that land, and you have a property that's worth a good twelve thousand. You ought to write the hotel down for another twelve thousand. I know that old Magruder, here, must clear a good two thousand a year out of it. Or maybe he clears three thousand. So at that rate it's worth twelve thousand of any man's money. Besides that, you have to consider the cost of the barns and the sheds and the fencing, which is all extra-fine quality and built to last. And there are all the other improvements, such as that blacksmith shop—which make a sure sale, they're so convenient, besides adding, I should say, several thousand dollars to the price. Now, for my part, considering all of the improvements and the horses and equipment all the way through, I'd write this place down for a thirty thousand dollars' value, Phil. And your half of it would be fifteen thousand, of course, which is what Magruder, here, is offering to you in this paper."

He tapped the sheets with a semi-legal frown.

What came to the mind of Phil Slader, then, was perhaps purest foolishness of fancy, but, at any rate, it took a strong hold upon him. The whir of a bullet was still as loud as a trumpet in his ear, past which it had sung that same day from the rifle of Magruder.

He merely said: "Doc, it won't do. I can't take so much money from you! Can't possibly!"

The face of Magruder wrinkled with something very closely akin to suspicion, but he forced himself to smile at once. Leaning back in his chair he said:

"Talk to him, Harry. The kid thinks that it's too much. You convince him."

Harry Mansell grinned and remarked: "If you want me to convince him, really, I think that it would be an easy thing to do. For one thing, he's been doing a man's work around this place for the last ten years or more, and I don't know that he's been troubled with a man's wages during that time."

At this unexpected turn in the conversation, Magruder cleared his throat painfully, but Harry Mansell pretended not to hear, and he continued:

"Besides, you have to consider what you've done to the place, youngster. It was just a thistle patch and hardly more when you took hold of it. Land not worth a thousand dollars at the most. The way it stands today, it's your work. And you've built the new barn and the sheds and you've made the tools or most of 'em and repaired the old running stock until it's as good as new; you've bred and raised the horses that are pulling the plow for you today. So that, take it all in all, it looks to me as though you're responsible for a lot more than half of the property as it stands. However, any way that you look at it, I would say that you're entitled to what's in these papers. What do you think yourself?"

"I don't know," said Phil Slader. "What you say may be true, but I have other plans. And I may not be here very long. I'd rather finish up here and call it quits. Doc has taken care of me for fourteen years. Fed and clothed me."

He looked down at his ragged clothes with a smile and then he added: "I don't want your money, Doc. That's all, I guess. And—so long, gents!"

So he walked out of the room, and as he closed the door behind him he could hear the voice of Magruder muttering:

"There you are! He's queer, you see. Something always on his mind. Growed up, now, and he wants to spread his wings. Old nest not good enough for him. Turns down a fortune. Think of it! Fifteen thousand at twenty-two!

135

What one of us had that much at his age? But you heard how he talks?"

Phil Slader had heard enough, and he walked softly on down the hall. He could tell, from what he had heard and seen, that another shadow had fallen upon his reputation, and he had been written down, again, as a "queer" one.

What interested him most was the attitude of Magruder. He could not attribute that offer to mere generosity. There must be something else behind it. Knowing Magruder as he did, he knew that it must cost the big man the blood from his very heart to even consider parting with half of his property. Therefore, what was the ulterior motive which spurred on Magruder to this act of generosity or justice? And before such witnesses, who would spread the report of it over all the country in a very few days?

He paused on the veranda and let the heat of the sun fall strongly upon his face and throat. It seemed to him that he needed that healthy fire to burn away the shadowy thoughts which were rising in him.

A flash of red and gold beside him made him turn, and there stood a slender, dark-faced man in Mexican jacket and high, peaked sombrero that must have weighed many pounds. The red was his silk shirt, none too clean, and the gold was the braid around the crown of his hat.

"You have a match, señor?" he asked.

"Here," said Phil Slader, passing a package to the foreigner.

The other lighted his cornucopia-shaped cigarette. As he smoked, he took out a little watch charm from his pocket, a little, golden Agnus Dei, and began to spin it back and forth upon his delicate forefinger. There were other little decorative aglets about him, from the fringes of his sash to the bells that tinkled behind his heels.

"You live here, señor?"

"I live here," admitted Phil.

"I, also," said the other, "have come to work for Señor Magruder. I am Diego Pasqual."

"Pasqual, I am Philip Slader. I'm pleased to know you.

136

But what sort of work are you going to do for Magruder?"

"I? I cannot tell. I do things with cattle. I can ride herd, and other things. I do not milk cows—I do not saw wood —I do not plow. No, those are not things for a man. But otherwise I am ready to do a man's work. We shall see!"

He said this with a faint smile in his eyes, and there was no doubt that he meant the insult to sting. However, though the whole line of loungers leaned forward to see in what manner he might act, it was not in the mind of Phil to allow himself to become entangled in a brawl. He merely shrugged his shoulders, and then he walked on down the steps. As he turned the corner of the building—indeed, even before he was out of sight—he could hear the voice of the Mexican raised unnecessarily loud:

"This plowboy, he does not defend himself, no?"

Trouble—trouble—trouble! And more mystery, too? For what on earth could Magruder want with a hired man of this type and on such a place as this?

He had his explanation a little later in the day, when Magruder came out to him as he worked to repair the broken windlass on the windmill. He was very sorry, was Magruder, that his protégé had chosen to refuse the proffered grant, but Phil cut him short.

"You can't understand me, Doc," said he. "And I can't understand you. Let's not try any longer, but tell me what the fellow out yonder—Diego Pasqual, or whatever his name is—tell me what he's going to do for you, or have you bought a ranch for him to ride herd on?"

"Pasqual? Ranch? Ride herd?" asked Magruder, chuckling. "No I'll tell you about Pasqual. He's no good. There's good Mexicans and there's bad ones, the same as Yankees, Phil. But there's difference: When they're good, they're pretty near saints. A good Mexican, who is your friend, will do anything for you. But if a Mexican is bad, he's pretty bad. That's the way with Pasqual. My friend, you understand? I happened to do a good turn for him a long time ago, and so he's square with me and he's honest with me. But he's a bad actor, that Diego is. You steer clear of him, kid. Got a nasty tongue and he doesn't care how he uses it, not him. You steer clear of him. He'll only be here

137

for a few days. I want him to do a little dealing for me in the poker games that start up here now and then because he's got a rare talent for that sort of thing. 'Diego the Silk Hand'—that's what they call him in his own country. And he's silky with the cards, right enough. Diego the Silk Hand!"

And he laughed heartily.

One part of his speech proved true enough. For this Diego Pasqual proved to have a most virulent tongue. But as for remaining only a few days, he seemed to make himself so welcome to Magruder at the poker table that he remained on and on. And he proved a thorn in the side of Phil.

However, there was another bit of news that occupied all the mind of Phil Slader at that time. It came over the telephone, in the first place—just the hint of the news and no details—that Lon Kirby had been taken.

The next day it was in the newspaper in all its grisly details. Lon Kirby had been taken, indeed, and in a fight which would go down in history among the great efforts of the desperadoes. He had been shot at and dropped as he was leaving a house in the mountains. He had dragged himself into a grain field, and there a posse had worked in to get at him. One of that posse was killed. Three others were badly wounded and two more were incapacitated for further action before the ammunition of Lon Kirby gave out. Then, they had reason to believe, he tried to kill himself with his last bullet, but his bullet lodged in the weapon, and so Lon Kirby was captured.

They had carried him into the house, tied up his wounds, and carted him at once to the nearest jail, eight miles away. It was a marvel that the jolting trip had not shaken the little remaining life out of him, but he had managed to survive and now he was fast regaining strength.

But what remained before Lon Kirby? Death, of course. No jury in the world would refuse to convict him for some one of the murders which were listed on his slate. In the meantime, a treble guard was being maintained over him, day and night, to rob him of the least possible chance of escape. No, it seemed definite that Lon Kirby was to hang.

And when he was dead, what of the money which he had left buried on the bank of the Crusoe?

Phil had forced himself to keep from thought of it up to this time. Now and again, as Lon Kirby had prophesied, the thought of the buried treasure rushed suddenly upon him and wakened him in the middle of the night with a beating heart. But, on the whole, he had kept the money pushed firmly out of his mind. Now, however, he could not resist the thought of it, and of something that went with it, linked together with a mysterious closeness: Nell Newell. For he knew that she had meant what she said. Money was more than a word to her. And if she had noticed him before, what would she do if he came with a big fortune in his hands?

CHAPTER 25

PHIL HAD A strange interview, five days after he read the details of the capture of Lon Kirby. He had ridden to Crusoe to buy a pair of new collars to replace some which had been gradually worn beyond all patching. As he stepped out of the saddler's shop, a shifty-eyed little man touched his arm.

"You're Phil Slader, kid?"

"I'm Phil Slader."

"How are ye, Slader? I'm 'Blinky' Rosen, y'understand?"

Phil smiled at him, much at a loss.

"Come on!" snapped Blinky. "Take a tumble to yourself. I'm wise, kid. I'm wise. I come from the big chief, y'understand?"

Phil shook his head.

"Bah!" said Blinky. "Loosen up, kid. I'm on the level. What do you want out of me—a letter, eh?"

And he sneered with much malignity.

"Hold on," said Phil. "You're talking to the wrong man, I think. I don't know any big chief that you speak about."

"You're deep, eh?" said Blinky Rosen. "Oh, I used to be deep, too, when I was your age. I used to be deep as a well, till I found out that it didn't buy me nothing. But look here, kid. I ain't made any mistake. You're Phil Slader. I got the description from him myself. And what he wants is iron boys—a flock of 'em. Ten grand is what he wants. He says that you're to kick through with it. You hear me talk?"

"I hear you," said Phil, "but I don't understand."

"I thought you wouldn't," said the other, sneering. "I told the boys that this would be trying to fly a kite on a calm day. Never raise that much wind for a guy that's where Lon is now. However, I've made my try. You turn him down cold. Well, it'll never win you no good name in the business, kid, and you can lay to that!"

The first flash of his possible meaning crossed the mind of Phil Slader. It was Lon Kirby to whom the man referred. And Lon Kirby, in desperate need, had sent this man to receive money from the hidden store—had sent him to Phil Slader to receive ten grand—underworld talk which meant ten thousand dollars.

It was an exquisite compliment, in its own way. It meant that Lon Kirby, even in his desperate need, dared not trust to any of his cronies the discovery of the hidden loot, for fear lest they should take the whole body of the money and convert it to their own uses.

140

He had sent this emissary, instead, to find Phil Slader and to receive from Phil's hand, then, the amount of money which he required.

It threw Phil at once into the deepest sort of a quandary. That money was stolen, as he well knew. And if he became a partner in the distribution of it to other thugs, would he not really share in the guilt of the stealing of it or incur another form of guilt almost as black? Would he not be at once dabbling in the very sort of soot which he had striven all his young life to avoid with such a particular care?

Yet he felt that there was a strong bond uniting him to the thug. On the one hand, his life had been in the hands of Lon Kirby, and that life had been spared, and the whole of a great treasure left by the outlaw at the mercy of a young boy whom he had seen on one occasion and no more. On the other hand, it was from Lon Kirby that he had received the gentlest and what seemed to him the truest portrait of his dead father, and therefore the best and tenderest strain in him was profoundly touched.

He raised his head from these thoughts and he found that Blinky was regarding him with a quizzical and half-sympathetic grin.

"I know," said Blinky. "I've been where you are, though never so bad. I've had to loosen up with three grand at one time, to a pal that had his back against the wall, and it sure hurt. But I never regretted it afterwards. Neither will you. It pays to go square, kid. You been deep. Nobody ever guessed that Lon had a side-kicker. Nobody ever dreamed that he would of picked out a kid like you for a pal if he did want one. But if you try to go too deep—if you try to double cross Lon—you'll go to the devil for it. I tell you and I know, because I know the gang! Understand? But take your own time—take your own time!"

"I'll see you to-morrow," said Phil Slader.

"To-morrow it is. Only—remember that the chief has to scramble. Time ain't too rich with him, just now. He needs cash and he needs it bad or he would never of sent me out here for it. But I'll see you here in town to-morrow. When?"

"About nine in the morning."

"About nine. There's a nine thirty that goes back to town. I hope that you got that in your mind. So long, Phil!" And he slouched up the street with Phil standing in a daze and staring after him. On the whole, it was the hardest moment in his life. He had been in tight places before. The bullet from the rifle of Magruder had been one thing, and the danger of Lon Kirby was another. But, after all, when there was only a matter of physical danger to encounter one could rally one's muscles and harden one's spirit to encounter the crisis. This, however, was far, far different. This was a matter of quite another strain.

For, look as he would, he could not see what was the proper thing for him to do. Cold reason told him that the best thing was to go straight to the sheriff and tell him everything and turn the money over to him. That would be the perfectly legal thing to do.

But what had legality to do with this? For, surely, there was a morality higher than that of the mere technical law. He had stood, in a way, indebted for his life to this same Lon Kirby. And now it was necessary that he make some return, if possible.

But he could feel the world of crime in which his father had lived stretching out its arms toward him—and in his heart a wild and rising temptation. How simple it would be to take a single step through the door into the wild freedom that lay beyond! To cast off all weights and burdens of petty conscience and become winged with his own strength and liberty!

He turned slowly up the street, pausing many times. And so, before he had gone fifty steps, a heavy hand fell on his shoulder, and he looked aside into the face of fat Sheriff Mitchel Holmer.

"How are you, Holmer?" Phil asked.

"Pretty well," said the sheriff. "Took off three pounds, last month. Getting thinner every year now. Gunna have a human figger before I die, kid. But that ain't what I want to talk to you about."

"What is it, then?"

142

"Back yonder," said the sheriff, and he hooked his thumb over his shoulder.

"Well?" asked Phil, frowning.

"You know what I mean."

"I don't."

"I tell you, it's poison, kid. You may not believe me now; but I tell you that I know. I know the whole slimy gang of them. They ain't fit for you, kid. And don't you let them pull you down. I tell you, I know Blinky like a book, and the cur takes a lot of knowing. But just now— why, kid, it turned me sick all over when I seen you standing up there and talking serious to him. No matter what he wants you to do, lemme tell you that he's wrong— wrong—wrong as the devil!"

"Maybe he is," admitted Phil Slader. "Maybe he is."

"It was nothing honest, Phil?"

"No," said Phil. "In a way it wasn't honest. It was the sort of a thing that a man could go to jail for, I suppose."

The sheriff nodded.

"I know, kid," said he. "I know exactly how you feel. There's some things that can be put up to a man—and particular to a young man like you—that seem pure and all right. Even though the law looks black on 'em. Well, I know that the law ain't always right. There's times when it does wrong. Only what I say is that the kind of right that's outside the law don't pass through the hands of a skunk like that Blinky. You take that from me and write it down in big red letters, because I know!"

Phil Slader shook his head.

"I'd like to talk it over with you, sheriff," he said. "But it's a thing that's between me and my conscience, and nobody can help me."

"You and your conscience?" said the sheriff. "Well, kid, at your age, I know where that argument will end up. But I tell you that you got to watch. Because if you once start sliding, you're the kind that would go a long ways down the hill! And here's another thing, Phil. Mind you, I don't want to throw myself in your face, but I've got to tell you this. There's a report come to me that for the first time in your life you've been acting ugly around a chap out at

143

Magruder's place—a Mexican—name of Diego Pasqual. What about it?"

"Acting ugly to him?" echoed Phil Slader. "Darn it, sheriff, I've had to bite my tongue nearly out to keep from talking back to him half as bad as he's been talking to me. Who told you this?"

"I can't pass it on. Only—I tell you plain, Slader. You ain't a kid any more. Folks around here, some of them, have been waiting to see you go wrong. Heaven knows I hope that you don't. But I tell you this for your own good. No matter what sort of a corner that you might get into, the moment that you so much as show the butt of a gun or the handle of a knife—you're done. Folks will say that Slader is loose again—bad stuff! And after that—why, you know what I don't want to say!"

CHAPTER 26

HE KNEW, indeed, what the sheriff did not want to say. Perhaps Mitchel Holmer might have used more words, but he could not have said more clearly than this: "If you get into a serious fight, no matter how much you may be in the right, the instant that you strike a blow, public opinion will be solidly against you. The instant you strike, you had better flee!"

Such was the interpretation which he placed upon the

sheriff's words, and they were all the more sharply brought home to him because he knew that of all the people in that county where he had been raised, there was none who was more of a friend to him in his heart than this same Mitchel Holmer.

He thanked the sheriff for that warning and started back toward the farm. But what chiefly burdened his mind was who could have brought that lying word to the sheriff concerning the manner in which Phil was treating the Mexican, for he who sent that message was pretty sure to have some specifically evil intention against Phil Slader.

He wanted above all an undistracted mind to use as an alembic for the testing of his thoughts, but here he was drawn in two ways—toward the problem of Magruder and the Mexican and, on the other hand, toward the problem of Lon Kirby and the treasure. The second matter he put first, because it had wholly to do with conscience. He felt that it would be a crime to obey the request of Lon Kirby; he felt that it would be a sin to refuse him. With young men sins are perhaps a bit more dreaded than crimes. The law is often considered an enemy and not a friend until a man reaches middle age and has settled to his final work, with his properties gathered around him.

Not going straight home, he turned toward the valley of the Crusoe River and, forcing his way through the difficulties and the damp odors of the marshes, he came again to the beach at the edge of the river. The water had risen a great deal since his last sight of the spot. It was higher now, and he could see that the last rain had brought the watermark within a few feet of the stone. So he lifted the great rock in haste, fearing lest the stream might have soaked through to the paper money. But he found that the pit in the gravel was as dry as dust, and, inside its oiled-silk wrapper, the money was as secure as ever.

He counted the whole treasure over again, bit by bit, and a keen temptation gnawed at his very heart. So much so that when a squirrel chattered suddenly in a tree just above his head, he leaped up with a gasp and jerked forth his gun—the start of a guilty man!

A very strange affair it was, too—counting over this

bulky fortune which lay here by the edge of the river, buried with not much more security than a squirrel will bury a nut for the wintertime.

At length he stripped off the necessary bills—how small a part was the ten thousand of the whole mass—and with it made his way back through the marsh, spending a good half hour working to cleanse himself of the muck of that evil place. Then he went home. He passed Magruder as he went to the barn, and Magruder favored him with a smiling nod.

The graciousness of Magruder with the passing of every day was a remarkably interesting study to Phil Slader.

"You've been after fish, I see," said Magruder, pointing to the ineradicable stains upon the clothes of Phil.

"Yes," said Phil, keeping a steady eye upon the older man. For the thousandth time the eye of Magruder wavered and fell away from the look of the boy.

"Aye," said Magruder, shaking his head and sighing. "Still keeping things from me. Still being secret. Still thinking behind my back—why, Phil, what have I ever done to make you hate me like that?"

"You don't know?" asked Phil Slader, smiling.

"I don't know."

"You've made a slave of me for ten years. Or fourteen years, from another way of looking at it. Is that nothing, Doc?"

"Heaven bless you!" exclaimed Doc Magruder in the greatest apparent bewilderment. "D'you mean, son, that you hold that old agreement agin' me?"

"Sounds queer, eh?" suggested Phil.

"But, lad, ain't we been friends all of this time?"

"You see," said Phil Slader, "I got a slow-working brain. Doesn't function smooth and easy at all. What I chiefly remember is two things. The first is that you killed my father, Magruder. The second is that you held me ready to throw me over the edge of a cliff if I wouldn't promise to put in ten years of Hades for you."

"A bluff, Phil!" cried Magruder. "A pure bluff! You don't think that I would ever have tried to do what I threatened? No, no! But I was afraid that you would

146

maybe try your hand at running away again, and I couldn't afford to invest so much time chasing you all over the face of the hills. Will you believe me, kid?"

"I was free to go at any time during these past ten years?" said Phil.

"Of course—of course! Why, son, this here ain't the slave days, and it ain't a slave State. Of *course,* I couldn't hold you, and I wouldn't hold you! Couldn't do it by law and wouldn't try it outside of the law. Believe me, because that's the whole fact!"

Phil Slader rubbed his knuckles across his chin.

"I've still got three weeks to put in with you. Then we finish. We'll do more talking then, Magruder."

And he went on to the barn.

When he came back toward the hotel, he found the usual half dozen idlers gathered on the veranda of the hotel, and there was Diego Pasqual as the center of unusual interest, standing with a graceful hand draped upon his hip, while in the other hand he practiced the draw of his revolver.

He demonstrated with a delightful pride and a concentrated vanity such as made Phil Slader smile.

"Not the shoulder and not the arm—but with the wrist and the tips of the fingers," said Diego Pasqual. "Look, amigos!"

The heavy Colt leaped forth like a living thing and glided back again into its hiding place. There was a good deal of admiration for this demonstration of skill in a most practical art.

"Not for men—Oh, no!" said Diego Pasqual. "But when the head of the snake appears out of the hole—then you can shoot that head off, amigos. Do you hear me? You can shoot that head off before it is jerked back again!"

And he bent back his head and laughed. Plainly this was an art of which he was a complete master, and he was beside himself at having such an adequate audience. Then he saw Phil Slader coming up from the side. He turned on him with a gleam of malice in his eyes.

"You, too, Señor Slader," said he, "shall see what I

have to show my friends. Little arts of the draw—little arts of shooting. But you are the son of a very great man, señor. No doubt you could teach even Diego Pasqual a great deal!"

And he leered at Phil Slader with much assurance. ·

"Not interested," said Phil Slader. "I don't work with tools like that. Not interested a bit."

"Impossible!" said Diego Pasqual. "You say it only to insult me and my art, Señor Slader. But I am a man who cannot take an insult, Don Felipe. Do you hear? I cannot take an insult!"

He had worked himself into a wicked temper at once, and Phil Slader saw what seemed to him a most patent thing—that the Mexican had taken upon himself to force a quarrel upon Phil.

Of course, there might be no connection between this and the conversation which he had had only a few moments before with big Magruder. But, on the other hand, it was certainly odd that Pasqual should have adopted such insolent measures immediately after Magruder had made his last attempt to induce Phil Slader to remain at the hotel. An offered partnership and then a hypocritical appeal—such things could not but have some meaning, connected with the behavior of Diego the Silk Hand, or so it seemed to Phil.

But no matter how impertinent the Mexican might be, the warning of the sheriff, delivered that same day, still rang in the mind of Phil Slader.

"All right," said he to Diego Pasqual. "I'm not trying to insult you, Pasqual. If you're an old hand at this game, let us see your stuff. Why, I'll be your pupil, if you want! Where's something to shoot at?"

And he looked calmly around him. By the pinched smiles of the men on the veranda he knew that they considered he was taking water. But as for their opinion, he knew that it was hardly worth consideration.

Señor Pasqual kicked a tin can that rolled twenty paces away. "There is an easy target for a quick shot, Slader. Will you try it?"

148

"I'm not quick," said Phil. "But lemme see your own hand at this here game?"

"Willingly," said the Mexican. "From the hip, is it not, señor?"

And at the same time he snapped his revolver out and turned loose a rapid volley of shots. Four followed in rapid succession. Three landed so close that they spattered dust and gravel on the can and started it rolling. The fourth punctured it with a loud chime and knocked it flat against a stone.

"And now . . . ." said Pasqual, turning with a broad grin, while his flickering glance ran over the faces of the idlers and drank in their admiration.

So Phil took that revolver—standing for the first time in his life with a loaded weapon in his hand. He had shunned them all the other days. Many and many a time he had played, since his childhood, with an empty Colt. He knew the feel and the balance and the weight of the trigger pull and how to point the gun like a finger of the hand and how to draw a careful bead through the sights. He knew all of these things, and he knew, also, that the less skill he showed in firing his shot the better it would be for him. It was, in fact, a chance for him to demonstrate before the public eye that he was by no means the gun fighter that Magruder had made him out—by no means the secretly formidable warrior that many people believed him.

But, under the eyes of the keen, smiling Pasqual, he weighed the gun in his hand. It was a beauty, no doubt. A little lighter than Phil would have liked for a personal choice, perhaps, for it had been specially made more frail to suit the slender hand of the Mexican. On the other hand, its balance was so perfect that it fitted to the palm of his hand like his own flesh.

Phil liked the gun. He looked at the target, which was knocked some thirty paces away by the last shot of the Mexican.

And, as he fixed it steadily with his eye, he could feel a certain rigidity coming over him. His feet gripped the ground hard, his legs grew like stone, and all the nerves

149

in his body seemed to die except those in his right hand and in his staring eyes. It was as though the tin can had been placed suddenly under a magnifying glass, which drew it far nearer to him. It increased in bulk, and, staring at it, it seemed suddenly to Phil Slader that he could not miss.

Indeed, there was almost something of a physical projection from his eyes to the target, a strong line of attraction. The murmur of the voices on the veranda died from his ears. The trees and the dead grass passed from his eyes. All of this increasing tension in him has taken long to describe, but in reality it was extended over hardly a second's time. Then he raised the gun.

It seemed to Phil Slader that he raised the weapon slowly, slowly indeed. But his own nerves were now tensed to such a high degree that what seemed slow to him seemed to the others a lightning gesture. He did not try from the hip. For even instinct, no matter how keen, could not equip him with sufficient skill to shoot from the hip without much practice. But, the instant that the gun came even wih the line from his eye to the target, he fired. And as he pressed the trigger an odd certainty passed, thrilling, through his veins. He knew that he could not miss! It was as though a divine power had been given to him. The gun flashed up, exploded, and the tin can was tossed with a clang into the air.

There was a little gasp from the others. He handed the gun back to the Mexican and found the little fellow exclaiming in excitement:

"It was not from the hip—it was not from the hip, amigos! You have not played fair with me, señor!"

"Do you need to shoot from the hip to kill a man?" asked Phil Slader.

And he strode past the Mexican, and past the silent figures on the veranda, and into the hotel.

CHAPTER 27

IT WAS ALL very wrong, no doubt—all very, very foolish. Such skill was the last thing which he should have showed to the world. At a stroke, all that Magruder had said about him seemed true; Magruder had said that young Phil Slader, for all that he avoided guns in public, was practicing with them in private and preparing himself for his great day.

Now he had showed something which he himself had not dreamed that he possessed. But by the possession of it, he felt himself raised to a new level. Yonder by the edge of the river there was a great treasure which he could make his, if he chose. That treasure seemed a small thing to him, compared with the power which he had just discovered in himself. The bank notes were something which he could only take by an act of theft. But this new thing which he had found was a part of his own soul; the cunningest thief in the world could never take that from him.

The warning of the sheriff became a dim thing, of no importance whatever. And the Mexican, Diego Pasqual, was a person not worthy of an instant's consideration. All the problems of Phil Slader dropped into the background, and one grand and overwhelming truth remained—he had in himself the thing from which other men had shrunk.

151

There had been cause, then, for the manner in which other men had always treated him. They had felt in him the thing which he himself did not know.

He sat in his room with his hands locked around his knees, his head thrown back, his eyes closed, and a swelling joy in him, such as he had never known before. And he began to laugh, though he was one to whom laughter had never been easy. It came of its own volition, softly and sweetly flooding his very soul, filling his heart with waves of light.

Phil sat for long moments, that drifted by him with all the speed of falling leaves in autumn; he was unconscious of their passing.

The evening came, and still he did not move until the door opened softly, and he found himself looking up into the awe-stricken face of Magruder.

"What's the matter, Phil?" he asked huskily. "What's up?"

"Nothing," said Phil.

"Why, son, it's supper time, you know?"

"Supper time? Why, it's not four o'clock!"

Then he looked aside and saw the shadows of the evening and the brilliant rose of the sky in the west.

He was startled and, turning to Magruder, he found that big worthy pale with trouble and confusion. There was nothing that Phil could put into words to explain that odd sojourn in his chamber.

At the table he found Pasqual and four other men there. All eyes lifted and looked a fixed instant on him. Then all eyes flashed down to their plates.

They knew! The power of Jack Slader was reborn in the world, indeed. But there was more and more which they did not know, and which they could not know. That was singing in the soul of Phil. He controlled himself as he looked around the table and saw that they were conscious of the mastering weight of his glance, even when their own glances dropped to their plates.

Diego Pasqual was the one exception. He, indeed, finally forced himself to look up, but he was under a tremendous strain, and he left the table before the meal was ended.

It was a miserable repast for the others. Magruder made some futile attempts at conversation. But they were not picked up or enforced by the others. And the time passed slowly, slowly. Yet for Phil, all was happiness, and he could not help smiling even upon the bowed heads of the others. They only guessed at the thing that was in him. They thought that it was a dreadful and destroying angel; they could not know that he felt nothing but gentle kindness toward them all. Even Magruder, out of the greatness of this good which had come to him, he could almost forgive.

His sleep was deep and untroubled that night. The next morning, when he had finished caring for the livestock, he mounted his mustang and cantered toward Crusoe.

He found Blinky Rosen at the exact spot where he had left him, and at the appointed minute. Rosen grinned and nodded at him as he came up.

"I see that you got it with you, kid," said he. "I see that you got it with you. More power to you. You'll never regret it. I'm gonna go back and tell the boys that old man Lon is doin' business with a real comer from out this way. You never spent ten grand on a better business than this here. Y'understand?"

He took the money, seized the hand of Phil Slader with a hard claw, and wrung it. Then he turned and was gone. And Phil, raising his head, found himself looking fairly into the sad eyes of the sheriff.

He rode straight across to Mitchel Holmer.

"Holmer," said he, "why do you look at me like that?"

"Son," said the sheriff, "anything that makes a sneaking crook like that fellow Rosen happy, is sure to make me sad. I dunno what you gave to him, just then, and I'm not asking you. I really don't want to know. I'm afraid to know, Phil!"

There was so much justice and kindness mingled in this speech, that Phil Slader sighed. He wanted with all his heart to lay everything bare before the sheriff, but that certainly could not be. Therefore he said:

"Holmer, I got this to say. I like you a lot. I respect you a lot. I want your friendship. You're the only one of the gang that has any real use for me. And I'll tell you this: The rest of them are right when they think that I've got it in me to raise the devil. But I'm going to fool them and I'm going to run up to the stuff that you hope out of me, sheriff. Only I've got to have my chance. And I'll tell you this: If I get into a fight, it'll be because it's forced on me. You understand me, sheriff?"

"Forced on you, Phil?" echoed the sheriff, frowning. "And tell me, son, what fool would want to force a fight on *you?*"

"Pasqual!" exclaimed Phil.

"Pasqual? Phil, Phil, are you trying to prepare me for a fight with him? When I already been warned that you're after him? Are you going to try to tell me now, that Pasqual would try to pick a fight with you?"

And Phil Slader bit his lip, seeing that he had nothing to say which could be believed. He could not point to any deeds, except the strange conduct of Diego Pasqual the afternoon preceding. And that was certainly not enough. Because, afterward, Diego had been meekness itself.

So Phil rode slowly back toward the farm again. But he could not remain depressed. No matter what the sheriff might say or how much truth there might be in those sayings, the fact remained that he had found such an aliment for his soul that it was growing greater and stronger every moment of every day.

He passed, now, into a happy trance in which hours and days and minutes passed with almost equal speed.

A week later he heard the next astonishing news in the papers.

Lon Kirby was loose. No one could tell how he had managed it, unless there had been a systematic bribing of the guards and the attendants at the prison, for he had been watched with the most scrupulous care and with a constant changing of the guards who had the keeping of him. Yet in spite of all of their attention, he had managed

154

to get away from them, though his wound was hardly healed.

He had perhaps picked the locks of the vast irons which secured him. But though it was certain that he was a past master at such arts of trickery, it was hard to imagine how he could have freed himself without resorting to the covetousness of his keepers.

There was no doubt in the mind of Phil Slader, of course. He knew all too well what had happened, and perhaps there was very little of that money, which he had sent on by the crooked hands of Rosen, that was not spent in this jail breaking. He felt as though, with his own hand, he had reached out and plucked this man from prison.

Ten thousand dollars had done this. No wonder that Nell regarded money highly. Ten thousand had burst open doors of steel and stone and hewed through tool-proof bars and lifted a prisoner out into the safety of the underworld which had given him birth and which now had received him fondly back to its bosom.

He himself would regard money with a new eye, from this time forth.

In the meantime he prepared himself to face something of a duel with his conscience. For, if he were guilty of the release of the bandit, then every crime that Lon Kirby committed hereafter could really be laid to his own door. It was by no means a comforting thought!

CHAPTER 28

IT WAS TWO DAYS later, in the night, that he wakened and heard the neigh of big Rooster, restless in his corral.

It was hot in the room. And since he could not sleep again, he got up and dressed for a visit to the stallion. But he did not go to Rooster this night, for when he came near the corral, he saw two shadowy figures against the bars of the fence and against the clustered stars near the horizon.

It was Magruder and Diego Pasqual—he could distinguish their voices—speaking Spanish, a language with which Phil was only slightly familiar. He could make out, however, that they were speaking about the horse. Diego was holding forth at length and with enthusiasm, about the good fortune which such an animal would bring to the man who could master him.

"Not so much luck, either, Diego," said Magruder, breaking into English. "Man with a horse like that under him would be too much tempted to raise the devil. He could do pretty much what he wanted and then get away from trouble. That big gray devil could carry two hundred pounds at a gallop all day long and never know that he had been busy. That's what he looks like to me."

156

"Is that what the boy is waiting for—to learn to handle Rooster before he starts?" asked Diego.

"Of course it is. I've told you that before. But he'll never handle Rooster and neither will any other man until they make men in bigger sizes than any that I've ever seen."

He added after a pause: "And what are *you* waiting for, Pasqual? Is the job going to be any easier by waiting for another time?"

"I have tried already," said Pasqual. "But I could not get him to do anything. You know that."

"I know that I've paid you good money and that I'm still paying it, Pasqual. And I'm tired . . . ."

"Hush," said Pasqual, "you may be heard!"

And he turned around with a guilty start. But Phil was secure behind the corner of the wagon shed, and nothing was seen.

"No danger," said Magruder. "He's sleeping like a top. He's sure to be . . . ."

The rest of this sentence was lost to Phil, for after the warning of the Mexican both began to talk in soft murmurs, no more intelligible to Phil than dim humming. Phil, at last, stole softly back to the hotel and into his room. He did not attempt to sleep. But lying down on his bed, he folded his arms under his head and strove to think this matter out.

Whatever the skill of Diego Pasqual was at the gaming table, it was plain that he was not kept at the hotel on that account. He was hired, in the first place, to make trouble for Phil Slader, and Magruder was reproaching him for having wasted so much time before executing his mission. That explained, accordingly, the manner in which Pasqual had repeatedly attempted to pick a quarrel with Phil in front of witnesses.

It gave Phil, moreover, a fairly sure proof that the bullet which Magruder had fired at him, those weeks before, had really been intended for his head, and not for that of Lon Kirby.

He had been in peril of his life all of this time, and he shuddered at the thought.

157

That he must leave the place at once, was clear. And when he left it, would he not be removing himself from the opportunity to get at the root of Magruder's bitter fear and enmity? He dreaded Phil Slader with all his heart, and that dread must be founded upon the knowledge that he had murdered the boy's father, not destroying him in fair fight, as the world had been led to believe.

Magruder feared, then, lest Phil should discover the truth. But how could that truth be learned, unless there were some hidden witness of the crime who could relate it to Phil, himself? Why might that witness be? Removed from the hotel and Magruder's self, what chance would Phil have of learning the facts of the case? He thought of these things with a sigh.

Then he must have dropped off into a half sleep. Certainly when he roused it was from a semitrance to keen wakefulness. A little whisper of cooling air crossed his hot face, and he knew that the door of his room was opened.

That was not very strange, for the latch of that lock was weak, and any gust of wind, striking against it in a certain fashion, was apt to press it open. However, though there was a faintly stirring draft at the present moment, it seemed most odd to Phil that on this heavy, sluggish night there should have been enough force in any gust to open the door.

He did not sit up; he merely turned his head. And then it seemed to him that he saw a movement in the black shadows which filled the room. Ordinarily, he would have put it down for nothing. But that night he had heard something which sharpened his suspicions to a razor edge. Fear is an amaranthine blossom which never fades; and fear had been thrust into the very soul of Phil Slader on this night. So he was fully awake in an instant. Perhaps there was nothing, yonder in the darkness. Again, might it not be the stealthy form of Diego, the Silk Hand?

Phil Slader lay in his bed and thought he heard a faint ticking sound, as of a man's weight crossing the floor little by little. He endured it until he could endure it no longer. There was no weapon in reach. Even the chair was too far from the head of his bed to be used as a missile. But he had the weight of his body to strike with—and, with a convulsive movement, he hurled himself from the bed and straight at the danger point in his fancy.

In his reasoning mind, he expected to get nothing for his effort. But as he plunged through the blackness he heard a sudden snarl, like the cry of a beast, close to the floor. A gun exploded, and the darting point of flame showed him the convulsed face of Diego Pasqual, set grimly for a desperate deed.

Where the bullet went, Phil Slader did not know. His own effort had placed such a roaring in his ears that he could hardly have heard the humming of a cannon ball. Then, true to his mark, he struck Diego Pasqual, and they both rolled, crashing against the farther wall of the room.

The gun exploded again, as they slid across the floor. And Phil, reaching out in haste, closed his hand upon the coat of the Mexican. It was like catching at the slippery bark of the willow twig. For Pasqual shed that coat instantly and leaped for the door, screaming:

"Help! He murders me! Help, Magruder—friends—oh, Heaven help me!"

For, fast as he sprang, Phil Slader was coming swiftly behind him. Diego might fly like a good sparrow hawk, but there was a long-winged falcon behind him. He plunged through the doorway into the hall, raising the wild echoes before him.

Already those echoes were turning to real voices, as the guests in the hotel wakened in alarm. And it seemed to Phil that he could distinguish the bull-like bellow of big Magruder in the distance. He had no care for that. He had crossed the ambit of his old world and he was reaching into a new one of action.

On the stairs the Mexican half turned, with a second revolver in his hand, and tried a chance shot at the pursuer. The bullet went like a whip lash snapping past the face of Phil Slader, and he threw himself into the air and hurled down at Diego.

He struck him halfway down the stairs, and they fell to the bottom, head over heels. Cold steel met the hand of

159

Phil Slader. He wrenched it away—and now he was armed and most excellently armed, at that!

Diego, fighting like a madman, tore out his knife and drove with it, but a hard fist caught him on the body and knocked him flat against the wall. Phil fired—not at his man but into the air—that the flash of the bullet might show him his work. It gave him a winking glimpse of Diego Pasqual flattened against the wall, but, knife in hand, he lunged in at Phil again. This time Phil fired at the darting body. It was either that or receive the blade of the knife in his own body. He fired, and Diego fell with a loud scream upon the floor.

Phil leaned over him. "You brought it on yourself, Pasqual!" he said. "Will you tell the rest of them that?"

"I'll tell them anything—bring me air—water—Don Felipe—I am dying! I shall tell you everything—and the truth of how your father died. Only—Don Felipe—water—air—help!"

His scream was horribly strangled and then a burst of voices and lights rolled out into the hall—Magruder's voice and others with him.

"It's Slader!" shouted Magruder. "He's murdered the Mexican. I knew that it would happen. I warned the sheriff, and he wouldn't do anything. Boys, will you stand by me? Will you help me to get hold on this young devil who . . . ."

"Get hold on him, Magruder?" cried another. "Man, are you clean mad? Capture Jack Slader's son? He'd have lead fed into half a dozen of us before that could happen. No, tag that young skunk with a .45 chunk of lead and see if that will put him to sleep. There never was a Slader that was a good citizen until he was dead. Boys, come on—we're gunna stop this stone right now from rolling along and gathering itself into a regular slide that might wipe out half a hundred men, in its time. We're with you, Magruder. You lead the way!"

"This way, then! Phil, Phil! Are you down there? D'you hear me? The doors are double locked at the end of the hall. You can't get out that way. Will you come up here and surrender?"

"I'll come up and surrender," said Phil, "when I know that I'll get a fair deal. I want you fellows to understand that this greaser jumped me in my room, in the black of the night."

There was a yell of mockery and rage from the others. And then the great voice of Magruder thundering:

"You hear him, boys? Kill a man and then sneak behind a rotten excuse like than? Diego, are you dead?"

There was only a faint groan from Diego Pasqual.

And Phil felt that there was no longer any use in fighting against fate. He had done his best, he told himself, and plainly it was foredoomed that he should lead one of the lives of the hunted.

"Magruder and the rest of you swine!" he shouted suddenly at them. "I've tried to get a fair deal, and you won't give it to me. Now I tell you that I'm not going to chance myself in your hands. I'm going to get loose from this house, and Heaven help the first of you that gets into my way. You hear me?"

CHAPTER 29

HE WAS HEARD—a wild roar of anger and hate told him. And he shrank from the sound with wonder and dismay. There was no reason for it, he told himself. He had dared to defend himself from a midnight murderer; therefore was he to be set upon like a wild boar by a pack of dogs and torn to pieces?

But he understood. It was not he, himself, but bad blood that they hated. And he was not to go straight, no matter how he tried. Crouched back against the wall, he felt evil rising in him in a flood, wonderingly strong and wonderfully sweet. It was an added power rushing through his body and his brain.

In his immense surety he had time to lean and say in the ear of Pasqual: "Tell me how my father died, Pasqual, and I'll forgive you for trying to murder me. I'll be your friend—I'll stay here now and bandage . . . ."

There was only a faint gasp from Diego Pasqual, and Phil Slader knew that it was a dying man who lay at his feet. So his last opportunity of learning the truth, it seemed, was gone from him!

He shut that disappointment away from his mind. There was something else for him to consider, and that was the manner in which he might escape from this unlucky house.

So, first of all, he ran to the end of the hall and tried the doors. They were fast locked. He sent a bullet into the lock, but still it held, and a shout of triumph rose from three or four throats of men outside. He heard the rapidly approaching hoofs of many horses.

This must be reënforcements for the enemy, which already outnumbered him so vastly. However, he felt no weakness. The more they penned him in with strength and with numbers, the more a savage ferocity rose in him, and the more clearly his brain saw what he must do.

Magruder was back yonder in the hall, bellowing directions, telling one to guard the windows—another to run to help at the front. How many were now left in the narrow throat of the hall itself, at Magruder's side?

At any rate, that was the only point which remained for Phil to attack, and he determined to rush it. First he pulled off his boots. Then he ran back and hurled his shoulder against the doors at the end of the hall. They bulged and sagged under the shock, and an excited yell rose from the outside:

162

"He's coming out! He'll bust those doors down the next try! Stand ready, boys. Don't shoot too high—shoot low—shoot for the legs and you're more apt to hit the body!"

That was Bailey's voice—Bailey, who only the day before had walked over the new alfalfa field with him and had admired with much apparent sincerity the manner in which the new plants were sprouting. Ah, well, Bailey and all the rest were of one piece. They could not understand. And God forgive Jack Slader for this heritage which he had left to an involuntary heir!

One more shock would burst open those doors, as those on the outside knew. They had their guns ready, no doubt. A breath of silence fell over the night, and far away, through the darkness, a rooster, falsely prophesying the end of the night, crowed loud and long.

Once more Slader threw himself at the doors, but rather to make a great rattling and confusion at them than to attempt to force his way through them. Then he turned and raced down the hallway on silent stocking feet.

He went up the stairs like a sliding ghost and, as he reached the top of them, he saw Magruder on his knees, a double-barreled shotgun ready in his hands—and two men standing tall and stark behind the proprietor of the hotel, all ready to turn this night into one of carnage.

He paid no heed to the two. It was Magruder who thirsted to murder him, for many reasons. He fired straight into the face of the big man—and saw his hat jump, so he knew that his bullet had missed. But the flare of fire, and the spitting smoke blinded and choked the big man. His shotgun swerved to one side, and, as both the barrels roared at once, the recoil flattened Magruder on the floor of the hall. And now there were only two men between Phil Slader and freedom on this side.

He was not in haste. He picked his places to strike and then he struck home. His revolver was empty; he laid the long, heavy barrel of it alongside the head of the man to the left and seemed to feel the skull sag under the power of that blow. He turned and sank his left fist into the body of the second man, and so both were down—and

163

one shape lay motionless, while Magruder and the other lay gasping, choking, moaning.

They were writhing about among a veritable cluster of weapons, each dimly marked by a streak of light, and Phil Slader took what he wanted—a rifle and a revolver. Then he ran on down the passageway.

How slow were those fellows from the front of the house! Why was it that they were not already around at the back of the house to cut off his retreat?

There was no one before him. But, from the inside of the house there was a steady and a rising roar, and from the front of the building men were yelling in a vast confusion to each other.

Footfalls beat and echoed through the halls and chambers of the hotel. But no one loomed in sight of the fugitive.

If that were the case, he would profit by this confusion to give himself one more chance at something which he prized almost above liberty itself. He reached the corral of Rooster, and in another instant the saddle was on the back of the big horse; the bit was slipped with a click of steel between his teeth; the bars were thrown down, and here was Phil Slader sitting in the saddle with the black night before him and the greatest horse ever seen in the Crusoe Valley, between his legs. A thunderbolt and like a thunderbolt, a hard, hard tool to manage!

The confusion at the hotel had ended to a certain extent. For now Magruder was on his feet again, and, being on his feet, there was his bull voice bellowing forth directions and sending back his helpers to the work.

Yonder ran a shadow. And there came another.

"He's in that corral—on the gray horse—he'll never ride that horse. We got him, boys! Get in front of the gate—Charlie. We got Slader—Magruder, come on!"

At this moment Phil Slader touched the flanks of the gray monster with his heels and loosed the reins just a trifle. The gray stallion left the corral like a streak of jagged lightning—jagged indeed, for he bucked his way through the corral and through the gate and, with enormous bounds, he plunged, sun-fishing across the open

164

space beyond, giving for a target to the men of Magruder a dancing will-o'-the-wisp that flaunted across the starlight—now here—now there.

It was magnificent pitching, but worse than useless to Magruder unless it landed Phil Slader on the ground, for in the meantime it was making a hit impossible with revolver or rifle. He himself knew, for the barrel of his rifle was turning hot in his hand, and there were the others, firing as rapidly and as straight as they could, to no purpose.

But Phil Slader was not to be thrown from his saddle on this night of nights; he knew it with the very first bound that the stallion gave. He had been a worthy foeman of the stallion before. But on this night he was his master—now and forever. No matter how Rooster took veritable wings and knotted himself into quaint devices in the mid-air, Phil Slader still was sitting in the saddle as they reached the trees.

There the stallion changed his tactics and rushed furiously, straight ahead, hoping to brush off his rider, against some low-hanging branch. So doing, he put a hundred yards of black night instantly between Phil and the guns of his human enemies.

CHAPTER 30

THAT DANGER WHICH Phil Slader now enjoyed in place of the guns of Magruder and the rest was hardly a trifle less dangerous. For half a mile the gray horse raced through the woods, weaving back and forth and striving his best either to scrape his rider off against a trunk or to catch him against some low-dropping branch. And a dozen times there were close shaves. How the big horse managed to weave his way back and forth through that tangle of trees without crashing headlong against some one of them, Phil could not guess. It was almost as though the monster had the power of seeing by night as by day. For he dodged quicker than a football player, running through a tangled mass of opposition down the field.

They came out from a hundred dangers into the open field beyond. At least one great gain had resulted. The noise of big Magruder and the rest had not even begun behind them. A great handicap was offered in favor of Phil even as the chase began.

However, now that firm ground and the open presented themselves, Rooster passed into another frenzy of bucking, hurling himself on his back upon the ground and then flinging himself to his feet and into the air again, turning end for end in full leap, and crashing down to the earth again.

He was a tiger in horseflesh, but another tiger in human form was on his back. Twice before Phil had tried his hand with the stallion; and each time he had learned something of the savage ways of Rooster. But now it was a different matter. On the one hand, the tricks of the stallion seemed somewhat trite; on the other hand, there was a new strength and confidence in Phil, and he countered every buck and every pitch with slashing quirt and biting spurs.

Then Rooster dropped suddenly from the air to the ground, not like a falling rock, but like some softly winged creature. With his ears pricked against the stars, he started forward at a gallop lighter than the fancy of a child or poet had ever pretended in a steed of the imaginings.

He had ended his battle as suddenly as he had begun it. He had recognized his master, just as Phil Slader had known that the great horse would do, in case a master ever sat in his saddle. No longer would the gray horse stand with high head and wistful eye fixed upon the far horizon. For the man from the sky had come at last. And he, Phil Slader, was that lord of men. He was the man from the horizon, to sit like a king of men upon this king of horses!

Do you wonder, then, that he put back his head and laughed, rejoicing almost drunkenly while the black earth leaped away behind him, and the stallion gathered speed and speed from some magic wallet which the god of wings had given to him? For it seemed that the store of the stallion's strength was totally inexhaustible, and all that he needed was more asking in order to gain more having.

A chasm opened before him, a dark gulf which Phil knew to be a dry slough that never ran with water, except during the heaviest winter rains. The sides were steep, and the bottom was lined with hard and slippery rock. A fall into that pit would be death for horse and for rider also, and he drew in a little on the reins anxiously.

But the gray horse shook his head impatiently and

tossed his crest. It was as if he asked: "Why will you have me turn aside for such a trifling matter as this?"

"Take it, then!" gasped Phil.

And he loosed the reins—it was like being hurled, so suddenly did the speed of the big horse respond. The sharp wind cut like ice, stinging the face and the eyes of the rider. Then Rooster rose in the air. And the black gulf lay below, an endless stretch, it seemed, with a glint of starlight in an ominous little pond beneath. They hung in midair; they swooped down; and here was the firm ground receiving the shock of those formidable hoofs, which spurned that earth away again as he raced off with recovered stride.

Phil Slader shook his fist at the stars above him. Whatever happiness was in their twinkling eyes, there was a greater fire in his own soul. A fence jerked up before him like something rising from the ground by life of its own. He had no hesitation now. He merely loosened the reins a trifle once more; again there was the dazing burst of wind in his face as Rooster lurched away; again they took wings in the upper air—and the obstacle flashed back unregarded behind them.

What other horse had ever been like this? A hot tide of gratitude and joy rose in his heart. He could have sung, and it would have been a paean in praise of Rooster.

All that had ever been extravagant and foolishly beautiful—if such a term could be used—was now matter of fact. All the tales of super horses and of supermen could be believed. It was easy to lift a mountain—to move a city—to crush a hundred—for the deeds of mighty Rooster made all checks, all boundaries, all ambits of whatever nature, seem like imaginary things. All that one willed and wished was possible!

He pulled down the great horse to an easy canter and then to a trot. It was not like the trot of other horses, any more than his gallop was the gallop of others—but a swift and gentle gait in which the strokes of the hoofs were cushioned and softened by the flexible fetlock joints, playing through whole inches of give and take. Fast as a pounding cowpony's canter, that trot carried them along, a beautiful and effortless gait which propelled them on as though they were afloat on a swift river, gliding without friction beneath the stars.

The rider listened keenly to the breathing of his mount. All was as he could have wished but not as he dared to dream that it would be. He was breathing deep and hard, of course, but there was no sign of labor in the lungs. At this fleet trot the great horse could recover whatever little strength he seemed to have expended in his bucking, in his breathless gallop thereafter. And far away, far away, the pursuit must be floundering in the darkness of the night, more and more hopelessly lost!

Other thoughts rose in Phil then. First his mind dwelt on the perfection of that matchless horse and pondered on the grace and ease of motion which drifted them along as by witchcraft and not mere bone and muscle. He fingered the thought of the gray stallion, as some skilled virtuoso might finger a glorious violin. The more he dwelt upon it, the more there was to wonder at and rejoice in. And he said to himself that there was nothing to which he might not aspire on this night.

Where was he riding now? What instinctive sense had guided him in this direction across the mountains? He knew, then, as he examined his mind. He was riding toward her who had invited him to come the moment that he had the horse beneath him. He was riding toward Nell. It took his breath a little as he realized it, but it rejoiced him also. And he made the big horse gallop joyously on again.

Twenty miles, or was it thirty? He followed a road that climbed and wound about through the forest, wet and fragrant with the last rains, and then a road that fell away to the sweeping plains where the father of Nell was coining wealth and happiness for himself and for his son. But not for Nell. No, the things for which her heart hungered were not the things which could be got in return for fat steers and tonnage of hide and tallow. Something, bigger, greater, brighter must be included in her destiny than ever came from the soil of this world no matter how cultivated.

Perhaps he would be bringing the miracle to her. He laughed again. For the joy in him would not down.

So he came down to the place where the new building on the Newell ranch had been raised, and as he approached the house, he wondered at its size. He had heard much talk, here and there, of the mansion which rich John Newell was erecting on his property, but it had never occurred to him that the building could be of such dimensions as this.

It was all of stone, too—a fine yellow limestone which, in the starlight, seemed as clear and as pure as whitest marble itself. Vines had been trained along its sides. Already the edge of newness had been worn away enough to give the house charm. Men said that the total purpose of John Newell in the building of this house was to provide, in the first place, a fitting residence for the heir to his money and, in the second place, to keep his daughter home!

And even this could not accomplish the purpose! At what expense, too, had this rising cattle baron excavated the place for the lake which now flowed near the walls of the house, and how had the lawns been made to grow, whose sweetness was now so eagerly sniffed by the great gray stallion?

As Phil studied these things, he remembered more fabulous figures that he had heard, concerning the cost of the two great artesian wells which Mr. Newell had sunk in order to create this little green sketch of paradise. He would believe now the things which he had doubted before.

He respected the bigness of the rancher's labors. He admired him for the success which had made the erection of such a house possible. But he did condemn John Newell most heartily for creating such a labyrinthine place in which to find the lady of his heart in the blackness which was the end of the night. There was no great space of time left to him. Before long there would be an edging of gray toward the east, and on any ranch which was run by Newell, one could be sure that the workers would arise at the first hint of the day! The interim belonged to Phil Slader to find the girl, if he could, and to see her, if he dared.

170

CHAPTER 31

IT WOULD BE pleasant to say that Phil Slader felt some pangs of conscience in this matter of breaking into a locked house by night, but one must record truly that nothing troubled him. He left the stallion tethered under a fine stone pergola from which the climbing vines draped long tendrils. Already one of these was in the mouth of the gray horse when Phil Slader left him.

He stood with a smile and scanned the imposing bulk of the structure before him. And I think that the thoughts of Phil at the moment were more adventurous than amative. The amatory impulse will lead young men far astray, but I doubt if it has ever led them as far as the mere love of mischief and danger for its own sake.

Well, on the ground floor would be the living rooms, and above to the front was doubtless the chamber of Mr. Newell and his wife. Behind that, perhaps, would be the place of young Sam Newell. How mad with suspicion and rage he would be, if he were to guess that such a man as this stood beside their house on this night! And here toward the rear, where a little balcony stood before a window, where big boxes supported a little host of green things, shadowy against the stars—this was surely the place that they would have chosen for their loved and spoiled daughter!

He was glad now that there were no riding boots on his feet. He laid his grip on a drainage pipe that ran down from the projecting eaves above, and up the side of the house he clambered as expertly as any sailor running up toward a cross spar. Then he reached the balcony and swung himself onto it.

There he waited until his panting should have subsided a little, for there was no hope in trying to enter a room in secrecy when he was breathing as heavily as a Newfoundland dog on a summer's day. At length, he was ready. The great window yawned wide before him—bless all such believers in the virtues of fresh air—and now he was stealing through into the chamber itself.

He crouched on the floor and made his survey until his eyes grew a little accustomed to the pitchy darkness of the interior. It was not so pitchy black, either, for by degrees he could make out the outlines of chair and bed. Something gleamed near the wall—he stole toward it and found a rack filled with fishing rods.

It was not the chamber of the girl but of her brother. Phil found the glitter of the polished doorknob, opened it with care, blessing again such soundless latches as these, and stood in the dark of the hall beyond.

Another door opened to the right. He tried it and ran his nose into the edge of a shelf! This time he had entered a linen closet. All the while the precious moments were stealing away from him.

He left that door ajar, to shock Mrs. Newell or the housekeeper the next morning, as the case might be. And then he tried the next door beyond, and the instant that it was opened a delicate scent of perfume crept out about him.

Like a light and chilly wine it passed through him. This was she, indeed! He knew it by the very sense of the air which he breathed in that room. A streak of white yonder —that was her bed. And he leaned above it presently.

On the starlit whiteness of her pillow, her face was like a shadow—a semi-translucent shadow, it seemed to Phil, as though the light which was in her every day was still burning, however faintly, in the night.

He straightened again and tried to speak her name, but a sudden little contraction of his throat shut all the sound away. Then he leaned over and brushed her cheek with his lips.

Aye, she was a sleeper, sound enough! She merely stirred, and then groaned a little and stretched her arms above her head.

Her eyes must have opened, however, for though he did not stir, he heard the frightened catch in her breathing.

"Nell," he whispered, "this is Phil Slader."

She lay quite still for a long moment, while his heart stood still. It occurred to him for the first time that she might scream out and call for help, if he came upon her in this fashion. Far better for him to have committed a hundred foul murders, as far as the Western ideas of Western men would be concerned, than to be discovered like this in a woman's room!

He set his teeth upon the thought.

"Phil Slader," whispered the girl, "what in the name of Heaven?"

He waited, not attempting any answer.

And then she sat up in her bed and caught a dressing gown around her shoulders. "You've done something, Phil."

"Yes," said he.

"I knew it. I knew that it would come. Who was it?"

"Fellow who tried to knife me while I was in bed."

"Ah! When?"

"To-night."

"And now you're here!"

"Yes."

She waited again, and he could feel her eyes upon him.

"Go over there to the window. It's open, I think. There's a balcony outside. Go out there and wait a minute."

He obeyed without a word and stood beneath the stars again. He could trace the source of the perfume now. It came from flowers which grew in the window boxes along the balcony and—farther away—he could see the corner of that other balcony to which he had climbed those few moments before.

But what a riot of excited happiness was in him! It was not like conquering gray Rooster and whirling through the night as never a man before him had ridden. It was more than a greater sense of victory, a greater sense of conquest. And still he hardly knew. He could only guess—that she was excited, too—that she was not angry, at least, because of his coming.

He had hardly reached that point in his thoughts when the whisper of soft slippers passed through the French doors and here she was standing beside him.

"Now tell me!" said the girl.

He did not answer.

"What's wrong?" she asked him.

"I never guessed . . . ."

"What?"

"That you were so small!"

"I know. High heels make a silly lot of difference, I suppose. Have you come here to talk about high heels, Phil?"

Yes, she was laughing at him and laughing so heartily that she could hardly keep her mirth inaudible.

"By Heaven!" said Phil, "you're a cool one."

"I'm not cool. I'm all in a flutter. D'you think that I've ever been waked up before by young men in my room at night? Phil Slader—hurry and talk, talk, talk! How do you know that you're not being followed?"

"I know that I am."

She stared at this.

"Then if they find you here, Phil!"

"They won't find me here—not unless I stay a long time past sunrise."

"You took some short cut to get here?"

"The fastest short cut that anybody ever used across the Crusoe."

"What was it?"

"I don't want to waste time talking about that. I want to talk about something else, Nell. I haven't a lot of time before the dawn begins, and I suppose things are stirring around here, not long after that?"

"You know dad—of course. Only—great heavens, what a lot there is to say, and no time to say it in! First, who was it?"

"His name is Pasqual!"

"I know! The Mexican! The Mexican! Thank heavens that it wasn't a . . . ."

"It don't make much difference, I suppose," said Phil. "A man's a man, yellow or black or white. But where I'm concerned, it makes no difference at all. Anything to give them an excuse to hang something on me. If it had been a fellow with a price on his head, it wouldn't have made any difference."

"You're bitter, Phil."

"Do I sound that way?"

"Aye, bitter from the heart of you!"

"Well, I don't know that I mean it that way. Only, first of all, I wanted to tell you the facts, Nell. The rest of them—well, they'll simply write me down a gun fighter and the son of a gun fighter, and they'll say that it's just the bad blood in me, working out the way that it was sure to work out in the long run. You know what they've said before and expected of me? Everybody knows. I'm like a mad dog. They've just been waiting for the poison to show—waiting for me to bite!"

"Of course I know. And of course I've heard the talk. But you don't have to explain to me."

"I do. I want you to know all of the facts just the way that they happened. They'll tell you lies, of course. But this is gospel. I waked up—just the way that you did a while ago, except that I had my clothes on. Something that I had overheard between Pasqual and Magruder earlier in the night was enough to keep me ready, you know. And while I was lying there, I heard a sound, I thought. And I threw myself at it. Well, it was Pasqual. He missed me, but the flash of his gun showed me his face. He got into the hall. I caught him on the stairs. And in the hall below he tried to knife me, and I killed him with his own gun. You understand?"

175

She had drawn back a little from him, studying him.

"Turn around here where the starlight falls on your face, Phil. Somehow, the words all by themselves seem to make a difference. I can see you going after him more like a tiger than a man. It—scares me a little!"

He turned obediently and faced the stars. And she stood close before him, looking up.

"I was hemmed in in the lower hall. They had the way blocked behind me. Magruder was there. About a dozen more were scattered around. I made a feint at the locked front doors, and then I snaked off my shoes and ran back through them."

"Phil! Phil! And not . . . ."

"Didn't hurt any of them bad. I wish I'd killed Magruder, though, the cur! But I only knocked him down and a couple more, and got through. And so I came to you to tell you that these are the facts, no matter what low lies they try to make you believe about me. You won't be able to say that they lie. But you'll know down in your heart that they *do* lie. And that's all that I care about. Not what a million of the rest of them may think—but only about you, Nell! I want you to think straight."

"I'll never doubt you!" said the girl.

She took one of his hands and pressed it with more strength than he dreamed was in her.

"Thanks a lot," said he. "But don't say that. I may do something pretty bad after this. Only I haven't done anything up to this time. I'll swear that I haven't, and you'll believe me—and that's all I want."

"Did you come here just to tell me that?"

"No, I came for something else. You mighty well know that I came for something else, Nell. Why the devil should a man ride thirty miles otherwise? Or why the devil should he want one girl to know the facts about him?"

A smile flashed across her face.

"You're a rough talker, Phil!"

"Because I'm a rough man. You can write that down in red and believe it, Nell. I'm rough from this time onward. I tried to go smooth and I couldn't do it. But I came here first of all because you ordered me to."

176

"What in the world do you mean?"

"When I rode Rooster."

"You've done that, too?"

"Yes."

"I knew that you were different all the way through. But that's it. You've ridden him, and he's made the change."

"There was a change before I ever got on his back. I'm not just a kid any more. I'm a man. You understand me, Nell?"

"Yes, I understand you, of course. You *are* a man."

"That leads up to the rest of it. You know what the rest is."

"Why should I?"

"Be square and fair. You *do* know."

"Maybe I guess. I hope that I guess!"

"Humph!" said Phil Slader. "There's only one trouble with you."

"Thanks. And what's that?"

"You're only a girl. Darn it, Nell, if you were a man, I'd take you away with me to-night, and we'd go through the night on the fastest horse that you've got. You and me could be such pals that we wouldn't care what the rest of the folks were thinking about us or doing about us!"

"I know," said Nell. "Oh, I've felt the same way about it. I've wanted to cut loose and tear. Except that to-night —why, being a man, I never would of been able to drag you clear over here."

"I suppose not. Matter of fact, this thing has been sticking in my mind ever since I first saw you, Nell."

"Tell me what, then?"

"Why, you know what I mean. I love you, I suppose."

"I hope that you do—a lot."

"And I do—and a lot! Such a lot that it scares me. I was a good deal set up about being free, until I came here. And now it makes me feel pretty weak."

"How?"

"Lonesome as the devil. I thought that it was a pretty big night and the stars were pretty grand, and Rooster was the finest thing under the stars, and Rooster belonged to

177

me, confound him! But—it doesn't seem to amount to a snap now! Well, Nell, what's the answer?"

"What do you want me to answer?"

"You don't love me. I'm not fool enough to think that a girl could love a man after seeing him twice, ten years apart. And I wouldn't want you to tell me, even if you did. Partly because it would make me so desperate to get back to you. And partly because you shouldn't anyway. You're not apt to see me again for a mighty long time."

"Hush!" said Nell. "You talk like a regular chief mourner. Matter of fact, Phil, seems to me that I've seen you about as often as you've seen me."

"I suppose so. But the difference is that you were something to look at. And even when you were a little kid, you were so darned sassy, Nell, that you were pretty easy to remember and think about, you know."

"You have a queer way of telling me that you love me," said Nell. "I've thought that a man would polish up his talk a little when he told a girl such things. But you just curse and tell me that I'm a tomboy, and ought to be a man, and I never heard such talk, Phil. Honest, I never did!"

"Nell," said he, "there is something coming over me."

"What is it?"

"I feel that I'm about to lay hands on you, and . . . ."

"I suppose I should scream," quavered Nell. "But I don't suppose that I will!"

"You are trembling all over, Nell. Are you afraid?"

"Silly!" said Nell. "But can you make love *al fresco*, like this, without getting a chill?"

"I am going to kiss you, Nell—if I may."

"If you don't," said Nell, "I'll hate you till my dying day!"

CHAPTER 32

WHEN PHIL SLADER looked up from the face of the girl, he was facing the east, and across the edges of the eastern hills he saw a thin line of light creeping. Only a hint—a shadow of a shadow of brightness, if you will—that made the mountains stand blacker against the sky. Perhaps the stars were a little fainter, and a wind was rising.

But he knew that the day was beginning, and that life would soon start here—and with that beginning of life, if a man were seen leaving the room of Nell Newell . . . .

He gave himself one last glance at her face, and he paused with his hand on the railing of the balcony.

"I got just this to say, Nell," said he. "This here is all romantic, as you might say, and very foolish. But I don't want to hold you to nothing. I want you to be just as free as the wind. I've come riding along and told you that I loved you. And no matter what you've said back—I'll forget it. You hear me? And never blame you when you see that it's no use being true to me."

"You talk," said Nell in a trembling voice, "like a great idiot, Phil."

"I talk like I had a morsel of good sense. They'll clap a price onto my head inside of twenty-four hours. They'll have me wrote down a little blacker than the ace of spades, you understand? And inside of the week they'll begin to tack other crimes onto me. Things in the same day and thousands of miles apart—but every man on a gray hoss that does anything wrong—he'll be me—and every young man with black eyes—he'll be me. I know it. But I don't care. They'll shut the door on me—but, by Heaven, I'll make them know that I can still get into the house. So long, Nell!"

When he reached the stallion, below, he rode the big horse out from the vines and looked up, and he saw her standing there and waving to him. The heart of Phil Slader went weak with sadness and with yearning. He told himself that, after all, this might be the last time. The law and all its millions of hands would be working hard enough to make it the last time. And every mile that he rode back toward her would be a mile of deadly danger. He waved his hat toward her, and then he turned the head of Rooster back toward the mountains.

It was still only dawn when he was in the upper foothills. He was among the mountains themselves when the sun arose. There he made a camp. He could have pushed on. His strength and the might of the stallion seemed hardly sapped at all. But he did not wish to work Rooster until he was jaded. Rooster, as he stood, was a king which no mustang could live with for half a mile without breaking its heart. But Rooster, tired, might be a horse that another could run to earth from a fresh start. And that was the chief strength and great reliance of Phil— Rooster's matchless burst of speed.

He spent a chilly morning until the sun was warm. Then he drowsed until the prime. After that he journeyed on again, heading well to the north along the upper ridges of the mountains, and keeping in what covert he could. But when the evening came on, it came with a sharpened wind and a sudden fall of rain.

There is nothing so depressing as rain. Snow has a wildness and a thrill about it. It is beautiful to the eye. A cold rain bites to the marrow of a man's soul and his body also. At least, so it was with Phil Slader, and he was a gloomy man, indeed.

180

Oh, he was rough enough and tough enough to have suited the fancy of the most exacting, but when it came to facing a night in some ramshackle camp of his own devising, his spirit failed him.

Besides, did they not tell such tales of his father? Jack Slader did not ride from wilderness to wilderness. He rode from house to house and from camp to camp. And at nine places he bought what he needed. At the tenth he took it by the force of hand.

He forced the stallion on over the next rise of ground, and there he found a little yellow star to guide him. It proved to be the kitchen light in the window of a little shack. When he knocked at the door a little, old, bent woman and a little, old, bent man were revealed to him. Heaven alone could tell what their business and their life might be, that kept them here in the upper reaches of the wilderness, or how their pinched bodies could outlast another winter.

They were glad to see him. The old man took him to the barn and gaped and shook his head at the tall stallion.

"A mighty upstanding hoss, stranger. I had a colt ten year back that had something of the look of him, I tell you. But not quite the same, I got to admit. Not the same cut to its legs. But he don't look tired none for a hoss that has carried you all day long over ground like this. A mountain hoss. I see that's what he is. Nothing like mountain hosses—aye, and mountain men, too, some say. I've heard it said, I mean to say!"

He took Phil back to the house, still chattering idly as they walked. And so they came into the kitchen again. Of course, they had a spare bed, and, of course, any man that came to them on a wet night like this . . . .

The woman had gone that far when Phil stepped into the full light of the lamp, and out of the nerveless, red, and wrinkled hand of his hostess the iron spoon fell with a clatter to the floor.

Her husband turned to her in amazement. "What ails you, Bess?" he asked her.

She pointed to the young stranger aghast.

181

"Ain't you got eyes in your head, man? D'you see what you've brought in under our roof? The red-handed murder of the both of us, I'm thinking! Oh, Harry, Harry, don't you see, man? It's young Phil Slader come to murder and rob us of all that we got! It's Phil Slader, like his daddy's ghost, come back to us!"

The old man turned to stare in his turn. And he, too, turned a sickly white.

So the news had come here, too. Oh, how busy the sheriff and the rest must have been to spread it so far, and so soon! He would have at least one willing volunteer to help him—Magruder!

"Old folks," said Phil, "I've not come up here to plague you or to rob you. I'd like to get a supper here from you. And—tell me what harm my father ever did to you when you saw him! Was he ever in this house before me?"

"He sat in yonder chair," said old Harry. "And yonder are the holes in the wall where Deputy Racham emptied a gun, trying to kill him, before he killed Racham!"

It was a grisly feeling that came upon Phil, then, as though he had been shunted back suddenly through the years, and had come to the place where his father had stood before him, not in time but in the flesh. More than a ghost—his father's self, just as famous Jack Slader had been in those other days.

He saw another thing, just as clearly, and this was the impossibility of forcing the ordinary run of people to believe that there was anything in him different from other desperadoes who had ranged through the mountains.

And indeed, was there? He was no brute, no beast of prey, but surely other fellows before him had just as many claims to the same distinctions. They were as gentle and as goodnatured as he had ever been, but still, the tiger had grown in them faster than the other elements, and so, at length, they had become public menaces. And he would become so in time!

He sat down at the little table in the corner of the room and he would have had them sit with him. He wanted to share their supper—not simply be fed like a horse in a stall. But they seemed afraid to sit. They moved like

182

frightened ghosts about the room. They placed food before him with trembling hands. They spoke to one another not at all, or else in hushed voices. They knew not, good souls, that this was more sad to the heart of Phil Slader than leveled guns and well-aimed bullets!

He could not even finish his meal—for the terrified eyes of the old people were poison to his very soul. He started up, at last, and hurried from the room. He took gray Rooster from the horse shed and he rode wildly off through the rain. The wind had come up sharp and steady. The rain was turning to rattling bursts of hail, but this dreary weather and the wild mountain way and the blackness of the night all seemed to Phil Slader preferable to the wretched silence in that house.

He found a half-sheltered nook among the trees, after a time, and there he made his camp for the night, trying to sleep and finding it a miserably wet, chilly business altogether. However, as the hours drifted on, it began to seem to Phil that a stormy night was not half so dreadful to those who were out in the midst of it as it was to those who remained indoors and only listened to its howlings through the windowpanes.

There was not much real sleep for him on that night; and when the morning came, he was prepared to find himself a haggard, nervous, and weary man. But he was not. The rest that comes to us under an open sky is twice as precious as that which we enjoy indoors. Even Rooster, in spite of all the ill use and hard wear which he had had in the past day, had his crest as high and his eyes as bright as ever they had been before.

So Phil mounted and they went on together. They drifted through the highest and the wildest part of the range on that day, for he could guess that the word would have gone out, by this time, and that scores of hunters for fame and fortune would be heading toward him. So he kept a sharp lookout and rode warily.

And yet when he saw a winking eye of yellow before him through the sharp cold of the mountain dusk, he could not avoid riding in toward it again.

CHAPTER 33

IT WAS A MORE promising abode for the night—in the estimation of Phil Slader—than that which he had approached the last evening. It was an old shack of the most ragged structure, leaning at a perilous angle on the side of the mountain, as though hardly more than the weight of a man's hand was necessary to thrust it from its place and start it toppling headlong down the hillside. It had a staggering chimney which proceeded by means of several crazy elbows up the side of the building and extended a very little distance above its roof.

Its windows had long ago lost all of their glass except a very few broken fragments. To shut out the air of the night and the storm, there were boards of various kinds nailed across the apertures. However dilapidated it might seem to be, nevertheless it was a building to the taste of Phil Slader. He regarded it with much satisfaction and, leaving the stallion behind a clump of great rocks, he slipped forward on foot to make a closer examination.

When he peered through the chink of the first window, he saw a scene of enough confusion to have satisfied the heart of the very devil. The whole first floor of this building had been turned into a single room, not according to any plan, as it seemed, but just as fancy or laziness moved the inhabitants to kick down the partitions and use them for kindling or for cooking wood. At all events, everything except the ragged stumps of some of the posts had been broken off, and the unsupported ceiling sagged dangerously. So much had it curved, that all of the plaster had broken off, save a few bits. Most of the rough slats were revealed.

The furnishings of the great ugly room were just what would have been expected, if the contents of a junk heap had been carelessly mixed and exposed to the day. There was not a sound stick of wood in the lot or a bit of cloth upholstery that was not honeycombed with holes. The table was the most imposing bit that remained. It had given way to the weight of various occasions, but every time it had been propped up once more. Three of the original legs were gone. A sagging box now served as one of the legs, and two rough-cut sapling lengths supplied the place of the others. But there stood the table, and so long as it was there, it furnished something around which the interest of the room could be rallied.

Three men had gathered at the board. There was a wan old man with an evil, twisted face; there was a youth with a handsome Italian cast of countenance and a gay scarf twisted around his neck; and there was a man of middle age with a face which was partly bulldog for firmness of will and strength of purpose.

Phil Slader examined them in no great detail. He did not have to. For he felt that if here were not three outcasts and rascals who had been forced to flee from the society of the rest of the world, then his eye was unable to put together the facts which it saw. Evil was written in large capitals, he knew, on the face of every one of these rascals.

And therefore they were fit company for him!

It gave him a sudden stab of pain to think of it. It was the proof of the distance which lay between him and the law-abiding world, of course.

He left his post at the window and searched back among the little ruined sheds, which stood behind the shack. He was not surprised by what he found there. For each of those three vagabonds in the house, there was a fine animal standing in the sheds—longlegged, beautiful animals, with the look of blood and speed written at large over them.

Ordinary honest cowpunchers had no use for horses like these. Of what use would these long legs be, to be sure, when a man wanted to work cutting calves from a herd? How could these beasts manage to do the twisting and the dodging that would be necessary to follow the windings and charges of a mad-headed yearling? No, they were not meant for such work as that. They were intended, purely and simply, to cover the greatest amount of ground in the shortest possible time. They were useful exactly as the gray stallion was useful to Phil Slater. If he had wanted any further proofs of the nature of the three men who were in the house, he felt that he had them here.

He was about to turn from the investigation of the last horse when there was the faintest of stirs behind him, and he whirled. He had not been long in danger on the trail; but instinct taught him to bring his Colt into his hand as he whirled about.

A big, rosy-faced man was stepping into the doorway—a man with a round red pair of cheeks, curling white hair, and a pair of shaggy white eyebrows.

"Hello, hello, hello!" said the fat stranger. "Have you come to put up at my hotel for the night?"

"Your hotel?" asked Phil Slader.

"I'm Don Remy," said the fat man. "I suppose that everybody knew me by description if they didn't by looks. It ain't every county that can boast of a two-hundred-and-eighty-pound man, is it? Oh, yes, I'm Don Remy—I'm all that there is of him!"

He laughed again and reached out a ponderous arm. His hand did not fall on the shoulder of Phil, who had slipped smoothly away.

"There you are and there you ain't," said the fat man. "But what for are you side-stepping me? I ain't a sheriff and a posse, am I?"

"Look here," said Phil, amused and a good deal puzzled by this speech, "why should I want to dodge a sheriff and a posse?"

186

"Why for should you be here, then, if you *don't* want to dodge some sheriff or other? Why, son, you wouldn't try to pull the wool over the eyes of 'Daddy' Remy, would you?"

He looked Phil over with an appreciative eye. "You look familiar to me, though. Look like somebody that I had seen before. But not lately—not lately. I'll have to comb around in my memory and see what turns up! I'll have to see what shows itself about you."

"You'll find nothing," said Phil. "I've never seen you before."

"Tut, tut, young man!" said the fat fellow. "Don't tell Daddy Remy that his memory is wrong. You know as well as I do that I'm *never* wrong. I always remember. In the end I can always remember, and I'll remember you, son, and every word that I ever said to you and every look that was ever on your face in my seeing. I can remember *anything*. Why, kid, you look as though you didn't believe me!"

He did not seem offended, however, but waved his hand toward the blackness of the great outdoors. "Where's your hoss, kid?"

"I'll get him, eh?"

"Yes, you get him and bring him in. And I'll shake down a feed for him."

"Wait," said Phil. "It must cost you a lot to cart hay and such stuff up here!"

"It costs me a lot but it pays me a lot," said the fat man. "Why do you ask, son? Are you thinking of starting up an opposition shop against me?"

"I wanted to say this," said Phil Slader, "that I haven't got any money."

"Ah, ah!" said the other. "I understand. Most of the boys don't have anything when they get this far away from nowhere. While they got plenty of coin, they can afford to pay for protection down in some town. But when they get up here they're flat. However, don't you bother yourself none. I been a hotel keeper for thirty years. And in the first twenty years I'll tell you what—I made enough coin to let me settle down up there and here I've been for the past ten years, keeping open shop for the boys, and never charged a penny in all that time!"

He rubbed his great hands together and beamed upon Phil Slader. But as for Phil, he stared fixedly into the face of the fat man and marked a strange thing. For while the lips of Daddy Remy were stretching and grinning, while his voice was swelling with laughter and good cheer and his cheeks were puffing and dimpling with mirth, his eyes remained as large and steady as the eyes of an owl—great yellow eyes that met the glance of Phil Slader and encountered it without blinking—the very first man in all his life who could meet him look for look.

"So get in your horse, son," said the fat man. "And I'll have the feed ready for him. And then let out your belt to the last notch, because there's enough chuck in that house to fill your belly, not matter how lean it may be!"

Phil Slader went obediently forth and found his horse and brought it back, and all the while his mind was busy with the riddle of the fat man who kept open house—open house in this tumble-down, desolate shack—to the haphazard guests who might chance to come to him.

When he brought in Rooster, the eyes of the fat man glittered under his white brows like yellow diamonds.

"Hello," he cried. "Is *this* your style, son? Is *this* your style? Why, here I've been thinking that you were simply a fellow who had misplaced a few dollars that belonged to his boss. Or maybe that had taken a liking to some of the yearlings on the next ranch to yours—but it seems that I'm wrong! Very wrong! Why, my son, when I see the looks of this horse—when I read his eye—I should say, bless me, that there must be a dead man behind you on your trail, eh? A dead man lying back there some place, eh?"

He approached Phil Slader with a prodigious wink and prodded him in the ribs with a stiff thumb.

"Aye," said Don Remy, "I'd like to remember, if I could, where I've seen that face of yours. But amnesia is my trouble. Darned if I can remember all the things that are loaded away in my head. Have to search for them. Have to comb them out fine to get at 'em. However, we ain't gunna leave this hoss here. Bring him along behind me!"

He brought Phil out of the shed and up the hillside to a little cluster of tall shrubs. Through these they passed and Don Remy opened a door, set aslant on the face of the ground, and showed a black cavity beneath it. Through this he passed and presently lighted a lantern which revealed a snug little stable with stalls for three horses.

"All dry as you please," he said to Phil. "Underground, but not damp. Smell the air and see for yourself. We'll leave him here. Not that they can't find him here, the thieves! But to get him out they'd have to make such a lot of noise that we'd hear them."

When they had put the stallion inside, Don Remy took Phil outside, closed the heavy door, locked and double locked it and gave him the key.

"There we are!" said he. "And if they try to work a passkey on this lock, they'll have no luck. I'll tell you why —I made the lock myself!"

With this he broke again into his booming laughter and then led the way back to the shanty.

CHAPTER 34

THE THREE had finished their meal when Phil and the landlord appeared. The old man was nursing a tin cup of black coffee; the other two were smoking cigarettes. They greeted Phil Slader with nods and most casual glances. So long as he faced them, they acted almost as though he were not in the room. But the moment that his head was turned, he knew by an extra sense, which all men possess, that their glances were prying restlessly at him.

The host went at once to the big stove at the back of the room, and from some big pots which stood upon it he ladled out an immense portion of the tramp's favorite dish—mulligan! That, with a huge half loaf of stale bread and a great cup of night-black coffee, composed the portion of Phil and he devoured it with a hungry man's relish. He was halfway through with his silent meal when a gesture of the fat host made him look up with a start. The forefinger of Don Remy was leveled like a gun at him.

"Jack Slader!" he exclaimed.

It made the other three jump.

"Good heavens, Dad," said the young-faced man. "Jack Slader is dead, for fifteen years! What are you talking about?"

The host blinked. "Dead for fifteen years! Dead for fifteen years! Oh, well, but there's something in it, because my memory doesn't lie. Look at him, 'Buck!' Remind you of anybody else?"

The gentleman of the Italian cast of features, looked long and earnestly at Phil Slader. "I dunno," said he at last. "I dunno that I've seen anybody before with just that look. Why d'you ask?"

"I'm trying to place him. That's all. Look here, kid— have you got any of the blood of the Sladers in you? Hey, Buck, didn't Jack Slader have a son?"

Here there was a rattle at the door, and it yawned open with a loudly whistling draft of wind. Into the room stepped the slouching form of 'Blinky' Rosen. And Phil Slader drew back into the shadow of a corner.

Blinky flashed a glance over the others. "Hello, Buck," he said, "you lucky devil! How are you? Whew, ain't it cold?"

He banged the door behind him and strode to the stove. "Well, Pop?" said he to the fat man.

"You razor-faced rat," said Daddy Remy, "what did I tell you the last time that you was up here?"

"Easy, easy!" said Blinky, spreading out protesting hands. "Go easy, Dad. Don't you get reckless, now!"

"I told you to get out and to stay out and to never come back! And I meant it. Curse me if it don't rile me to see a gent that is built like a man, pull a knife. Curse me if it don't!"

Blinky spread his hands closer to the stove and wrung them together, and he merely grinned at his host.

"D'you hear me?" cried Remy.

"Say, boys," whined Blinky, "ain't there none of you that'll pass a good word for me, maybe?'"

"You know the rules, Blinky," said Buck. "The fat boy is the whole show up here. If he says go, you go. That's all, I guess. And if you been flashing a knife around these parts, I don't blame him none."

"Is that so?" said Blinky Rosen with a sneer. "The gent that you carved up back in Chi was a . . . ."

"Shut up," cried Daddy Remy. "It's agin' the rules to pull up old things by the roots. Besides, what he done in Chicago ain't no affair of mine. What he does here is what counts with me. I say, get out and get quick, or I'll have the boys roll you out and dress you down, you . . . ."

"Aw, tame down—tame down!" growled Blinky. "You would think that I was a disease and catching, the way that you talk. Lemme tell you that there's a gent coming in that will have a word to say for me. I'll wait here until you've persuaded him that I had ought to go."

"Who is it?" asked the host curiously. "You little tin-pan bread stealers, you little pocket pickers nowadays, you don't scare me. There ain't many names among the lot of you that I would take my hat off to . . . ."

"Shut up, you fool!" said Blinky Rosen. "Shut up, will you? It's the chief. And he's back as the devil. He's feeling mean! He might hear you."

"Kirby!" said the host, whistling long and softly. "Kirby!"

"Him!" said Blinky, nodding.

"Tell us how that deal was managed," said Buck.

"Let him tell you himself," said Blinky, "if he wants to talk about it. But I don't. And underground like that— why the darker it's kept, the fresher it'll be for them that have to use it. I don't talk about that. Let the chief do the chattering, if he wants to. And here he is, now."

At this, the door was wrenchèd open, and Lon Kirby strode into the building, with that rolling stride which comes to sailors and to cowpunchers. He glared at the others, he nodded to big Don Remy. And then he stood with his hands in his pockets and glared around him.

The old man was still nursing the last of his tin of coffee. But now he rose and offered the stool on which he was sitting.

"Glad to see you again, Lon," said he. "So's all of us. There was a time, not far back, when we didn't think that there was going to be much hope for you. But here you are! They can't beat old Lon, I guess!"

Lon Kirby regarded him with perfect indifference. But he took the stool and sat with his long sinister chin dropped upon one fist. Blinky Rosen busied himself in bringing a steaming portion to his master, and Phil Slader, withdrawn to the farthest, coldest and most shadowy corner, noted with some interest that there was no longer any talk of removing Blinky from their midst. There seemed, suddenly, to be only two men in the room—one, the giant host with his strange yellow eyes, like the eyes of an owl that hunts by night, and Kirby. The others were as nothing.

There was no doubting the excitement which pervaded the atmosphere. It was like a breath of mountain air in a desert place. There was a native strangeness in Lon Kirby. Even the fat man was a good deal worked up. No matter what he had had to say about the great men of the past and the pygmies of the present, it was plain that he made an exception in the favor of Lon Kirby. He belonged, clearly, to the heroes!

Blinky Rosen, in the meantime, freshened the fire and helped himself to food. The silence was broken only by the occasional moan of the wind outside, and the crackling of the fire as the flames rushed up the chimney. A warmth began to pass through the room and reached even to the farther corner, where Phil sat watching.

Lon Kirby, having eaten, said to the old man who had given up the stool to him: "There's a place over by the fire, oldster. Why don't you take it?"

This amend for past discourtesy seemed amply sufficient to make the other nod and grin; but he did not move from the spot where he stood. He merely said:

"Pay me for that stool by telling us how you managed to get loose, Lon. Tell us that, will you?"

Lon Kirby turned a sneering, wolfish face toward the other. "I'll tell you about that, old man," said he. "I'll tell you the strangest story that anybody in this here world ever run up against. I found an honest man!"

He said it with a peculiar emphasis and a raising of his eyes, so that it was plain that there was more than a sneer in the remark.

"An honest man," said big Don Remy with almost equal solemnity, "is something that I've heard tell about and never have met up with."

The fierce eyes of Kirby flashed across at his host. "That's one time that you ain't lying," said Kirby, "one of the few times that I've heard you open that big mouth of yours without flopping out a lie. Well, it's true. I met an honest man."

"But how the devil would an honest man get you out of prison?" asked Buck, the Italian.

"You wouldn't know," said Kirby with his evil eye fixed upon the handsome youth. "You wouldn't even be able to guess, because honesty is something that you don't know much about, old-timer. It's a foreign land to you, right enough."

Anger showed in the eyes of Buck, but it was only an amorphous light, not fixed and formed with resolution. Lon Kirby was plainly too much of a man to be answered back in that assembly.

"But honesty," went on Lon Kirby, "can do more things than any of you would guess. It was that honest man that reached out a hand a thousand miles long. He smashed down the walls and he busted open the doors and he

193

twisted the tool-proof bars like they was just straws. And so he took me out as safe and as sound and as easy as you please."

"All right," said the host, after a bit of silence, "we'll admit that the honest man could of done all of these big things. But still we're a long ways from understanding just why any honest man should of took such a whopping big interest in you, Lon?"

"You wouldn't be able to guess that. But I'll tell you what an honest man does. He pays you back ten for one. I done a little favor for him. And then he turned around and paid me back like this. Paid me back by setting me free, by Heaven! Free! Free!"

He closed his eyes suddenly and ground the stiffened fingers of his right hand across his throat. And deathly silence fell over that room.

They knew that, in this moment of delicious agony, the soul of Lon Kirby had felt the grip of the hangman's noose from which he had escaped by miracle.

CHAPTER 35

"AH, WELL," said Kirby, speaking with his eyes still closed and his long, ugly face white with emotion, "there's no use wondering and gaping over it. Here I am safe—safe—safe! And where did they have me?"

"I know," said the fat man.

"Aye," said Lon Kirby, "you ought to know!"

"Shut up, will you?" said Don Remy, growing very pallid and flabby of cheek.

"What's the matter?" asked Kirby. "Ashamed of having beat them right from the death house? Not me, old kid. I'm proud of it. They'll never choke me with a rope and they'll never send me up Salt Creek, because when I die, I'll die with a gun in my hand. Something tells me that. I'm bad. Sure, I'm awful bad, friends. But I'm good enough to deserve to die like a man instead of a rat!"

It was a most amazing thing to Phil Slader to listen to this outburst of superstition and of childishness. He felt that he was opening sudden and unexpected doors and viewing all of these men in new lights, looking deep and deeper into their souls.

"And where's the honest man?" asked the host at last.

"I'm trying to get on his trail now," said Lon Kirby. "I'm trying to get onto his trail, but I got only a small chance. I'm trying to find him, now!"

"On a trail?"

"Yes."

"What d'you mean, Lon? You mean that he's not too honest to be afraid of the law, too?"

"They trapped him," said Lon Kirby. "They done a dirty job and trapped him. And the meanest and the lowest skunk in the world was the one that had a hand in it. Will you guess who I mean?"

"The meanest and the lowest skunk in the world?" said the host. "Who is it, boys?"

He turned blandly to the others, and each had an instant answer, for men in their callings are sure to have precious friends and more precious foemen.

"There's a low-down elbow in St. Louis," said the old man, "by the name of Chivvers, that I would . . . ."

"Some day when I get a chance," said Buck, "I'm going to take a year off and go to Alaska and get me a big Canuck that is up there bluffing folks into thinking that he's a man, when he's only a low-down pup! I'm going up there and I'm going to get him, and I'm going to get him good!"

"I tell you what . . . ." began Blinky Rosen, with a whine. The voice of the host cut in: "Shut up, all of you. There's only one man that's lower than anybody else. None of you know him. I don't think you do, anyways. But I been told about him, and the name of him won't never get out of my throat. Magruder is his name."

"Magruder!" shouted Lon Kirby. "Where did you get that name, you old ragpicker? Where did you get hold of that name? Do you know him, too?"

"Oh, I know him too, right enough! And you, Lon? Is that your man?"

"Yes."

"Then you've picked out the lowest rat in the world, right enough."

"I know that as well as you do. Well, Don, it's strange that you should have known of him, though."

"Why not?"

"After all," said Lon Kirby, "he's pretty famous. But anyway, it was a dirty trick of his that sent the kid away. The finest and the straightest gent that ever lived—and now he's gone to the devil. They sent in a murdering greaser to get him. And he got the greaser instead. Ten bunches of wild cats—that's all that he is. And now he's gone to the devil—too young to know how to travel through this stuff."

"What stuff, Lon?"

"*This* stuff. If he was here, wouldn't he be in a fight inside of ten minutes? But tell me more about what you know of Magruder. I'm gunna kill that man, Remy. So you might as well tell me what you know. All that I got for a fact is how he crooked the kid and then I know that he killed Jack Slader in a fight."

"In a murder!" said Don Remy.

"Murder?" repeated Kirby. "Yes, I always guessed that that was the way of it. But tell me how you know. Were you there? I thought that they was alone."

"They was alone—they thought. But I'll tell you the facts. There was one other man that knew the whole truth. Or rather, he wasn't a man either. But only a little kid. But he could stand up and tell you a story that would

196

of turned your blood downright cold, Kirby. Even yours!"

"Go on!" said Lon Kirby.

"No," said the host. "When you come to be my age you don't want to think about things like that. And I won't tell that story again, not even to please you, Lon. No sir, I can't do it. But I'll give you my downright word for it—that Magruder is the meanest and the lowest skunk that ever breathed. You guessed him right. And if it was him that sent your kid on the trail—why, then, maybe the kid *is* honest, after all, but . . . ."

Then Phil Slader, who had remained in the dark of the background as long as he could contain himself, arose and stepped forward.

"I'll tell you what, Remy," said he, "I'll give you a good excuse, now, for telling that story. I'll give you reason for telling it now, if you never tell it again."

"Hello," said Don Remy. "Here's the kid come to life. I thought that you was asleep, back yonder!"

Lon Kirby burst in between them with a shout. "It's Phil! It's the kid! It's the kid!" he shouted. "Remy, it's him! I tell you, Remy, I'll be your friend for life for turning up this kid for me."

"Curse me white and black," said Remy. "I don't know him from Adam. But don't tell me that he's your honest man?"

"Honest?" said Kirby. "I tell you, gents, that this here is the gent that the word was made to fit, and that it don't belong to no other. Kid, I'm so darned glad to see you, that you wouldn't believe it. Sit down—sit here—curse my heart, but this is fine!"

He gripped Phil by the shoulders and, leaning close to his ear, he said: "I went back to the spot. I moved the rock and I found every penny—except that stuff which you had sent to me by Blinky, the rat. Why, Phil, I would go to perdition and back for a man like you!"

He was so thoroughly excited that he would hardly allow Phil Slader himself to say a word.

"I've got to tell him why I have to hear the story," said Phil. "Let me tell him that, Lon, will you?"

"I'll do your talking for you," said the outlaw. "Remy,

open up, and say what you got in your pocket. I got the pleasure of introducing to you the son of the finest man that ever lived—a kid that has got the promise of being all the man that his dad was before him. I want you to shake hands with Phil Slader, Don."

"It's the son of Jack," said the fat man, grinning. "Yep, and I knew it and I picked him. Tell Kirby if I didn't pick you, Phil? And as for Magruder—well, it's a nasty yarn. But you're the one gent in the world that has the right to hear it told just as it was spoke out to me by a Mexican—a skinny young card sharp he was, with a right eye that turned out a little—a very handy kid at a knife or a gun either."

"And his name was Diego Pasquual?" asked Phil Slader.

"Diego Pasqual!" shouted the host. "Why, this here is getting a little too spooky! How come that you ever heard of that name, kid?

"Shut up, you fat fool!" said Lon Kirby. "Lemme tell you that Pasqual is the name of a gent that is pushing up a headboard with his forehead in the graveyard down at Crusoe. They planted him just the other day. It was him that went in to sink a knife in the back of Phil Slader, here; and it was him that Phil Slader got all ready for the long sleep, y'understand?"

Remy emitted a long, soft whistle, though his lips were so thick and unwieldy with fat that it was less a whistle than a moaning sound. "It was Diego that tried that?" he said. "Well, that was the speed of Pasqual. He was made real fine and handy to try a knife play in the dark. It was the sort of a game that he would shine at when he wasn't dealing crooked poker. Son, I begin to see that maybe my friend, Kirby, ain't so very far wrong about you. I begin to see that maybe I'll have to back him up in what he's been saying. Diego come for you, with Magruder sending him. Is that straight?"

"I think that it's straight," said Phil. "I've got almost a sure proof of it. I know that I overheard them that same night, and Magruder was blaming Diego for not having done the job for which he was hired and brought to the farmhouse."

198

"Very sweet!" said Remy. "That's the kind that Magruder is. Deep—and dangerous and mean. And now, old son, I'm going to tell you the story just the way that I got it from the greaser—and that was about five years ago, when I was taking a little vacation trip down into Mexico, y'understand? I had started out to . . . ."

"Leave out the trimmings and give us the bald facts, will you?" asked Kirby.

The fat man began to cram his pipe with black tobacco from a capacious pouch, and as he stuffed and lighted it, the fire of the narrator's ardor began to kindle in his eye.

"I'll give you just the facts, if you want them that way," he said, "because I can see that the kid, yonder, is breaking his heart to know what I got to say!"

CHAPTER 36

"I'LL CUT OUT all of the little things that go into the making of this here yarn," said the fat man, "and I'll come down to the facts that there I was, one day, sitting in an upper level of an old mine. I had come busting through from one side, on the search for an old silver pocket that my lead was pointing at. When I got through, there I found a young Mexican just polishing off the last of that ore! He had just outguessed me and he had got away with the cream of the stuff.

"I was just able to laugh, instead of braining him, and

we sat down and had a smoke together. And we got to talking about the funny coincidence that it was—that old mine having laid there for hundreds of years, just the way that it was when the Spaniards got through with working it with Indian labor, and then along comes two gents and they starts in and works up leads. And almost at the same minute, they arrives at the same pocket.

"We was talking about that, and about other coincidences, that led up as how I had seen a strange thing in Chicago, where I had run into, on the street, a pickpocket that had gone through me in a street crowd in Singapore. And I dipped into his pocket and the first thing that I pulled out was a match safe that belonged to me!

"Well, when I got through talking about that, we turned on to more spooky subjects, and finally the Mexican kid, whose name was this same Diego Pasqual, turns loose and tells me the strangest thing that he had ever seen in his life.

"He said that a long ways back, fourteen or fifteen years, he had gone up north and he had a job working for a gent that has a shack on the edge of a river."

"The Crusoe, eh?" put in Phil Slader.

At that, the fat man lifted his big, yellow, expressionless eyes. "The Crusoe it was," said he and frowned, as though he would have liked to stop all further interruptions. "The Crusoe it was, right enough. There this Diego Pasqual settled down, and he was working pretty peaceful and contented and more industrious than he had ever been before, in his whole life. And he says that his boss was the best and the easiest gent to work for that he ever met with in his life."

"It was my father," said Phil Slader.

"It was," said the host; "it was your father."

He tamped his pipe down with another scowl. "The kid had a good reason, of some kind, for not wanting to ramble around none too much. This was a good, wild, quiet spot. And the kid wanted wildness and quietness. Just what he had done back in Mexico, I don't know, but I think that it had something to do with running a knife between somebody's ribs back in old Mexico. Anyway, there he was, happy and comfortable, with nothing much to do except some fishing, a little cooking, now and then, and sweeping up the shack. And all the time, his boss was extra special kind and easy with him.

"Well, things went along like this, all hunky dory, for a long time, until finally the trouble busted on them right out of a cloud, as you might say. For he come back from a trip up through the hills, trying to get berries, one day. And he had a hat filled with the berries right up to the brim. His arms was aching with that load, and he was hurrying down before the sun and the heat of his hands should have made all of these berries begin to wither up, y'understand?"

He paused again to lean back his great bulk against the side of the house, and the broad boards creaked and bent under the heavy weight which was thus thrust against them.

"Well, when the kid come through the door of the shack and started to close it, something grabbed him from behind, and he was pretty near choked. There was a gag jabbed into his mouth. And then he was throwed in under the bunk.

"He lay there, choking and nearly dying. Fact of the matter was that he would have died, and the big fellow that was there in the shack with him, leaned down and took a look at his face and then shrugged his shoulders—not giving a hang whether or not the kid lived or died!"

There flashed back upon the mind of Phil Slader a certain moment when he had lain in the trail, tortured by the sun, and the calm, indifferent face of Magruder above him.

"That was Doc Magruder?" he suggested.

"Aye, that was Doc Magruder. And Magruder looked the kid over, as I've said, not caring whether he lived or died, and perhaps preferring that he should of died and so been out of the way. But he couldn't quite make up his mind to murdering the kid. Anyway, the kid didn't choke. He managed to shift that gag a little by working the muscles at the root of his tongue, and then he could lie there and breathe more comfortable, though still feeling more than half stifled all the while.

"After a time, the day began to turn dark, and the kid, staring out from under the bunk, saw the big Magruder sitting there with his revolver in his hand, all ready and fixed. Then the revolver didn't seem good enough for him, or sure enough as the darkness got thicker. So he took up his rifle, and he oiled that up, and looked to the loading of it, and he sat there with the rifle, ready to shoot the minute that the door opened.

"Well, after a time some voices come down, echoing across the water, pretty loud, and there wasn't the voice of the owner of the shack in that number."

"Jack Slader owned that shack, then?" asked Phil.

"You've spotted all of the names," admitted the fat man. "Slader's voice wasn't among those that was paddling down the stream in a canoe. But they landed near to the shack, and they come up and opened the door of it.

"Everything was pitch dark inside, and some of them was for coming in and making themselves at home; and then somebody spoke up and said that he thought he knew who owned that shack, and that it would be a poison-bad business for anybody to be found in there by the owner. When he mentioned the name of Jack Slader, that was enough. They didn't even so much as light a match to look around in the shack and to see what was there.

"Well, when they went off, the kid could hear Magruder groan with relief, because he had been pretty scared for fear that he might have been found there, rifle in hand, waiting to do a plain murder—even if it was only the murder of an outlawed man.

"Now things went along like this for a time, and the kid could hear the new party of folks settle down not far off, and he could hear the blows of their axes as they chopped down the trees that they wanted for their night camp or for their fire. A rifle popped here and there, as though that some one of them might be off shooting at rabbits by the moonlight—which it is as good a time to kill rabbits as any that I ever knew about. Anyway, those sounds from the near camp sounded so cheerful that the kid began to feel that all of this might turn out pretty good.

"And, just then, the *back* door of the shack was pulled open, and somebody stepped in as silent as a shadow. You see, what had happened was simply that Slader had heard the camp so close up to his, and he was going to sneak into his cabin and see that the strangers hadn't disturbed anything there. And he took the back entrance as a matter of course, in case that any of the gang might be watching the front door. He stepped in, and must have seen the shadow of Magruder bulking there like a shadow inside of a shadow.

"Magruder had shifted his position. He was watching only the front door at that moment. He tried to whirl around, but he had the grip of Jack Slader on him, and any of the old-timers that rode through the mountains in those days, could have told you what the Slader grip was like, I suppose."

"There!" murmured Lon Kirby with his lips, whispering. And he pointed a sudden hand.

They saw young Phil Slader sitting with a thick bar of iron between his hands—a ponderous bar, used by Don Remy for the purpose of shifting and freshing the fire in the great old stove. It looked like a gun barrel, melted down into a single clumsy rod.

The rod, under the enormous pressure of the hands of Phil Slader, was bowing into an arc. As he had listened to the tale of his father's peril, he had sought this dumb employment of his strength as an outlet for his emotions.

The host, staring in the indicated direction, looked askance at Phil, and then across to Lon Kirby.

"It's the Slader grip," said Lon Kirby. "And now you've seen for yourself."

"I've seen!" said Don Remy. "I've seen. I dunno that his dad could do a thing like that—but he could do enough. And he mastered Magruder and laid him flat on the floor of the shack. And Magruder, he began to gasp and ask what it all meant, and beg for his life like a whipped cur . . . ."

"Are you sure of that?" broke in Phil Slader.

"I'm telling you what the greaser told me, word for word. Nothing changed from what he said!"

203

"All right," said Phil Slader. "I didn't think that Magruder could be as low as that—but now I'll believe it!"

"Son," said the narrator, "this here which I'm telling you, it's a study in lowness and meanness, and you got to get yourself ready to believe a lot more things than this, before I'm through with you, because I'm going to show you how Magruder was the lowest and meanest skunk that ever stepped and that ever breathed!"

CHAPTER 37

BY THIS TIME the interest in the shack, which had been at a high point long before, had grown to a feverish intensity. And they pressed on into a close and closer circle. The center was Don Remy, and the rim was composed of six eager listeners, all bent upon hearing an incredible thing.

Then said Don Remy: "This here is a yarn that I don't like to tell. I've just hinted at it before, but I've never given out the facts. And I'll never do it again, because it makes me pretty sick, y'understand? Anyway, this is the way that the layout was:

"There was the greaser kid lying there under the bunk, scared to death, but pretty happy because that his boss had come along and got the upper hand with Magruder. He was only hoping that Slader would wring Magruder's neck or give the kid a chance to do it for him.

"But the kid couldn't move. He was tied hand and foot.

And he was tied by Magruder so hard that he had turned numb, long ago. There wasn't any sensation in his arms and his legs below the shoulders and the hips, and so he just lay there, unable to move, without nothing living in him except his brains. He lay there and he saw his boss light a candle wick that throwed just enough light to see a ghost's whiteness, as the saying is. And when Jack Slader saw the face of Magruder, he was a good deal cut up, and he says: 'Doc, by Heaven, I can't believe that you really have tried to murder me! I can't believe it!'

"Magruder, he just tried to wriggle himself through the floor, and he began to beg again and he told Slader that he hadn't meant him any harm. But Jack Slader just smiled. Jack was never any man's fool. And you can't very well explain away sitting in the dark of a man's shack with a rifle bare in your hands. That takes a good deal of explaining, and a lot more than Magruder had the tongue or the wit for, and yet he was always a powerful liar, according to what I've heard."

Here Lon Kirby put in: "I hate to interrupt you, Remy, but it makes me boil a little to think how many honest folks in this here world really believe with all of their hearts that that snake, that Magruder, really waltzed into the house of Jack Slader and had the nerve to fight him, hand to hand, and had the nerve to beat him and kill him."

"Wait a minute," said Remy, "because you've got to understand that they're partly right. He *did* fight Jack Slader in his own house, and he did kill him. And this was the way of it.

"After Slader had looked down at Magruder for a time, he says to him: 'Folks know that I've been a friend to you, Doc. And over yonder is some gents that I've got a mind to call in and let them hear the story of what's happened between you and me, so that they can make up their minds for themselves as to what had better be done with you!'

"Even Magruder, that had no shame, he felt shame at this, and he begged Jack to kill him if he wanted to, but not to turn him over to the boys to hear what sort of a murdering skunk he had tried to be on that night.

"And Jack, he was always a goodnatured gent that loved to have a joke and that loved to have friends around him. He was plumb kind and gentle, the way that I remember him, and he couldn't keep malice against nobody. He says to Doc that he wouldn't call in the others. And with that, he cuts the ropes with which he had tied Magruder's hands, and he lets Doc loose and free to stand up. But Magruder wouldn't stand up. He just sat on the ground and asks Jack:

" 'What d'you aim to do, Jack?'

"Slader says: 'I aim that you are going to have as fair a chance as though you deserved it, which you don't, and which you know that you don't!'

" 'I don't deserve anything,' says Magruder. 'Only—what do you mean by a fair chance?'

" 'A chance to stand up here and get an equal draw for your gun, Doc.'

"Well, at that Magruder just melted back into the floor, and he says: 'It's murder!'

" 'You lie!' says Jack Slader. 'And you know that you lie, because I've promised you that I'd give you an even chance and not take any advantage of you, and there was never a Slader yet that would break his word!'

"Well, that didn't ease up the spirit of Doc Magruder none. He pointed out in a whimper that there was nobody in the world, hardly, that could stand up to Jack Slader in a gun fight from an even start, and he told Jack that it was simply murder to ask him to do such a thing, and Jack couldn't argue him into standing up and fighting like a man.

"It threw Jack Slader into a terrible temper. When he got mad he was a devil to face, and you can believe me when I say it, because I've seen him raging, a couple of times. It was something worth remembering.

"He says to Magruder: 'I've treated you like a brother, Doc, you rat. And now you've come here to gnaw away at me and get fat on my death. You came here to murder me.'

" 'No,' says Magruder, 'only to capture you, Jack!'

" 'You lie,' says Jack Slader, 'because you know that

206

I'll never be captured alive—but they'll have to take me dead! You know that, and that means that you came here to do a murder on me. I loathe your rotten heart, Magruder. I would like to burn you inch by inch, and in another minute I'll swear that I'll do it, unless you stand up here and fight me like a man. Hand or knife or club or gun—I'll take you any way that you say!'

"Magruder, he sat there on the ground, turned into ice, he was so badly scared, and he kept shaking his head and moaning with every breath that he drew, like an unhappy puppy that wants to get out of its kennel. And he says:

" 'There's nobody that can stand to you, hand to hand. You know that. You got the strength of a devil in your hands. And you got the speed of a devil in those hands, too. No, if you're going to murder me, Slader, go ahead and do it—because I won't raise a hand to help myself!' "

At this point in the story, there was a sudden snarl of disgusted disbelief, and the sound came from most of the men in the room, but the fat host merely shook his head.

"I felt that way, too," said he, in perfect sympathy with his hearers, "but the greaser swore that that was the way that it was, and I had to believe him. After all, it was to his advantage to make the yarn better than it really was and not worse—as I'll explain to you in a minute more.

"Well, when Magruder showed that he wouldn't fight that way, like a white man, Jack Slader yanked a revolver out of its holster in that flashy way that he had of handling a gun, and he seemed about to shoot Magruder on the spot. And would you believe what Magruder done?

"Well he crawled across the floor of that shack and he put his arms around the knees of Slader and begged him not to kill him!"

Here the host was forced to stop and wipe his brow, and every man in the room was looking down to the floor, in silent rage and horror that such a creature should ever have been able to call himself a man.

"Slader listened and tried to kick him away, but when he saw that Magruder wouldn't turn into a man, whether he were kicked like a dog or not, he finally said: 'I'll give you a handicap, Magruder, if you'll start fighting and stop whining!'

" 'What can you do for me?' asks Magruder.

" 'I'll let you have your gun in your hand while my gun is still inside of the leather,' says Slader.

"But Magruder wouldn't hear of it. After all, the way that Jack got a Colt out of its leather was a caution to watch, and Magruder didn't hanker to take any chances, as you'll see later. He kept on whining and begging Jack to give him a chance to prove that he was a friend and not an enemy, until finally Jack Slader says to him:

" 'I've thought of a way that even a skunk like you could never refuse. We'll take off all of the guns that we have on us. And then we'll put just one gun on the little table there, in the middle of the room, and then we'll step back one step from the table, and at the signal, when we've counted three, we'll dive for that gun. You hear me?'

"Magruder all at once showed a little sign of life, after this. He stood up and let the thing be done, and the Colt was put on the table between them. But when they stood there and Slader begun counting, Magruder lost his nerve again and fell on his knees and said that it was murder and that he wouldn't fight. Then Slader asked him what he could want more even than this. And Magruder said that everybody in the world knew that Slader was as fast as lightning on his feet, and that there wouldn't be anything to such a thing. Because Slader would be sure to reach that gun first.

"After that, Slader seemed beat, for a minute. But he was plain raging for the fight, as the greaser told me. He couldn't wait and hold himself off. Finally, he was fool enough to consent to move back a whole pace further away from the table than Magruder.

"After that, he began counting, and you would say that Magruder now had enough advantages to play the rest of the game fair and square. But he didn't. He wanted to crowd every advantage that he could into this game before he would play it at all. When the count was only at two, he left Slader flat and dived for the gun. Even at that, he was only a flash ahead of Slader.

"He just had time to twich the gun around and shoot at Jack, as Jack reached for the Colt. Two inches more, said the greaser, and Slader's hands would have been at the Colt, and, of course, that would have meant the death of Magruder.

"But that goes to prove to you that Magruder has brains. He's a big and a hard-fighting man, as everybody knows; but he had the wits to know just the difference that lies between him and such a man as Jack Slader. He counted it down so fine that he managed just enough handicap to beat Slader—and to kill him. Because that's the way that your father was killed."

At this, all eyes shifted suddenly to Phil, and there was a real pity in the glances that fell upon him.

"But it seems very strange to me," said Phil, "that a man like my father could have laid dying and asked any favor from a cur such as Magruder had just proved himself to be!"

"Why not? Only him and Magruder knew how much was owing to him from Magruder. And he thought that maybe Magruder might have something like a conscience. Anyway, that's what happened. And then there came the sound of the feet running and voices from the camp outside of the shack and Magruder remembered about the greaser. He looked daggers at the kid and would have murdered him if he dared. But there wasn't time for that. He had to work fast even the way that it was. And so what he did was to slash the ropes with which he had tied Diego Pasqual. After that, he reached into his pocket and flashed a whole handful of gold pieces before Diego's eyes. Then he crammed them into his pocket and threw him out of the room.

"The greaser was only a kid, but he was enough of a wise head to think about the money while he was lying on the ground, and he knew that if he kept his mouth shut, he could drain the white man the rest of his born days by blackmail. And that was exactly what he did. He laid low, and he heard the others run into the shack; but he kept his mouth shut, and he told me that he had made

209

Magruder pay through his nose to his dying day. Aye, but Magruder, in the end, found a way of making Diego pay back."

CHAPTER 38

So the story which Phil Slader had waited fourteen years to hear was told to him in detail, at last; told to him, as he could not help noticing, not by honest men but by thieves, who were standing him as friends in this all-important moment. He went up to the fat man and gripped his hand.

"Remy," said he, "I may live a long time or a short one, but I'll never owe any man more than I owe you right now!"

And he started for the door.

"Wait a minute, Phil!" called the outlaw, Kirby.

"I'm stepping outside for just half a minute," said Phil. "And then I'm coming right back, Lon."

And he disappeared through the door.

"I wouldn't be Magruder now," said Don Remy, rubbing the fingers of the big hand which the youngster had just gripped. "My hand understands the way that that iron felt when he was petting it. Darn such a kid, I say! He don't know his strength! Kirby, how did you pick up with him? And what are you gunna do with him?"

"Give him a chance to do the thing that he's been

working for all of his life—give him a chance to go straight," said Kirby.

There was a universal muttering of assent around the room, for even the most degraded vagabonds and tramps have little pleasure in seeing an honest man brought down to their level.

"That sounds pretty sweet," said Buck, the Italian-born youth with the handsome face, "but I'd like to know what real chance there is that he *can* go straight, while folks are remembering that he's the son of Jack Slader?"

"You talk like you had good sense," said Kirby. "It's not easy. But there's a way that's growing up in my head— a way of handling the business so that the kid *can* go straight."

"Did the greaser really try to murder him?"

"No doubt about it at all."

"What makes you think so? The word of Slader?"

"No. You know that he hasn't talked about it to me. He hadn't had a chance when I made up my mind by the story of the thing just the way that I heard it. No, Diego Pasqual tried to sashay in and murder him when he was in his bed. I'd as soon try to sneak into the room of a wild cat and surprise it asleep. Anyway, that's what happened. But I got a way in mind of making Magruder confess that he sent Pasqual to do that murder. And I got a way in mind of making Magruder die, too, after he's made the confession. But it will take quick acting. Because I can see this: The kid has had enough taste of the wild life to like it pretty well. Give him another few days, and he'll start to be an incurable. I know the symptoms and I can see them growing in him."

"Go on," said Don Remy. "Tell us your plan, will you?"

"The first part is that we've got to stop the kid while he's here. Don, I'm going to leave that part of it to you and the boys that you got here with you. I want a five-hour start. And after that, you can let the wild cat scratch his way loose. Only, you'd better be in hiding when he gets away, because he's liable to make some fur fly. Can you hold him, Remy?"

"And you'll do the rest?"

"I'll do the rest."

"I don't like my part of the job," said the fat man. "If I had a hoss that would carry me, I'd rather ride down to Crusoe and do the work with Magruder than handle this young devil. But—since there ain't any other help for it, I'll do what I can."

He stepped from his place to the wall and took down a Mexican lariat, made of rawhide, nicely sun-cured, supple with oil. He shook the noose open and stood close by the wall, with the corner of his eye fixed upon the door.

"Kirby and Buck," he growled at them, "you be ready to tackle him and tackle him hard when he comes in."

They took their places instantly and they had barely stepped into them when the door opened, and Phil Slader stepped in, busy in settling his hat more firmly above his eyes. That moment the heavy rope left the hand of the fat host. It shot through the air with a faint humming whisper and, brief as the time was, Phil Slader heard it and leaped forward.

Instead of settling around his shoulders, the rope caught him by the neck, and the jerk of big Remy landed him flat upon his back—flat upon his back, but with a gun already in his hand. He had flipped the Colt back for a snap shot at Remy, when Kirby reached the fray in true football style, literally hurling himself through the air and upon the prostrate form of the boy. His strong hand gripped the wrist of Phil, and Buck, at the same moment, cast himself upon the other arm of the fallen youngster. As for Blinky Rosen and the others, they cast themselves upon the legs of Phil, and he was buried under a human avalanche.

In a moment, he was helpless. The rawhide rope was worked around his arms, tying them securely to his sides, and then he was hoisted into a sitting posture with his back against the wall.

He had not spoken in surprise or in protest since this brief work of treason had begun. But now his black eyes burned like coals at Kirby and at Don Remy. Kirby occupied the focal point of his attention; Phil realized that none of the others, by themselves, would have dared to initiate such an attack against him.

Lon Kirby stood back, dusting his hands and nodding with satisfaction. "Here we are!" said he. "Damned if I had hoped that it could be done so quick. I thought that one of us would be pretty sure to catch the devil while we was trying this little game. But you got a fast hand with a rope, Remy. I got to tell you that. You done a fine piece of business, just now! Kid, I'd like to explain all of this to you, but I can't. I give you my word that we have in mind nothing but your own good. I'd like to ask you to believe that we don't mean you any harm, but just the opposite. And now—I got to start!"

"Kirby," said Phil Slader. "I've played a square game with you ever since I first met you—and I'll still play square. I'll tell you man to man what you ought to know— that I got business that takes me to see Magruder, and that if I miss him because of what you've done here, I'll go on your trail, Kirby, and I'll never stop till I've run you down, curse you! You hear me talk? While your friends keep me here, how can I tell but what some other gent might pull a gun on Magruder and bump him off?

"If that happened I'd never live a happy minute the rest of my life. I've waited fourteen years to see a clear path ahead of me to the killing of Magruder."

There was such a world of emotion pent in these words that Lon Kirby blinked as he turned to Don Remy. "You see what I mean, Don," said he.

"I see what you mean, and we'll do our best to keep him here. But work fast, Kirby. Work fast, I say!"

"I'm off now," said the outlaw.

"Good luck!" said the host.

Outside, in the stable, Buck stood at the side of the famous outlaw.

"Well?" said Kirby, jerking the saddle onto the back of his horse.

"I've done my share of rotten things," said Buck. "But I'd like to have a chance to square up some of them now. Let me ride along with you, old-timer. If you miss with Magruder, maybe I would have a mite of luck."

But Kirby merely dropped his hand on the shoulder of the youth and pressed it.

"Why, Buck," said he, "I take this to be right kind of you, and it's a thing that I'll remember for a long time—no fear of that! But what I want you to do now is to stay right here and help Daddy Remy to take care of that Slader who's inside. He may keep your hands full. Will you stay and do that, Buck?"

"I'd rather go along with you, chief," said the youngster.

"I tell you, kid," said the outlaw, "that the biggest half of the job is the one that you're staying behind to finish. So long, Buck. Best of good luck to you!"

He swung into the saddle. Outside the shed, the horse fidgeted among the sharp rock for a a moment, daintily, getting into its stride, and accustoming its feet to the hard going. Then it struck off with a bold canter that rocked the outlaw rapidly out of sight.

But Buck turned back into the hostelry—if it could be given that name. There he found Phil Slader sitting still with his back against the wall and letting his bright black eyes rove ceaselessly across the faces of the others, as though he were writing them down in letters of fire in his memory, to be consulted again upon another day, to the cost of them all!

The Italian stood beside Daddy Remy and said: "It looks to me as though we'll have to keep a guard over that kid day and night."

"Two guards, Buck," said the fat man; "two guards, son. I'm one—and I'll never close my eyes so long as he's in this here house. And one of the rest of you will keep awake in four-hour stretches."

"And in spite of that," said Buck, "I've got a sort of an idea that maybe he'll be able to give us the slip."

"Humph!" said Remy. "You talk big right now as though you had almost your full share of brains, kid. And you've said what's in my mind, right enough. Buck, you can have the first watch. We need eight hours guarding of him, at least so that old boy, Kirby, can have enough start."

"Eight hours?" gasped Buck. "Why, a four-hour start to Crusoe . . . ."

"Shut up!" said the fat man. "You'd know what I meant if you'd seen the horse that this kid rides."

CHAPTER 39

THE HORSE "that this kid rides," however, was constantly in the mind of Lon Kirby as he rode fiercely down from the mountains toward the town of Crusoe and the farm of Magruder beyond it. His own mount was a good one, but it was a matter of principle and almost of conscience with Kirby, never to hesitate in changing a good tired horse for a fresher and poorer one. Ten fast miles are often better than twenty slow ones.

He had a hundred and twenty miles before him, and he took the best course for the spot. He covered a solid fifty miles of rough going before the dawn had showed its hand in the east, and then he stopped at a ranch house and wandered into the horse pasture.

There was not much light, but even by the stars, Kirby could tell a good horse from a bad one. That rancher was relieved of a strong-standing young gelding whose canter in the pasture gave token of speed on the road. The fine animal which Kirby rode was left here to take the place of the other. Then, with saddle changed, he drove away toward his mark again.

Perhaps he could have taken a slightly more direct course by dipping down into the valley, but after the sun rose, he ran the risk of being seen and recognized, for his face was published abroad in that section of the land, though it had never reached the dangerous popularity of Jack Slader's, say. However, he could not afford to take too many chances on much-traveled roads. Therefore he dipped to the side and kept among the rocks and the copses of the hills as he pushed on.

In the mid-morning, he reached a schoolhouse, with all the school children inside, busy at their work. And, since there were no windows on one side, from that side he approached the building. He left the strong young gelding here and took to himself an excellent gray mare with a promise of endurance in her pony-built body.

She was not a very good animal, but in a school yard one could not be too particular. She served him very well, at that, pounding along with a racking gait from mid-morning until mid-afternoon. And in the middle of the afternoon, he left the pony-built gray and took in her place a cow pony, with no points at all, except to one who knew that difficult and dangerous breed. Kirby knew them, and he was not disappointed in his choice. It had the gait of a broken wagon, but it knew not exhaustion, and it held to a gallop or a sharp trot all the time between mid-afternoon and early evening. When the sun went down, it brought the outlaw through a clump of trees in the sight of the twinkling lights of big Doc Magruder's hotel.

Here the outlaw paused and considered matters. He was exhausted by the long, long ride. His body was shaken to numbness by the pounding which he had received in the saddle. In addition to all of this, he had not closed his eyes during two entire days.

He decided that this was the time to make haste slowly. He lay down on the edge of that copse and slept soundly for an entire hour. When he awakened he was thoroughly chilled, but his muscles were relaxed, and the journey down to the hotel would take care of the cold. So he mounted and flogged the mustang to a furious gallop, and in the midst of a cloud of dust, he drew up in front of the veranda of the hotel. The idlers were gone to supper. There was only a Negro servant idling there, and he called to him:

"Run inside and tell the boss that I'm in a powerful hurry to see him, George!"

George disappeared through the door, and Kirby was instantly out of the saddle and standing in the gloom beside the doorway. He heard the quick, heavy step of Magruder approach, in another moment, and as the proprietor reached the threshold of the building, Kirby stepped out before him gun in hand.

There was no attempt at resistance on the part of Magruder. He thrust his hands above his head when he saw the flash of the gun in the dusk.

"Well?" he gasped.

"I've come for a little friendly chat," said Kirby. "Will you come with me, Magruder?"

"I've heard your voice before," said Magruder. "Who are you?"

"You're wrong," said the outlaw. "You've never heard my voice before. Walk ahead of me, Magruder, and start for that shed behind the barn. We'll have our talk out there."

Whatever the faults of Magruder, he could recognize the inevitable when it stood before him in such a form as this. He marched ahead without a word of protest until they reached the shack behind the barn. A lantern hung inside the door, and with the hard muzzle of the Colt in the small of his back, Magruder obeyed the command which forced him to take down the lantern and light it.

Then, with the light on the peg once more, he turned and recognized the long, pale, ugly face and cold eyes of Lon Kirby.

"Kirby!" he said. "Kirby, by all the gods!"

"It's Kirby, well enough," said the outlaw.

"Where did you drop from?"

"Out of Hades, so far as you're concerned," said the

217

outlaw, smiling. "I've brought you a piece of paper and a fountain pen, and I want you to do a little writing for me."

He passed the writing materials to the other.

And Magruder, shaking his head in the wonder at what this could portend, uncapped the pen and prepared to write at Kirby's dictation.

"Begin: 'I hereby state and confess that when I met Jack Slader, I killed him by an unfair play . . . .'"

Magruder groaned. "But that's a lie, Kirby!"

"Son," said the outlaw, "I've got the whole story from the mouth of Diego Pasqual. Diego didn't die as soon as he should have died, so far as you're concerned!"

Magruder closed his eyes.

"Start in," said Kirby, "and write down the facts fast and hard—about how you got there and tied the kid—and how Slader came in—and how you played the dog until he gave you the chance to do a murder on him. Then say how you paid Pasqual to kill the boy. Write it all down, and write it fast. Because they may come asking for you, at any minute."

"Is that all that you want out of me?"

"Ain't that enough?"

"Enough, Heaven knows. I can never live in this country after this thing is known, Kirby!"

"I hope not. And you can't—not if you got any shame in you. But go ahead and write, old-timer!"

And Magruder wrote, and his writing drew a groan from him now and again as he penned the shameful words. He finished and he passed the paper back to Kirby and saw him pocket it.

"No," said Kirby, "there's one more thing. You've got a pretty sharp taste for money, Magruder. You like it pretty well, and you'll fight to get it. Now I'm going to give you a chance to get the price that they've put on my head. I don't know what they've boosted it to since I got away from the pen. But it'll be high enough to be worth your while."

"I don't follow you," said Magruder sullenly.

"Think again. You're going to stand there in front of

me and make a fair-and-square try for your gun, while I try for mine. The best man lives, and the loser dies. You understand?"

The glance of Magruder flashed from side to side.

"But if it comes to begging off," said Kirby, "begging won't do with me. I've come to kill you, Magruder, not so much because I hate a dog like you, but because I don't want the hands of a decent man to be dirtied with your murder. You got a good chance, I ain't chain lightning and sure death with a gun the way that Jack Slader used to be. You've got a fair and equal chance against me. Here is my gun back in the leather. Here is yours at your side.

"Start, Magruder, and give me the sign by making the first move!"

CHAPTER 40

MAGRUDER, THROUGH the long moment that followed, found the eye of the outlaw and strove to master it, but the glance of Lon Kirby was utterly cold and steady.

Then, listening sharply, Magruder heard far off the steady drumming of the hoofs of a galloping horse—a horse that moved with a long cadence. It came rapidly down the road toward the hotel. He raised his left hand slowly toward his forehead and rubbed it slowly toward his forehead and rubbed across the perspiration which had gathered there.

"Kirby," said he, "I would like to make you an offer."

"Offer away," said Kirby. "But in ten more seconds if you don't . . . ."

In speaking those words he made a slight gesture with his right hand away from the hip where his holster hung, and that was enough for Magruder. It was only a small advantage, but he could not hope to get a much greater one. His own hand jerked up and brought the Colt from its holster; and Kirby flew for his own weapon.

By a fifth of a second he was too slow. The gun of Magruder spoke first and filled the shed with the roar of its explosion. There was a tingle along the side of the head of Kirby as the bullet grazed the mark for which it had been aimed. Then the .45 slug from the Colt in the hand of Kirby tore through the body of the bigger man, and he sank to the floor, clutching at his breast and staring at Kirby with horror as though the outlaw had been turned into an incarnate devil, come for the soul of a condemned man.

"You've got it, Magruder, I think," said Kirby quietly.

"Yes, yes. I've got it!" gasped Magruder. He clasped his head with his hands, and they came away crimson.

"I've got it, Kirby, and God have mercy on my soul!"

"What Pasqual said was true, then?"

"All true! All true! And if—and if—"

He broke off, gasping and staring, and Kirby flashing a glance over his shoulder, saw the form of Phil Slader standing in the entrance to the shed with a terrible twisted look of baffled rage upon his face.

"Keep him away!" moaned Magruder. "Will you keep him away, Kirby? I'm dying! But not by him. I been ready and prepared and watching him all of these years. And he's never got to me—save me from him now, Kirby."

"He won't touch a dying man, Magruder," said the outlaw. "He's not your kind of a rat, Magruder. Here's a flask of something that will help to let you out more easy and cheerful. Drink it down, Magruder!"

"No, Kirby. I'll live yet," said the dying man, groaning. "Tie up the wound—I can't die now. I can't go down with all that I have on my conscience. You hear me, Lon? It ain't my body that you've killed. It's my soul—and I need —a chance to repent—and—make . . . ."

"And there," said Kirby, as the voice ended, "is the finish of the only gent that I'll never regret killing."

"Kirby," said Phil Slader, "back in the house of Remy I gave you warning that if . . . ."

"Hold up, Phil," said the outlaw. "I won't have trouble with you and I don't deserve it. I've got this to tell you. I've invested in a lot of bad actions and trouble of one kind or another ever since I can remember, hardly. And now what I want to do is to help to balance the books, a little. Phil, hold off till I've had a chance to talk to you a little—and until I've had a chance to write out something that's worth your having!"

Sheriff Mitchel Holmer had, among other things, been the man who had brought famous Lon Kirby to the prison sentence from which he had escaped by the miracle of bribe money. But matters were not all as the sheriff would have had them. His hold upon the affections and the respect of the men of his county was so strong and steady that there was no danger he would lose the next election— or the ones after that until he chose to retire, for that matter. Still, the conscience of the sheriff troubled him, and he wondered if a cleaner and more active man might not, perchance, be able to keep affairs in order in that county more thoroughly than he had done.

For the crowning stroke had been the murder of Magruder, found lying in the shed behind his barn. And men had seen a rider on a great gray horse swinging through the dusk of the evening—so what could be more patent than that Phil Slader had committed the crime?

He was pondering this, and wondering, indeed, how he could phrase a letter of resignation—and what comments people would have to make upon such a letter—and how he would be able to resist the foolish persuasions of his wife. He was pondering upon all of these things, when his door opened, and he saw against the black of the outer

221

night, the form of the man he most wanted in his hands. Phil Slader himself!

It took the sheriff something less than a fifth of a second to cover Phil Slader's heart with a Colt. But the youngster raised his hands slowly above his head and stood smiling at him.

"Take your time, Mitch," said he. "I've come to surrender. Take your time. I left my guns behind me. So you won't have to bother with them. But reach into my breast pocket, while you jam your gun into me and take out the papers that you find there!"

The sheriff was cautious, and he was watchfully suspicious, as well, but when he had removed the papers and regarded a little red smudge upon the corner of them, he gave a groan of interest. A moment later, he was exclaiming: "But if Pasqual—bless me, Phil, are you clean handed in this game?"

The paper seemed to answer all his questions. Presently he was sitting helpless in a chair and staring at Phil Slader with eyes wide.

"Put down your hands, Phil," said he. "And then tell me what sort of magic you used to make a crook like Kirby do a straight thing like this—a confession that *he* killed Magruder. But for that matter, when these things are published, Kirby will be a popular man for that killing! But tell me—what about yourself?"

"I've come back to work my way along," said Phil, "and I've got my ambition laid out straight as a road before me."

"And what is that?" said the sheriff.

"To marry the finest girl in the world, in the first place," said Phil. "And, in the second place, to learn how to show some of the folks that we call crooks, how to come back to the straight ways of doing things. That's my business in life. Because where honest folks wouldn't *let* me go straight, the crooks *made* me do it!"

Max Brand® is the best-known pen name of Frederick Faust, creator of Dr Kildare™, Destry, and many other fictional characters popular with readers and viewers worldwide. Faust wrote for a variety of audiences in many genres. His enormous output totalling approximately thirty million words or the equivalent of 530 ordinary books, covered nearly every field: crime, fantasy, historical romance, espionage, Westerns, science fiction, adventure, animal stories, love, war, and fashionable society, big business and big medicine. Eighty motion pictures have been based on his work along with many radio and television programs. For good measure he also published four volumes of poetry. Perhaps no other author has reached more people in more different ways.

Born in Seattle in 1892, orphaned early, Faust grew up in the rural San Joaquin Valley of California. At Berkeley he became a student rebel and one-man literary movement, contributing prodigiously to all campus publications. Denied a degree because of unconventional conduct, he embarked on a series of adventures culminating in New York City where, after a period of near starvation, he received simultaneous recognition as a serious poet and successful popular-prose writer. Later, he traveled widely, making his home in New York, then in Florence, and finally in Los Angeles.

Once the United States entered the Second World War, Faust abandoned his lucrative writing career and his work as a screenwriter to serve as a war correspondent with the infantry in Italy, despite his fifty-one years and a bad heart. He was killed during a night attack on a hilltop village held by the German army. New books based on magazine serials or unpublished manuscripts continue to appear. Alive and dead he has averaged a new one every four months for seventy-five years. In the U.S. alone nine publishers issue his work, plus many more in foreign countries. Yet, only recently have the full dimensions of this extraordinarily versatile and prolific writer come to be recognized and his stature as a protean literary figure in the 20th century acknowledged. His popularity continues to grow throughout the world.